About th

John Mower was a primary school teacher ... ...e last 15 years training new teachers into the profession. The world of education and the wonderful characters, both children and teachers, that he has met during this time have inspired him to write this novel.

John's first novel, *First Class*, was also a comedy and was set in a primary school. It told the story of a newly qualified teacher and his attempts to control, inspire and teach a class in their final year before moving to secondary school.

John lives in Hemel Hempstead with his wife Claire and their two grown-up children, Nicholas and Megan.

Dedication

This book is dedicated to all the students that I have taught over the last 15 years.

John Mower

Hot-Fussing

Austin Macauley Publishers™
LONDON • CAMBRIDGE • NEW YORK • SHARJAH

A CIP catalogue record for this title is available from the British Library.

ISBN 9781398400900 (Paperback)
ISBN 9781398400412 (ePub e-Book)

www.austinmacauley.com

First Published (2021)
Austin Macauley Publishers Ltd
25 Canada Square
Canary Wharf
London
E14 5LQ

Acknowledgements

This book would not have been written without the support and ideas of Vicki Fitt, who has helped to structure the story and develop the plot from the outset.

A massive thanks also to Grace Carter who has provided the invaluable 'student take' on the story, as well as her unwavering support throughout.

Thanks also to Laura Wildgoose, Shannon Foy and Ellie Branford whose ideas helped to shape several of the storylines.

Finally, thanks to my wife Claire and daughter Megan for their ideas.

Chapter 1

Martin

The Dean droned on. Martin watched the sea of faces listening to him, trying to gauge body language. Nervousness − check, excitement − check, terror − certainly on that kid near the front row, and yes, there it was on at least five faces − boredom. Martin checked his watch. Fifty-three seconds. The Dean had been speaking for less than a minute and was already boring the students. Quite some achievement. Not that William Ranch, Dean of the School of Education, was especially noted for his repertoire of witty repartee, amusing anecdotes, and knob jokes, but even so, 53 seconds. Not that Martin minded, of course. He saw himself amid a slightly rose-coloured and, it had to be said, immodest light, as the kind of guy that students liked. The fun lecturer to Ranch's dull one. The kind of guy that they warmed to, opened up to, and were inspired by. Well, most of them. He supposed that Cally Harding felt differently. Not a good time to remember such aberrations, but the mind had ways of amusing itself when the Dean was clearly failing on that front.

He still felt entirely justified in the rather harsh tone of the email that he had sent her last year. After all, the students knew that they were expected to attend all lectures and seminars, and Cally had missed four out of the last five. Maybe he shouldn't have used the phrase 'growing up to do', but United had lost that night and he was pissed off. So was she. Spectacularly so. The problem was that in her frenzied attempt to forward the email and her own take on the matter to Jade, she had accidentally pressed 'return' instead of 'forward'. The term 'horrible little weasel of a man' did seem a little harsh, even if it wasn't meant for him to read. Fortunately, she was neither in his seminar group nor, thank goodness, his Surgery Set, and they spent the rest of the year largely ignoring each other. He knew he should have taken it further, perhaps even to the Dean of Students, but something stopped him. Cowardice on his part perhaps, embarrassment maybe (there really was nothing weasely about him) or simply that it was the best way for everyone involved to forget and move on.

Martin was awoken from his reverie with the sight he had waited for. One minute and 43 seconds. A new record. In the sweepstake before the lecture began, Martin had opted for two minutes and Richard for three and a half. He looked at Richard, who had seen it too. His face showed a mixture of delight that it had happened so early and mild irritation that he now owed Martin a beer. There was something about students, especially first-year undergraduates, that assumed that as long as the phone could not actually be seen, no one would notice that they were texting. But Martin was an expert at noticing the subtle and not-so-subtle body language of the surreptitious texter: the slightly unnatural position of the hands, the slight tightening of facial features and – the real giveaway – the glances down to the lap. Martin studied the texter now. Tall, blonde, probably straight out of school, but with an air of confidence, verging on the worrying for someone two minutes into her university career. She definitely had that air of 'I'm good-looking and I know it', and as he continued to watch her, she gave up any pretence at the subtle 'surreptitious glance' and simply stared at her lap. Ballsy, or what? He'd have to keep an eye out for her. But then she stopped and, instead of looking back at the Dean, looked directly at him. As he glanced round, he noticed, to his horror, that all 80 of them, and the Dean, were now looking at him.

'Martin?'

Oh my God, he'd already been introduced – hell, that was a short speech – and all and sundry were now awaiting his turn. The 'clearing of the throat' was always a sensible approach to take shortly before speaking to a large audience, but as he was already a few seconds late, he opted against this extra half-second of time.

'Hi everybody.' Damn. The high-pitched squeak that emerged from his mouth sounded horrible and was greeted by a few polite smirks and an audible snort from the blonde texter.

'Hi everybody. Sorry about that. Malfunction in the voice department. My name is Martin Summers, and I am the programme leader for the Bachelor of Education degree. Can I firstly reiterate the Dean's sentiments by welcoming you to our university? I thoroughly hope that the next three years will be both a rewarding and enjoyable experience for you and that, by the end of it, we will have 80 first-class primary school teachers to grace our schools. Beautiful butterflies will emerge. Let me start by talking you through…'

Anna

Anna now had to stop herself from laughing. That snort really was rather too loud, and it had gained her a few unwelcome side glances. But now she was itching to text Leah again with the 'beautiful butterflies' line – did he really say that? – but figured that she had better wait. She was pretty sure that he had noticed the first text and she didn't want to get off to a bad start. Actually, despite his rather unfortunate opening, she felt that this guy might be okay. He had a manner about him that was easy to listen to and was clearly now saying important stuff. So, they could choose their own seminar group and go straight there after this introduction. Okay, so what factors would determine where she would go? As she had arrived slightly late − damn those road works − she hadn't actually spoken to anyone yet. She looked round for potential friends. So many girls of roughly her own age, all looking earnest and intent. No clues there then. What about the boys? Of the 80 or so people in the room, it appeared that only about 14 were boys. Getting to know some of the better-looking ones seemed like a sensible plan. There were a couple of them together, just in front of her. Without asking them to turn around, she could not, as yet, award marks out of 10, although they looked all right from behind. She would follow them to their chosen seminar room and let fate take her from there.

Was that a fart? She sniffed again. No one else seemed to be stirring but she was pretty sure. A lifetime of living with three flatulent younger brothers, whilst not exactly making her an authority on the subject, had given her a nose for this − so to speak. It was not a really smelly one, but there was a definite hint of a tint in the air. Who would do that? Who could possibly think that it was socially acceptable to break wind less than five minutes into their first-ever lecture? Surely it must be a boy. The nearest guy to her, and well within distance, did look a little shifty, although she thought that was probably nerves. After all, he looked about 12. Maybe his mother had forgotten to tell him not to fart in lectures.

Gabriel

Gabriel was completely sure that he wanted to be a teacher. He had been for many years, ever since his nephews were toddlers and people remarked how good he was with them. He was also pretty sure that he didn't lack confidence, despite his youthful and, some might say, effeminate looks. He had been looking forward to this day all summer, to the time when he could move away from home and start the process of learning how to teach. And yet now, for reasons that he could not fathom, he felt terrified. Everyone looked so self-assured, so ready to be a student and so much taller than him. That girl behind him was already texting, for God's sake. Gabriel would have loved to have had the confidence, at that moment, to get out his phone and text his brother, just to show that he, Gabriel Morgan, was not the sort of guy to take no crap from no one. Who was he kidding? Not that he was some sort of goody-two-shoes or anything, but being even mildly subversive on Day One simply wasn't him. Instead, there was just a tangible, overbearing terror, such as when you wake suddenly in the middle of the night and are scared for no discernible reason. He was sure it would pass, but part of the nature of the terror was that he didn't feel that he could articulate it, however many helpful and reassuring kind responses – 'Don't worry mate, we all feel like that'– there may have been. Because – and this was the rub – he was a bloke. A bloke in a predominantly female environment. And of course, boys don't cry; boys don't turn to their seminar group during introductions and say that they are almost literally cacking their pants. Of small comfort – and he could not really articulate why – was that all of the three people at the front were men. He'd gathered that the first guy seemed to be in charge of the whole department and the guy talking now was in charge of their course. He assumed the third one, Richard something, was also a lecturer. He'd find out soon enough.

A further symptom, and one which perpetuated his fright, was that he was now unable to take in anything this Martin guy was saying. Martin had put up a weird-looking timetable on the projector and was brandishing words such as modules, credits and semesters, but none of it was going in. Gabriel decided, in the end, not to listen, figuring he would pick things up as and when. Instead, he took a look around him. Most of his fellow students seemed to be young, white girls, although the 13 other boys he had counted, as well as the smattering of different ethnicities and older students, was again, for whatever reason, a source of some comfort. His eyes focused now on one of these older ladies. She seemed considerably older than any of the rest – easily as old as his mother, with a kind yet scrutinising face and sensible short haircut. He wondered if her extra maturity enabled her to feel more confident or whether that focused expression hid someone who felt both self-conscious and out of place.

Mary

It was, finally, Simon's decisiveness which persuaded her to take the plunge. After all, he argued, by the time she graduated, she would only be 53, and could teach for a decade or more; easily enough time to carve out a second successful career. Mary knew that the unwavering support of her husband, both emotionally and financially, was key in making such a bold decision. She still felt a burden, though, despite his reassurances. With the kids now grown up and the mortgage nearly paid, this was absolutely the right time. Simon was well aware how disillusioned she had become in her current career, and how much she needed a change. But still. What if it didn't work out? What if the age gap between her and her fellow students was, ultimately, too much? She knew she had the academic qualities to thrive. She'd done well in school and effortlessly gained her professional qualifications, which had subsequently led her to her career in finance; and she had never struggled with time management. She didn't need to make friends and certainly had no desire to socialise with people younger than her children. But still.

Martin Summers looked the part. He was of medium size and build, and dressed appropriately enough, and he was clearly going to be a central figure in her programme. She was currently trying to gauge the man, whilst taking in the information that he was giving. Her initial impression was that he was trying a little too hard. This didn't seem quite the stage to be cracking jokes and sharing knowing glances with a sidekick, but she knew only too well the importance of reserving judgement. This was actually going to be one of her biggest challenges. She knew she was the sort of person to get easily irritated if others around her lacked her intelligence, enthusiasm, common sense or − and this was the big problem − maturity.

Alice's words the other day had really stuck: 'You do realise, don't you Mum, that most students revert to adolescence in their first term away? The girls will flirt, the boys will show off, and you'll have to fend off some very dodgy bad breath in those morning seminars. You're gonna love it.'

And that's before she got to placement. She'd spent three years being a parent helper when her children were young and had to stop herself, on a regular basis, from correcting the teacher's grammar, or from tutting at the inappropriate dress, or from commenting on the lazy ticks at the end of a piece of work or… It was more than possible that she would have some such specimen as her mentor. Now *that* would be a challenge.

Surgery

'Just to reiterate, there are three different formats here. You'll have lectures with all 80 of you, regular seminars in your seminar group of 25, and then Surgery, with just the six of you. As I was saying in the introduction, pastoral support is something that we value highly here. Naturally, you'll get plenty of academic support, but the purpose of the weekly Surgery is for us to iron out all those personal issues that may affect your studies here. You know, when your boyfriend breaks up with you, when you can't organise your time or when the parrot's died. That sort of thing.'

Martin's voice seemed to echo in this smaller and intimate room.

'Sometimes we'll arrange to all meet, and sometimes the space will be specifically for a drop-in, if any of you want to have a private chat. I'll email you in good time if I want you to prepare anything specific. As each lecturer has only six students in their Surgery, it does give us an opportunity to get to know each other really well. I'm sorry to say that you lot have drawn the short straw and been landed with me, but at least, as your programme leader, I should vaguely know what I'm talking about.'

Mary tried to think of any possible scenario where she would want to have a confidential *tête-à-tête* with this man.

'So, can I suggest,' continued Martin, 'that we spend this session getting to know each other a bit? Maybe telling each other a bit about ourselves, and sharing a few hopes and fears? Anyone like to start? Thank you. Donna, isn't it?'

All eyes turned towards the petite brunette. At 21, Donna hoped that her age and her penchant for highly-coloured clothing might hide all the turmoil going on inside of her. This unease had not been helped by the fact that she had arrived at campus two days after most people, due to a wedding commitment, and she already felt that she was 'catching up' socially.

'Yes. I'd just like to begin by saying I'm not normally like this. You know – quiet and looking a bit crap. Maybe what I'm trying to say is that I forgot how much I need my sleep. Don't get me wrong, I've enjoyed my first few days on campus, but I'm not entirely sure that vodka and I are going to last the duration together. But actually, more than that, it's the noise. I don't want to sound – you know – hypocritical or anything because I'm quite sure that I can be very shouty when drunk, but I really do struggle to sleep if I can hear noise. Actually, music. Well, specifically James Blunt. I mean, who the hell plays James effin' Blunt on their first weekend in halls? At 1:00 in the morning? I mean, God, if you don't want to be bullied. Sorry, rant over.'

It was Mary, sharp-eyed as ever, who noticed it first. However good you are at hiding it, telling body-language, a reddening of the face, is most certainly an involuntary movement. But now Anna had noticed it too and there was no way, from Mary's little knowledge of her so far, that Anna was going to let this pass…

'Gabriel? You seem to be looking a bit shifty there in your new jeans…?'

Mary knew that the next few seconds would say a lot about Donna as the realisation dawned on her, and to the girl's credit, she looked more embarrassed than sneering.

'Oh Christ, I didn't realise – I mean I didn't know – I mean, are *you* in room 19?' blustered Donna.

There really was nowhere to go, and Gabriel just sat there feeling six pairs of eyes staring at him.

'Yeah – really sorry I kept you awake. But I like James Blunt. I mean, he's a really good singer.'

Had he have stopped and planned that little speech for several hours, Gabriel realised, after the words had come out of his mouth, that this was probably the worst thing that he could have said at this moment and Anna, for one, was making no attempt to conceal the fact that she thought him a complete arse. Yes, there was a time and a place for extolling the obvious virtues of the admirable Mr Blunt, but now, as Gabriel very quickly realised, was not one of them.

The next two seconds were, arguably, the worst two in his life, as no one quite knew what to say.

Fortunately, Callum came and gave him a big-brotherly shoulder squeeze. (Gabriel felt, wisely, that it was a good idea not to say that this hurt a bit.)

'You know what, mate? When I was your age, I was playing flanker for the Wasps Academy. I'm trying to imagine the look on the guys' faces if I had had James Blunt blaring from my phone. You know what, though, good on ya. Anybody who listens to what they want and doesn't give a stuff about what anybody else thinks gets my vote. All boys together, eh?'

'So, Gabriel,' persisted Anna mercilessly, 'are you a flanker at the Wasps Academy?'

At this point – and, in Mary's view, at least a minute too late – Martin stepped in and took up the 'settling in' theme again, and the conversation limped on for a few minutes. By the time that Martin was finished and was proudly announcing about the programme social, to be held later in the week, he had just about regained his composure. His initial lack of this, however, spoke volumes to Mary.

As the session was being wrapped up, Mary had to remind herself of the mantra that she had promised herself that she would stick by. *Don't pre-judge. Give people time.*

But of course, that was harder than it looked, and pre-judging was most certainly what she was now doing. She was pre-judging Martin to be a little out of his depth when faced with, quite frankly, a nasty piece of work. She was also pre-judging this nasty piece of work but – and here she felt a little more virtuous – she was genuinely holding judgement about the two guys and that Donna girl. Whilst he'd clearly had a bad start, she judged that Gabriel probably had a bit more about him than met the eye.

And then there was that other girl. Kathryn, was it? The one who hadn't said anything. The one with the inscrutable gaze. There was something, and she absolutely could not put her finger on it, that told her that it would be Kathryn, and not Gabriel, who was going to find life tough at university.

Chapter 2

Kathryn

Kathryn's fingers hovered over the 'send' button. She had reasoned that by simply composing an email to her nan this would help. This would help her to make sense of a very foreign world, containing people so different from her. She knew that she shouldn't send it, but she was unsure whether she could stop herself. She was intelligent enough to understand the consequences: however veiled her words, it would be very evident that she was effectively saying that she didn't like it here, that she wanted Nan to come and collect her, and that she wanted the security that their private world had offered over the years.

She reflected now on the nine years that she had lived with her nan since her mother had died. One week of being away from home added clarity to that reflection as it reinforced the glaring differences between her and her fellow students. Because when she lived with her nan, she knew that, however much she felt lonely at school, she was only ever a few hours away from the security of her home; of the comforting knowledge of the routine of early-evening quiz shows with dinner on laps, of a game of cards or Scrabble, and of silent nights. However well she knew, when inspecting herself in the mirror, that she was carrying a little too much weight and that her thick glasses did nothing for her, all of this could be forgotten over a cup of cocoa.

How could she tell Nan she hated it here? She knew the inevitable responses – *You need to give it time; you need to carve out a life of your own; don't forget the promise you made your mum* – all of which were sound arguments and which the rational side of her fully understood.

But.

No amount of rational argument could disguise what she was feeling. And loneliness, fear and a certain amount of disdain are very powerful emotions. It wouldn't have been quite as bad had she been in halls of residence. At least there one could hide in a vacuum of anonymity and shut one's door. She almost envied that boy Gabriel, despite his obvious discomfort at the Surgery Set meeting. At least he didn't have to live with Anna.

Kathryn had been vaguely troubled when she couldn't get a place in halls, but she couldn't really articulate the manner of that discomfort.

16

She could now.

Living with five other random girls in a house was a quite horrendous experience, especially when Anna was so clearly intent on having things her way. Not that she had picked on Kathryn in the same way as she had taken against that poor boy, but there was a definite sense that if any of the other flatmates attempted to rock the boat, then Anna would stamp her authority with her unique quality of disdain. The other girls seemed okay, but the necessity of house rules, cleaning rotas, shared expenses, etc. – visible things that could largely be ignored in halls – only exacerbated her unease.

And then there was the programme social this evening. When her tutor first told them all about this, her first response, categorically, was that she wouldn't go. Even the nagging thought of Mum looking down on her and urging her to do so did nothing to shift her resolve. After all, she had told herself many times that she was not there to make friends. She had always wanted to be an infant teacher and she starkly saw this process as a means to an end, but already that means seemed considerably harder than she had envisaged it, and if, in three long years, she had made no friends at all and had hidden behind the safety of her door – well, that would be very tough indeed.

And then there was Mary, who had so kindly sought her out yesterday, who had almost confided in her and had stated that, for very different reasons, she did not want to go either but felt that she should. Whilst Mary didn't actually say the words, her implication was that the two of them could, despite coming from very different worlds, look out for each other. But even this was confusing. Was Mary offering to be some sort of mother-figure or some sort of friend?

So, she would go. She dreaded the thought of it, but she would go.

Callum

Callum looked in the mirror. God, he was handsome. Tall, muscular and with a mop of dark swept-back hair, he liked to see himself, in his less modest moments, as a would-be matinee idol. And this was good for a variety of reasons. First, and foremost, here he was the alpha male amid a sea of girls, where the ratio was about one guy to seven women. Well, that was good odds, even for your average bloke, but Callum had never had any problem attracting the fairer sex and was rather confident about his chances with such a weighted proportion. When his friends had asked him why he wanted to retrain as a primary school teacher, as opposed to using his undoubted sporting ability and five years of experience in sports management to become a secondary PE teacher, he had always responded with the well-worn line about the amount of girls to choose from on the primary course.

But his good looks, sporting endeavours and obvious charm hid the sort of insecurity that he had never really managed to articulate and which he had kept very much to himself for all these years. Being dyslexic had always presented academic problems, and he was genuinely dreading both the English and Maths modules awaiting him; but it was more than this. Callum had spent his life needing to be liked and still, at 28, this need had not dissipated, and as he stood in the toilets ready to join his cohort at the programme social, he was genuinely nervous about the prospect. In the first few days here, he had got on reasonably well with his seminar group and had flirted effortlessly with several of the girls, but he had not, for example, spoken with the four football-playing lads in seminar group B, or even Matt and Jamie from his seminar group, when he should have everything in common with them. Okay, so they were all straight out of school and a decade at this age is quite a lot, but still, how hard could it be? So, he would rectify that this evening and go and chat to some of them, but he would be lying to himself if he didn't acknowledge that, fundamentally, he was going to find this a difficult thing to do.

Martin

The programme social was a good idea. Clearly. What better way for students and staff to get to know each other and break some proverbial ice than for all of them to meet in a relaxed environment over a few drinks and some music? Definitely a good idea.

This was Martin's second year as programme leader and there was part of him that felt that it was now time to put his own personal stamp on proceedings: this social was totally his idea. But it was only now, as he surveyed the empty room a few minutes before the allotted hour, that he began to have serious reservations. What if nobody came? What if it was so boring that it had emptied by 9 o'clock? What if everyone got violently drunk? What if…?

'There you go, mate. Don't say that I never pay my debts. A pint of your Students' Union finest. Cracking stuff.'

'Cheers, Richard. Reckon I'm going to need this. Have I made a really stupid mistake here? Is this evening going to be completely shit?'

'God, no. My Surgery Set were full of it when I saw them today. I'd like to see that Charlotte Wilkins after sinking a few shots. She definitely fancies me.'

'Well, that will make the evening go with a bang, won't it? **"University senior lecturer snogs student after just three days. Call the *Guinness Book*** *of Records.*" Jesus, Rich, that's good, even by your standards. Can I come and watch when you explain that one to Ranch? Incidentally, is he coming tonight?'

Richard guffawed as they both pictured the rather lurid image of William Ranch, sporting his best disco kit, getting down and dirty with the new intake.

'Hey, ladies, come and have a dance with me. They don't call me Big Willy for nothing.'

Blokey banter. God, Martin was glad of that tonight, as he watched the door open and the first of the students entering the union hall. There was something vaguely comical, and perhaps a little sad, about watching Mary and Kathryn enter together. Kathryn wasn't exactly clinging on, but she may as well have been. He desperately hoped that she would relax into the evening and into the course. He had seen nothing yet that convinced him that she would be able to hack it in school. At present, quite frankly, she'd be eaten alive. He suddenly, amid a sea of pathos, felt a great deal for this young lady. He knew a little about her background now and felt very glad that she was in his Surgery Set. For all his bluster, he knew that he was a damn good lecturer, and he cared deeply for his students. She'd survive, this one. He was going to make damned sure of it.

'Okay, Martin. Put your bets on. No point doing this with my Set. Six normal, middle-class, white 18-year-old girls, who will all make adequate or good teachers, and will come out with a smattering of 2:1s or 2:2s. But your lot, what an eclectic bunch they are. Usual rules. We pick one student each that won't last the distance. My turn to go first, a no-brainer. Kathryn Wood.'

'D'you know what, Rich? She's yours. Me? I'm going for the dark horse. I don't know what it is, but there's something about that Donna Martindale.'

Kathryn

She knew, instantly, that it was a stupid thing to do. It's not as though she's never had alcohol before, but vodka? Really? It was all too confusing. She'd had no problem at all asking for a Coke when Mary offered her a drink after they first arrived, but when Donna offered, well, she sort of panicked. She had been slowly warming to the evening, and Mary, Donna, Callum, and Gabriel were being genuinely nice. Gabriel, in particular, looked as lost as she felt and that was strangely comforting. But then Donna stood and announced that it was her round. If only she'd gone the other way around the table. But she didn't. Callum, of course, asked for a pint of something and then it was her turn. Kathryn had never done 'rounds' and she didn't really understand them and here, all of a sudden, they were all looking at her and waiting for her to answer Donna's kindness and that was all a bit much, really. She envisaged Donna and Callum sharing a sly glance had she have said those dreaded words: 'I'd like a

Coke, please,' and Anna was close by with another group and was bound to be listening and Kathryn wasn't sure she'd have enough money when it came to her round and it just kind of slipped out.

'Er, a vodka and Coke, please.'

'Sure. Mary?'

'I'd like a Coke, please.'

That had been the closest Kathryn had ever come to swearing, and now she sat, 30 minutes later, not really knowing what to do. She'd had a few sips, but was pretty sure she couldn't finish it, and then what? It seemed like an age since Donna's round and other glasses were ominously close to needing refilling.

She forced herself to relax. At one point, Callum turned to her and smiled as he was telling a joke and she felt it. A twinge. Kathryn had never felt a twinge before, and of course, Callum was much too nice for her, but even so; a twinge is a twinge. Had Anna not walked past them, carrying a tray of drinks to a completely separate group just as Callum was really getting into the swing of things, well, maybe that twinge may even have graduated to a flutter.

Richard

At 29, Richard was the youngest member of the School of Education. Having taught in an inner-city primary school for six years, he had joined the university a year ago, and was, by his own admission, a cocky bastard. He knew perfectly well that most of his colleagues saw him as a bit of an upstart and as someone who, quite frankly, was far too familiar with his students. At six feet tall, he stood a good five inches over Martin, which, at times, such as now, made him feel just a little better about himself. And he loved that image – or at least he used to. He had learnt a very valuable lesson at the graduation ball last summer, when an inebriated young lady, who was letting her hair down after such a hard year, actually made a pass at him. A very public pass. Yes, he deflected it and nothing more had come of it, but in that moment, he had seen the eyes of all the other students on that dancefloor: eyes that suggested comeuppance, and that was a very scary moment indeed. Fortunately, as with tonight, only Martin of the academic staff was present, and he had spoken wise words indeed about lecturer-student relations. So, whilst Richard still enjoyed banter with Martin, they both knew that the 'I'm sure she fancies me' line was said in jest and with absolutely no hint of intent.

One of his pet loves was trying to read body language and predict students' characters accordingly. Whilst he liked his Surgery Set well enough, he had openly confessed that he wished that he had Martin's group, as they just seemed more interesting, and as if to prove the point, he had spent most of the evening studying them. In particular, he had studied Callum. All of the others had behaved about as he had expected them to. Donna, Martin's 'dark horse', was still a bit of an enigma and he saw no particular reason why she shouldn't sit with Gabriel, Mary, and Kathryn, and Anna seemed to be chatting up a group of lads. But Callum? Surely he would politely say hello to the rest of the Set and then ingratiate himself amongst the swarm of attractive young ladies or talk rugby with the group of lads at the bar. But no. If anything, Richard thought that he might be actually flirting with Kathryn − a million-to-one outsider, if ever there were one. Still, the night was young, or it would have been if, at that moment, Anna hadn't passed their table, carrying a round of drinks.

Surgery

At first, Martin took the view that he could just ignore it. Water under the bridge and all that. But the more he thought about it, the more he realised that he simply couldn't. What would they think? What would Mary, in particular, think? He'd always hated the idea of appearing spineless...

'Okay, thanks again for all coming. I know it's been a really long first week for you and before we try to unpick what you have learnt this week, I think we really need to talk about Wednesday night. I mean, em, well we're all, you know, in this together, and er, elephants in the room and whatnot. So, would, maybe, one of you like to start so that we can try to clear it up − so to speak − and move on?'

'He's a knob. That's what went on.'

'Yes, well, thank you, Anna, for starting us off, but maybe we should...'

'Maybe we should all agree that Callum is a knob.'

'It was an accident, Anna. I have said sorry,' sighed Callum.

'You've said sorry. Well, that's all right then. I don't need to worry about my bruised back. I don't need to worry about sitting in six fucking pints with my dress ruined, my knickers soaked and four guys getting more than they had hoped for that night when my legs spread up in the air as I slipped and fell. No need to worry because you said you were sorry.'

'I was sorry, Anna − I am sorry. I just, you know, slipped.'

'You slipped? You were sitting on a bloody chair, for God's sake. How the hell did you slip?'

'Well I was sort of embellishing my story. You see, there was this teacher − and this is true by the way − there was this teacher who had annoyed a kid in her class so much that he put a drawing pin on her seat, right, and when she sat down she sort of leapt backwards and...'

'Callum, I don't want to hear this old chestnut of a story. I don't actually want to know why you fell backwards, and I don't want to know about all of your hot-fussing just as I was carrying a tray full of beer to my friends, and I don't want to know how it was that you managed to send it flying, how you managed to send me flying, and how you finished my evening for me. No, sorry, scrub that. How you managed to finish *everyone's* evening, because Mr Health and Safety, our friendly bar manager, decided that the floor was simply too wet and sticky to let the evening continue. All I want, really, is for you to acknowledge that you are a knob.'

'It was an accident, Anna. And, actually, you didn't need to swing a punch at me.'

So, this was it. The moment had come. The moment that Kathryn had worried over for the last two days. The moment that had caused her to virtually vomit in the middle of the night. She hadn't meant to laugh when Anna had fallen over – she really must have hurt herself. Maybe it was the vodka. Maybe, even, it was the twinge, but it was too loud, and Anna glared at her as she got up and took a half-hearted swing at Callum, before bursting out of the room.

'Wouldn't you throw a punch, Callum?' continued Anna. 'Wouldn't you hit out if someone ruined your evening and people laughed at you? Wouldn't you…'

And so, it went on. And whilst Martin didn't exactly exude calm authority, the moment did pass and, all in all, it probably was worth bringing up as at least now, perhaps, it could be forgotten. But Kathryn didn't miss the slight glance her way when Anna was talking about people laughing at her, and she wondered if Anna was biding her time, ready to pounce, perhaps even in their shared house.

And during all of this commotion, Gabriel looked on impassively. Like everyone else, he saw venom on Anna's face, a brow-beaten expression on Callum's, and a mixture of dread, shame, and embarrassment on Kathryn's. But it was not at them that he was really looking. Because, in all of this melee, Donna, who had had nothing to do with the incident, looked on with something approaching absolute dread on her face. No one else noticed, not even Mary, but Gabriel did, and he resolved, there and then, not to listen to James Blunt that night, but to knock on her door instead…

Chapter 3

Donna

'Individual task, to be completed in time for your seminar on Friday 4th October:

"Think of a time in your life when behaviour has been an issue. This can be either when you were at school, from your observations so far in primary school visits, or from any other time in your life. The purpose of this exercise is twofold: first, it will give all of us some scenarios to discuss, which will allow us to consider why people misbehave and what we can try to do to prevent it. Secondly, you are training to be primary school teachers, hence you need to be confident talking to a group of people, so this exercise will give you the opportunity to present to an audience. Make it engaging. Make us laugh, make us cry, make us angry. Remember, how *you speak is as important as what you say."'*

Donna reread Martin's group email again and tried to make up her mind what to do. This, after all, was a perfect opportunity to get things out in the open, even to make light of the incident and her subsequent mistakes. She had already arranged to meet Martin privately in Surgery straight after the seminar and wondered whether it would be better to have already mentioned it or just to talk about something else. It was not as if she didn't have plenty of ammunition at her fingertips. Some of the behaviour that she had witnessed at school was quite outrageous. It was almost tempting to tell the story of when Felix literally got his penis stuck in a wine bottle in an RE lesson − of all subjects – just to watch the range of facial expressions as she embellished the tale. Whilst she had nothing against Kathryn, the slightly malicious side of her smirked as she imagined how Kathryn would react when she told of how he was forced to walk to the front of the class in full swing − so to speak – how attempts to dislodge the offending bottle failed and how, whilst crying in pain, Felix was taken to A&E, where he proceeded to wait for four hours trying somehow to preserve his modesty before the final excruciating extraction. But no. Eventually, Donna decided that all of this hilarity would simply delay the inevitable. If she were forced to leave the programme, however humiliating and disastrous that this would be, she decided that it would be better if everyone knew why she had gone, rather than the inevitable spread of rumours and speculation that would happen if she were suddenly to disappear. It was horrible, but she would tell the truth.

Anna

Anna completed her presentation to a few laughs, the odd gasp, and a smattering of applause. As she sat back down, she figured that she had pitched it about right. Her story told about the boy in Year 10, Danny, who had refused to do his homework. When instructed to then do it twice for insolence, he still refused. And so developed a stand-off that had shown, through Anna's eloquent reconstruction, just how badly her teacher had handled the situation. Mr Andrews had upped his demands on each refusal with determined, and it has to be said, unimaginative regularity until, upon the phrase: 'Okay then, you will complete the homework five times tonight, and that's my final offer.'

Danny had responded, with justifiable exasperation, with the immortal phrase: 'Oh, piss off Andrews, you sodding peanut-head.'

Funny, edgy, and well-told. Not anything like the appalling story about the spray paint, but within the bounds of seminar etiquette, and crucially, not painting Anna as the bad guy. Again.

Just before she had started the primary teaching course, Anna had asked her sister for advice.

'It's very simple,' replied Leah. 'Be the Top Dog. Establish yourself at the beginning as someone who you don't mess around with and then there's no chance that you'll be bullied. And you do not want to be bullied at university, believe me.'

Anna had spent most of her life looking up to her sister. Throughout school, she had often been referred to as the sister to the immature brothers, rather than the sister to the beauty queen. In Year 11, she and a similarly disenfranchised group of friends had broken away from a school disco and spray-painted the front of the school entrance with swastikas. The upshot of such madness was a fixed-term exclusion, a letter home to her parents and humiliation in front of the school by an apoplectic head teacher.

And yet, despite all the infamy and shame, her actions had also brought with them a badge of honour, not least from Leah who, in a rare moment of praise, had smiled, and said, 'Nice one, Anna.'

A psychiatrist would have loved it. They would easily have made the connections between Anna's erratic and unwelcome behaviour and her desire to gain acclaim, especially from Leah.

Hence, when she started her B.Ed course, she heeded her sister's words, but it was only when thinking about what to say in this presentation that she started to wonder. She had been dismissive of most of those around her, including her tutor. She had been cruel to Gabriel and intimidating towards Kathryn. She had made a public show of deriding Callum for what was, unquestionably, an accident. (Even though he was being a bit of a knob.)

And where had this got her? Had she been acclaimed, after two weeks at university, as Top Dog? Did fellow students look up to her and all want to be her best friend? In a moment of clarity she had realised, with a slight shudder, that most people were tending to keep a safe distance, rather than gravitate towards her. So, she told the story of Danny that didn't involve her and felt suddenly rather moved when she saw Gabriel clapping warmly at its conclusion.

Gabriel

Gabriel could never speak with the authority and ease with which Anna spoke. He had always considered himself quite good at telling stories to his friends and was often rather gratified by the responses that he received. But presenting in front of a group of 30 students, immediately after the confident and imposing Anna – well, that was another thing altogether.

Last night, his brother had texted him to ask how his first two weeks had been. Had they been a success? On the one hand, he did feel rather young and rather out of his depth. Anna, in particular, had made him feel remarkably small and nobody seemed to share in his penchant for the music of James Blunt. But he had been terrified when starting that he wouldn't make any friends and that he would hear fellow students plan Saturday night parties and neglect to ask him along. His brother had told him, perhaps unwisely, that in his first week at university, he had been so desperate for attention that he had stood outside the room of someone in halls and tried to pluck up the courage, for a full five minutes, to knock on the door to see if they would like to have a drink at the bar. Whilst this story had been tempered by the knowledge that this pathetic and rather unsuccessful method of trying to make friends had not lasted long, and that his brother soon boasted an array of friends, it did little to help.

'Yeah, thanks a lot for that, Rob. Just what I needed. Maybe I can phone you when I'm sitting on my own during the fresher's party. We can tell some jokes.'

But, actually, it had not been that bad. His seminar group were generally nice, and Callum, in particular, seemed keen to look out for him. He had been especially chuffed when Callum had confided some of his fears as well, such as his dread of the English and Maths modules, and Gabriel had delighted in offering his help. Yet, he had not really got what he really craved; someone who he could genuinely call his friend. At least, he hadn't, until he had knocked on Donna's door last week and she had opened up to him. Gabriel had never felt so proud of himself, and he hoped, with all of his heart, that Donna would not be thrown off the course before she had really started it.

His story was simple and brief, but as he started talking, he saw eyes that wished him well, and this filled him with confidence.

'Okay, so I was 12 at the time, and we had this English teacher, right, Miss Salmon. I actually quite liked her, but there was this boy in my class, Dylan, who she quite clearly didn't like and the more she showed this, the more he played up. What was funny about it all was that Dylan was not a dreadful child who sold drugs on the playground. He was actually really posh and ended up going to Oxford. The thing is, Miss Salmon didn't always speak very well, and Dylan delighted in correcting the grammar of his English teacher. If she said something like: "You and me need to have a chat about your attitude," Dylan would be quick to retort with the words: "Do you mean you and *I*, Miss?" One day, Miss Salmon had frustrated him by ignoring him all lesson when he had wanted to offer his opinion on *Animal Farm*, and he clearly decided to rile her to the point where she would snap.

'"So, year 7. Here is a list of books that we will be looking at after Easter, and I want you to choose one of them and read them over the holidays."

'"I've read them all," said Dylan.

'She then proceeded to offer a further 10 books. Each one was greeted by a sneer and the words, "I've read it." Eventually, she snapped and sent him, in disgrace, to the teacher's room behind the classroom. When she opened the door five minutes later to see if he was ready to apologise, she was horrified to see that he had made himself a cup of coffee.'

Gabriel had expected a reasonable response for his anecdote, but stood open-mouthed as people laughed out loud and clapped as he sat down, and as Mary winked at him before taking the stage herself, he genuinely felt, perhaps for the first time, that he was going to make it.

Mary

Alice was quite adamant. 'Mum, you simply have to tell that story for your presentation. It is absolutely hilarious.'

'And you know what, Mary, you've been dining out on it for the best part of 30 years and it always gets a laugh.'

'I know, Simon, but chatting over a dinner party and embellishing the details when a bit tipsy is very different to giving a professional presentation to fellow students. What if they are just too appalled? After all, it was from a different age and teachers just don't behave like that anymore. It also needs plenty of exaggeration and oomph for it to work. I'm just worried that I'm going to make a bit of a fool of myself. After all, I'm the mature one. Should I really be telling a story about a teacher hitting a child?'

'It fits the brief, Mum, and I think it will do you good to be seen as someone with a bit of fire in your belly. Go on, sock it to them. You'll bring the house down.'

And so Mary took the stage. She wondered, as she took a deep breath, whether the following few minutes would improve the perception of her from her peers or lessen it. She also felt a strange sensation, which was very new to her: one of complete terror. But she had rehearsed her words and knew, ultimately, that her story would command attention:

'Before I start this tale of bad behaviour, you all need to remember that this happened in the early 1980s, before most of you were born, and the teacher involved came from an era when caning children and hurling chalk around the room was the accepted norm.'

For all her nerves, Mary knew, ultimately, that she was a good orator and she was gratified to see that her opening gambit had everyone hanging on her every word.

'We had a teacher at my secondary school who was, quite frankly, mad. He had the eyes of a psychopath and this shock of white hair that seemed to travel vertically from his head, as if trying to get away. He was our woodwork teacher, and for all his scary appearance, was poor at his job and did not command the respect of his pupils. Like most classes, we had the requisite class clown who delighted in riling the unfortunate Mr Jones, especially when egged on by cute 15-year-old girls.

'One day, and I can't actually remember the exact nature of the riling, but Mr Jones suddenly completely lost it. In a moment of sheer rage, he picked up a wooden mallet and − I kid you not − smashed it down on the unfortunate Micky's knee. Well, I won't repeat the language that came out of Micky's mouth as he writhed about in agony, but I do remember him using the "F" word when Mr Jones helpfully offered him some whiskey to ease the pain. But it was what followed next that was especially astounding. As the class watched with a mixture of horror and amusement − you know what teenagers are like − Mr

27

Jones suddenly put his hands to his head and let out an almighty wail. His following words were ones that I'll never forget:

"'Oh, my God, what have I done? There goes another New Year's resolution!'"

Mary had planned to embellish this a little more, perhaps by imitating Mr Jones' likely words to his wife on New Year's Eve, 'Okay, so this year I'm going to quit smoking, lose some weight and stop smashing children over the knee with a mallet.' But the reception that she received upon delivering the punch line was such that she decided, wisely, to let it hang in the air. As she sat down to tremendous applause and genuine belly-laughs from the cohort she resolved, there and then, to take Alice out shopping the following day.

Martin

All in all, Martin felt that the session had gone well. It was definitely a risk letting the students effectively run the session, and having nearly two hours of unregulated material could have gone either way. Yes, he had tried to impose some boundaries by limiting each presentation to two to three minutes and by impressing the need to be engaging, but still, you never quite knew.

There were a few aberrations, of course, although some of these did actually add to the entertainment value, if not the purpose of the exercise. Jamie, for example, decided to 'be' badly behaved during his presentation, which just resulted in a series of awkward silences as everyone tried to fathom what on earth was going on. When he capped his performance by pretending to have some sort of hissy-fit, the atmosphere was one of complete incomprehension, and it needed Matt, his sidekick, to diffuse the situation, albeit at his mate's expense.

'What the bloody hell do you think you're playing at? See me after school for a detention.'

It was interesting, also, that so many of them had chosen to focus on an event from secondary school, despite training as primary teachers. Interesting, perhaps, but not altogether surprising, given how little time they had spent in a primary school before the course had commenced. Martin knew that the next few minutes were crucial in getting the students to start thinking about the nature of poor behaviour and of effective behaviour leadership.

'Well, thanks again to all of you for your presentations. Clearly though, there is no point in such an exercise if we can't learn something from it. Apart from some thoroughly interesting tales, what did we all learn from this? Kathryn?'

Only about two-thirds of the group had given their presentations due to time constraints, and Kathryn was more than happy to have been one of those to miss out. She had, however, listened earnestly throughout and felt that she wanted to contribute:

'It seems to me that nearly all the stories told today involved not only bad behaviour from the children, but bad teaching or poor relationships between the teacher and child. Perhaps what I have learnt most is the importance of developing mutual respect with the children.'

'I agree,' said Anna, much to Kathryn's surprise. 'I always thought that good behaviour management meant that the teacher was strict, and that the children didn't dare to misbehave. I don't think that anymore.'

And so, for the next ten minutes or so, the conversation flowed well, and the students seemed keen to contribute. Some of these contributions were a little simplistic, but that was what Martin would have expected at this stage, and he was genuinely pleased with the level of thought and reflection that was shown.

'Okay, everyone, we need to wrap this up in a few minutes. We've just got time for one more presentation. Donna, I know that you wanted to talk about something completely different, something that happened outside of school. We'd all love to hear your story.'

But it was only when 30 expectant faces turned towards her that Donna froze. She couldn't do it. She'd speak to Martin in a minute, but she couldn't talk to everyone else.

'I'm sorry, I just − I mean I don't think I can − it's just a bit − you know.'

And for the first time, Mary was impressed by how quickly Martin handled a potentially excruciating moment, this time for Donna, by quickly letting her know that it was okay − there was never any compulsion to speak, and ending the session a few minutes early.

Surgery

'Thanks for seeing me, Martin. It's taken me quite a bit of time to pluck up the courage to talk to you.'

'Hmm. I rather figured that you were feeling a bit anxious, Donna. Take your time.'

'Anxious. That's one way of putting it. Bloody terrified, that's another. It all happened a few years ago when I was 17. I was at a party with my boyfriend − just a normal party where everyone was drinking and having fun. And then the music started, and people began to dance and as the songs became livelier, so did the mood and − well, it really was an accident. My boyfriend was dancing and mucking about and this big guy ended up getting pushed and falling over. It was no big thing but − what with the drink and that, he started to turn nasty and tried to pick a fight with my boyfriend. Dominic − my boyfriend −

apologised and kept saying that it was an accident, but this other guy was having none of it and things started to get – you know – sort of ugly. Dom's not a fighter and this guy would have really hurt him, and everyone tried to calm things down, but the more they did, the madder this guy got.

'Sorry. This is a bit difficult. You may have noticed that I was looking a bit out of it when Anna was shouting at Callum last week. Well, it sort of brought it all back, as did the presentation on behaviour.

'Anyway, I'm not really sure what came over me, but this guy was right up to Dom's face and I sort of – well stamped down on his foot. I can't believe quite how hurt he obviously was – I mean, I was wearing heels, but even so. He was screaming and the police and ambulance were called, and he was taken to hospital. God knows how it happened, but he completely tore his ligaments and it took him six months to fully recover. His dad is some big-shot lawyer and he pressed charges and I ended up with – with a police caution.'

There was a moment's pause, as Donna paused for breath and then Martin said gently: 'It must have been horrible, but Donna, I need to know, did you disclose this on your DBS form?'

'DBS? Is that the criminal conviction one?'

'Yes. It stands for Disclosure Barring Checks. You filled it out on interview day.'

'I know. I remember. And at the time I thought maybe it wasn't important, as the conviction was spent and then the lady giving the talk said it was vital that we disclosed everything, but I'd already handed it in and there wasn't really another opportunity, and then I'd had my interview and it was time to go home. I know I should have emailed later, but I kind of hoped it would go away. You see, I'm just so ashamed even though I didn't mean it.'

And that was as much as Donna could muster, as months of worry and secrets finally caught up with her, and she started crying uncontrollably. Martin felt a wave of sympathy for her, but he knew that this was potentially serious.

'Listen, Donna. You've done the right thing in coming to speak to me, but I can't promise that things will be okay. Best bet is for us to be pro-active and come clean now, before the DBS forms are returned. I'll talk to the Dean and perhaps we can both talk to the Dean of Students. We'll give this our best shot, Donna, I promise.'

Chapter 4

Martin

'So, everyone, let me remind you about your school placements this year. You will have three "school experiences" over the course of the year. The first one, as you know, is next week and will last for just three weeks. It is not assessed, so you don't need to worry about passing or failing. It is purely for you to get a feel of being in a primary school setting, of observing good teaching, of having a little experience of engaging directly with children, such as by reading a class story, and of learning what it means to be a professional and to act professionally.'

To act professionally.

Martin was not quite sure whether he dreaded the inevitable or genuinely looked forward to it. He would oversee his Surgery Set, and he knew, with an uncanny sense of certainty, that despite all the advice and warnings, a lack of professionalism, in one form or the other, would rear its ugly head in the next three weeks and he would have to pick up the pieces. In all the years he had been here, there were always pieces to pick up, awkward phone calls to be made, and incidents to smooth over. But there was a part of him that couldn't help being vaguely amused by the sheer stupidity of the young student who just hadn't quite got it yet, and Richard and he would delight in exaggerated, jaw-dropping tales of professionalism at its worst over a beer in a few weeks' time.

Last year's clear winner was the irrepressible Marco, who, less than half a day into his first ever placement, had observed his teacher − a stalwart of the profession for two decades − and offered a three-point plan for improvement:

'First, the good points,' began Marco, without any trace of irony. 'You clearly have a nice relationship with your class and your lesson was well planned.' He then proceeded to advise the unfortunate Mrs Roe that stories were better told than read, that a greater range of facial expressions and voices would add layers of nuance, and that her interpretation of character had been flawed.

Whilst this was both horrendous and hilarious in equal measure, it was also a salutary lesson in learning from mistakes. By rights, Mrs Roe should have let the bouncers loose on him and had him hurled off the premises forever. But she was not a stalwart of the profession for nothing, and she recognised the sentiment behind Marco's appalling lack of tact. Indeed, she made a point of harnessing this, and now, a year on, Marco was thriving at the start of his second year and was the very soul of discretion.

So, Martin spent most of the next hour talking about dos and don'ts, about dress code, timekeeping, and such like, before wishing them all well in school.

'When we get back in a few weeks' time, we'll use Surgery to give you an opportunity to reflect honestly about how professional you have been. Remember, as you will be in a class with another member of your Surgery Set, learn together. Be honest with each other so that any mistakes are kept to a bare minimum. We will all look forward to hearing these reflections. Good luck.'

Callum

So, he was to be on placement with Anna. He had been taken aback a little to be placed with her. When told that they would be paired up with someone in their Surgery Set, he naturally assumed that he would be with Gabriel, as Martin had already spoken to the 14 lads and discussed ways in which they could all support each other in a female-dominated environment. Callum spent several moments thinking about this pairing and decided, eventually, that this wasn't such a bad thing. Of course, the incident at the programme social had hardly helped to foster a love-in, but when she had eventually calmed down, Anna had talked pleasantly enough with him and they even shared a grim smile when ruminating about the next few weeks. Indeed, it was she who had confided that she saw the process as being both scary and exciting in equal measure, a comment aired as if sharing some sort of personal vulnerability. Give her three weeks and sharing personal vulnerability may well upgrade to definite flirting. He really needed to stop looking in the mirror.

But her words had struck a resonance with him, not least because they were going to be in a Year 5 class. He definitely saw himself as someone who would eventually veer towards teaching older children, but the downside of this was that his dyslexia would be more likely to be noticed by the children, by their mentor and, of course, by Anna. How would she react when he misspelt obvious words or when he struggled to read out loud to them? Of course, there was to be no direct teaching on this placement, but if a child put up their hand for help, he would naturally need to step in.

They had all listened attentively when Gabriel had spoken to everyone about Donna's secret, shortly after their presentations, and he had felt a sense of real empathy with her. For whilst he had been officially diagnosed for both dyslexia and dyscalculia, and despite being strongly advised, from the onset, to disclose any disabilities or disorders, he had not as yet done so. Of course, Donna's situation was totally different to his own, yet there were also obvious parallels. At least now, as far as Donna was concerned, things were out in the open.

And then there was the whole professionalism bit which Martin had spoken about so forcefully during their preparation lecture. He knew that he would have to physically rehearse the professional smile, so that, when introduced to both the 60-year-old spinster and the busty blonde NQT, they would both receive a similar greeting…

He looked at his watch. Midnight. He knew he had to get up in six hours, yet sleep seemed like a distant luxury. At least he was to have a male mentor, and he fervently hoped that when he met this guy in the morning, he would see someone ready to support, rather than someone ready to judge.

Adrian

It was Rachel who had finally urged him to take the plunge and to move schools. He had spent four years at Green Acre Primary School, all of them in Year 6, and year by year, this comfort zone of familiarity had seemed harder and harder to come out of. Rachel had done the right thing: she had left after three years at Green Acre to become an Early Years Coordinator, and was now, just five years into her profession, an assistant head teacher. Whilst he was very proud of his fiancée, there was a definite sense of inadequacy that had seeped in over the last six months, and it was this, ultimately, that had made him change schools. He knew, subconsciously, that he rather expected to automatically climb up the ladder simply because he was a bloke. After all, male teachers always ended up as head teachers, didn't they? When Rachel, in her usual diplomatic fashion, pointed out that maybe there needed to be a proactive approach on his part, a sort of 'meet me halfway here', he reflected, with some honesty, that he had been coasting a little for rather too long.

So here he was, just a month into a new post and a new year group, with all the disorientation that this brings, being a mentor for the first time. When he had first met Anna and Callum on the Monday morning, he had felt a definite sense of unease. Here, for the first time really, were two adults looking at him as an authority, as the professional, as someone who knew totally what they were doing. Added to this, Callum was a couple of years older than he, which was disconcerting in itself, as was the fact that his mentee was both taller and better looking. When Rosie, a sullen child if ever there was one, had fluttered her eyelids at Callum at 9:02 on that first Monday morning, Adrian had felt genuinely pissed off. And then there was Anna. From the onset, he had been slightly wary of her. Again, both tall and good-looking, she had steely eyes,

33

which would have made a braver man wilt. What if he had to tell her off for inappropriate behaviour or for swearing in front of a child? He was quite ashamed to say that he thought he would find this really rather hard. But as the first week had worn on, she had acted with great professionalism and the sort of self-assurance that was, in all truth, just a little bit annoying.

Adrian knew that, as first year students, they had been actively encouraged to take notes when he was teaching, and whenever he had glanced over at them, they both had a serious and worthy expression on their face as they jotted things down, although this, in itself, was disconcerting. Many times during that first week, he found himself thinking about what he would write if he were in their shoes. He had always delighted in writing what he really felt rather than what was socially acceptable − his diary in his first year of teaching was testament to that − and he pictured, in one of his less confident moments, Anna doing something similar in the privacy of her own home.

But of course, such ruminations did not really reflect how he felt. He knew that he was a good teacher and it was only Anna's overconfidence that had occasionally brought his own insecurities to the surface. But now, sitting at home, drinking wine with Rachel at the end of what had definitely been a long first week, he allowed himself a mischievous grin as he thought back to Callum's 'Friday Special', as Anna had delighted in calling it. Adrian had suggested to them both that, as a way of getting used to speaking in front of the whole class, that they should both spend a few minutes at the end of the week talking about themselves, perhaps about an interest and maybe with a touch of humour added along the way. Anna, of course, had been spot on with tales of her dancing career, and yet again, Adrian felt just a little peeved as she held the audience so skilfully. And then up stepped Callum:

'Okay, so some of you may have guessed that I'm a rugby player − you don't get these muscles from reading books − and I used to play semi-professionally for Wasps. Er, they're a rugby team, by the way. Anyway, after the games, we used to all enjoy letting our hair down, and one day, on my birthday, I'd had a few drinks and this policewoman came up to me, and said she was arresting me, right. But, as I tried to wonder what I had done wrong, I saw some of the lads sniggering, and then she started fiddling with one of her buttons, and I realised that she wasn't a policewoman at all. You see...'

'Well thank you Mr Williams, that's, er, a really interesting story, and maybe, before you leave us, you can show us all some, er, rugby moves. Now, it's nearly lunchtime and I'm sure you're all really −'

'So, what happened then, Mr Williams?' piped up Sammy from the front row. 'Was she a stripper?'

And even then, in that moment of horror, Adrian thought he might be able to get away with it – after all, the lure of fish and chips was just around the corner – but then Anna had let out arguably the loudest snort he had ever heard, resulting in full-blown hilarity, as one very big rugby player suddenly looked very small indeed…

Anna

Anna's friend Tara, now in her second year of teacher training, had told her that this first placement, without the burden of lesson planning, evidence, marking, and the like, was the one to really enjoy, before it all got a little serious. And, as she looked back now over the three weeks, she was satisfied that she had done well, and hence she genuinely had enjoyed her first experience in school, especially after such a beginning. One thing that she had not felt very prepared for was that initial arrival on that first day. She had used the phrase 'scary but exciting', although, when she'd arrived at the school gates on her own at 8:30 on that first Monday morning, 'absolutely petrified' would have been a more accurate description of how she had felt. Even though the placement wasn't to be assessed, the sheer magnitude of being responsible for other people's children really hit her. And when she had witnessed a full-blown shouting match between two parents in the playground, this simply heightened her anxiety. Real people and real shouting. What if they were to direct this at her if she mismanaged a child?

But these concerns had not really emerged, and she was especially proud at the way that she had handled herself, given all that Martin had said, which made the nightmare on her very last day all that more annoying, as well as being embarrassing in the extreme.

Anna had asked if she could introduce a lesson to the whole class, so that she could begin to get a feel of class teaching. Adrian had been more than happy and explained to her that the theme of the lesson was exploring young children's books from different cultures and trying to infer as much as they could from the language, dress, clothing, etc. He had collected a range of picture books for the children to explore in pairs, and Anna's job was to explain what they were going to do, look through a few of the books with the children, and model the process of inference. She had genuinely looked forward to this and had spent some time the previous day examining a few of the texts.

'Okay, Year 5,' she said. 'Now I've given you an idea of the task, let's look at a few between us. This first one is called *Handa's Surprise* by Eileen Brown – you may have heard of it.'

Again, Adrian could only be impressed by the way that she skilfully elicited inference from the children, and she proceeded to do the same with *Arctic Wonders* and *The Well of Dreams*.

'One more then,' continued Anna, now really warming to her theme. 'This one is by Larry Ojolo Bulahao, and it's called *Ulani and the Giant Crap*.'

There was a moment, a moment of less than half a second when everyone in the room digested what had been said, cross-referenced it with the wording on the front of the book, and then with glorious realisation, allowed their faces to curl into smiles, before bursting into a collective howl of laughter. It was too much for Anna. An experienced teacher would have laughed it off, smoothly corrected herself, let the children have a few seconds to enjoy the moment, and then moved on. But Anna, not unreasonably, froze, and as tears started to well and the moment expanded into a pastiche of horror, Adrian quickly stepped in.

'Of course, Miss Mills means *Ulani and the giant CARP*, and this is a particularly fascinating tale from the Philippines about a magic carp and the importance of family values...'

Looking back at the incident now with a rueful smile on her face, she was, of course, incredibly grateful to Mr Gray for stepping in and saving her, but now that she really focused on the scene for the first time, she was certain that the level of hilarity on the faces of the children had been echoed, albeit for a mere moment, on the faces of both Adrian and Callum.

Well, let them have their little victories. She knew, as Adrian had told them both, that this was his first time as a mentor, and this had shown over the three weeks. She was good at reading faces, she knew that he had been just a little bit threatened by her and she could picture him, at that very moment, embellishing the story with gusto at the pub, whilst using the phrase, 'That will knock her down a peg or two.'

And then there was Callum. He had undoubtedly struggled over the last three weeks. Whether it was telling inappropriate stories or clearly flirting with young teachers, he definitely had a lot to learn. But it was more than that. There was something, and she couldn't quite put her finger on what, that he was hiding. Something that went beyond the sort of inappropriateness that was easily learnt from. For on three occasions, she had bailed him out. She had taken over when he was clearly struggling with a child's reading comprehension, she had volunteered to read to the class for a second time when clearly it should have been Callum's go, and she had moved in front of him and walked to the whiteboard when Adrian had asked for one of them to jot down the children's ideas during a discussion. He was scared of something, and Anna resolved to find out what it was.

Gabriel

All Gabriel could do was wait. Martin and the Dean of Students had agreed to meet Donna before Surgery to tell her the outcome of the student misconduct investigation, with the view that she could just quietly disappear if the news was not good. Gabriel was a mix of emotions. Their three weeks together in a particularly challenging Year 3 class had really cemented what was already becoming a firm friendship, and he was incredibly grateful to her for her continued support, when he had clearly struggled with establishing himself as an authority figure, whilst Donna had taken to the role with grace and ease. Which made all of this seem so unfair. Yes, she had made a mistake – twice – and yes, he was aware that university protocol needed to be followed, but he also knew, beyond any doubt, that Donna would make a wonderful teacher.

And she was also his friend. Whilst, of course, nobody would factor their friendship into any decision-making, the next few minutes mattered nearly as much to him as they did to her. In truth, he might have given up, when, at the end of the second week of placement, a young boy, who had suffered the most horrendous of childhoods, spat at him and called him a 'useless fucker'. Gabriel didn't think that he had particularly had the most sheltered of lives, but this personal attack, both physical and mental, had shocked him to the core. Of course, their mentor had done all of the right things, and the boy involved had been reprimanded accordingly, but if it hadn't have been for Donna and her insistence that he should rise above this and prove to everyone just how talented he undoubtedly was, well, he didn't honestly think that he would still be here.

And so, he sat and waited until eventually Martin's door opened. Donna emerged, burst into tears, and ran straight into his arms.

'It's okay,' she managed to say between sobs. 'I've had a grilling, and they made it very clear that the situation had been touch and go, but I think Martin probably managed to sway it. He had obviously seen something in me, and he has spoken to our mentor at school who must have said good things and – anyway – they managed to persuade the powers that be to let common sense prevail. It's over, Gabriel. Thank God, it's over.'

Surgery

'Thank you, Callum,' said Martin, after they had all listened to first Anna's and then Callum's exploits over the last three weeks. 'You have just got to give me permission to use that story next year when talking to the new cohort. I simply can't think how I neglected to warn you all not to tell tales of strippers to nine-year-olds.'

It was all good-natured enough, and Callum, to his credit, had been incredibly self-deprecating when relating his tale, but Anna was a little bit put out by the way that Martin seemed to equate her *faux pas* with Callum's story, using the old 'learning from our mistakes' yarn for both. And this, for her, seemed remarkably unfair. Hers was a slip of the tongue, nothing more and nothing less, whilst Callum's was misjudgement of the highest magnitude. But never mind. She could see the difference between them, and that was good enough for her.

'Okay, who's next?' continued Martin. 'Donna?'

'So, this should be really embarrassing, but d'you know what, I'm in too good a mood to care. I was in what must have been a deep sleep when someone nudged me firmly. In the second that it took to come to, I looked up expecting to see my boyfriend Dominic telling me to stop snoring, hence I was rather surprised to see Gabriel's face. It was only when I looked around that I saw the group of children I had been working with all giggling. I'm quite certain I've never done that before, but as I'm sure you can appreciate, I've had rather a lot on my mind recently and have barely slept.'

'Oh yes,' piped up Gabriel cheerfully. 'And you *were* snoring. Loudly.'

And so Gabriel and Donna shared some stories about professionalism, such as when Gabriel made the terrible mistake of using the scary Year 6 teacher's mug without permission, or when a child compared Gabriel's whiteboard writing to a baby's, until finally their tales had been told.

'So, what about you two, then?' said Martin, looking at Mary and Kathryn. 'How did you get on in your Reception class?'

There were at least three seconds of silence at this point, which was enough to tell the other students that everything had not been perfect, but all of them were a little surprised by what happened next.

'It was – difficult,' said Mary, at last. 'I always thought that I might struggle learning from both a teacher and teaching assistant who were half my age, and so it proved. I suppose that I can't really help myself. I know that I was a guest in the school, that I was there to learn and everything, but if I'm honest, I'm so used to managing people and being in charge and – well – I kind of made it clear that I would probably have done things a little – differently.'

Yet again, Kathryn was keeping quiet in a Surgery Set meeting, but this time for very different reasons. Before placement, her quiet demeanour was down to her simply being overwhelmed by everything, as well as her natural shyness and wariness of Anna. But this time, she was quiet, due to a combination of modesty – she really had thrived in the Early Years environment – and awkwardness. Because she knew, better than anyone else, that Mary's words really didn't tell the whole story. For Mary had been very difficult, indeed.

Their mentor was very nice − perhaps too nice − but Mary was constantly chipping in with ideas that, if truth be told, were more akin to criticism than anything else. And as for the incident with the poster, well, Kathryn's perception of Mary had changed in an instant, perhaps irrevocably. The poor teaching assistant, not trained as a teacher but hard-working and good with the children, had addressed her as 'Mary' instead of Mrs Peterson, and the look she received in return spoke volumes indeed. And then there were the tears. Kathryn was genuinely taken aback when she first saw Mary, after something that had clearly upset her, sobbing gently in the stock cupboard. Kathryn was proud of herself for her role in the supporting the elder lady − she even created the term 'crying closet' for her, a safe haven where Mary could let out her frustrations and inadequacies. But the simple truth was, that unless Mary somehow shaped up and learnt that, ultimately, she was the student, the learner, the inexperienced one, it would be she and not Kathryn who would struggle to survive the process.

Chapter 5

Grace

'So welcome to the English module, everyone. It's lovely to meet you all at last. As I'm sure Martin has explained to you, between now and Christmas you will be studying for English, Maths and Science modules concurrently, and I will be working with your seminar group as we begin to consider the importance of an excellent grasp of English for any primary school teacher.'

Grace had now worked at the university for ten years and she always felt that the students responded well to her teaching. Both passionate and extremely knowledgeable, she managed to inspire without ever losing a professional boundary with them, which she had always considered so important. Both attractive and well-dressed, she was a former deputy head who did not want to lose the immediacy of working in a classroom by becoming a head teacher. Grace had reached a point a decade before, when, still only 35, she had begun to wonder where her career would take her. Her own children were growing up, and there didn't seem to be too many obvious directions to move forward, given her desire always to remain at the chalk-face. But she had then mentored a final year student, Robert, who had told her, at the end of the placement, just how inspirational she had been, and that he had completely transformed his own core values about effective teaching and learning because of her support. And when Robert had added that she should apply to the post of English lecturer that was being advertised at the university, it did not take her long to come to the view that this, for her, was the way forward. She had never looked back since and had always been very comfortable in her approach.

But now, for the first time, she wondered. When Richard had joined the team a year ago, she saw him for what he undoubtedly was: a bit of an upstart who had no issue with, in her view, crossing the professional barrier with his students by being overly familiar with them. This influence had definitely rubbed off on Martin, and she, like most of the academics at the School of Education, had politely declined the invitation to attend the programme social at the beginning of term. Meeting with tea and cakes in the afternoon, as they had always done before – absolutely. But mixing for a whole evening in their first week and sharing alcohol? That had seemed too much.

And yet. She had happened to walk past when Richard and his Surgery Set were sharing anecdotes about their first placement and she had seen a natural and easy atmosphere, laughter, good-natured jibes, and a skilful lecturer generating a depth of reflection that was, frankly, highly impressive. Perhaps, even after ten years of successful lecturing, she needed to keep more of an open mind and maybe even take a few more risks.

'We are going to begin this module by considering one of the most important aspects of English, effective communication. As some of you may know, I am the admissions tutor here − I would have led the interview day for many of you − and hence I receive many emails from potential applicants. What I'm about to show you is genuine − I honestly haven't doctored it in any way, shape or form, apart from changing the name. After you have read it, have a think about where you think I'm going with this.'

Email from Carl:

Hi! i was wondering if you could send me some details of how to be a teacher and stuff. The thing is, right, that lots of people tell me that Im really good with chilrden and only last week I was helping to look after my girlfriends nieces and there Mum said that I was brilliant with them so I thought maybe that this is something that I could do as Im clealy a natural with kids innit.

Thank you
carl

Grace really wasn't sure how this gambit would work − she had nearly deleted the email after her polite reply − but the response, as she studied the sea of faces in front of her, was electric. Some simply enjoyed counting all of the errors, some started to play devil's advocate, one much older lady simply looked horrified and an athletic-looking man in his late 20s seemed to just be very thoughtful… Later, when reflecting on the seminar, she would concede that maybe this slightly riskier approach to lecturing may have more going for it than she had previously thought.

'So, this is what I'd like you to do,' began Grace, as the session came to a close. 'Go out into the real world. Have a look at the way that we communicate with each other. Don't forget that you can focus on any aspect, either written, verbal or non-verbal. You can work either with a partner or on your own, but come back ready to discuss the sort of things that children naturally pick up from their environment and, more importantly, what the implication is for them in the classroom and for you as teachers. You might also want to consider the relationship between communication and professionalism. I had another enquiry from a girl recently whose email address was naughtymisstommy @hotmail.com. The mind boggles.'

Mary

Mary sat with her glass of wine and tried to make sense of everything: tried to rationalise her confusion and why this whole process was so much harder than she had envisaged. When Grace had told them that they could work in pairs for this activity, she saw, as she had expected, Kathryn looked her way, but she knew, for a variety of reasons, that this was a task that she was going to work on by herself. It was now nearly a week since they had completed their placement: a week where she could fully reflect and assess what had happened. And no matter how she tried to spin things in her mind, the overriding emotions that she now felt were a combination of embarrassment and confusion. The more she thought about it, the more she winced. Whilst it was not in her nature to deliberately belittle people, especially those who were trying to help her, she simply couldn't stop herself. Mary had spent the last 20 years managing people and having high expectations that her staff had to adhere to, yet in the last three weeks, she had experienced the sort of sloppiness that she simply couldn't ignore. And then came the infamous poster incident, which really could have got her into trouble, and which, she freely admitted now, was not her finest hour. Mary was in a rather fragile mood anyway and had just spent a meticulous hour creating a detailed and carefully crafted poster that she was going to use as a stimulus the following day. She had planned a sorting activity for the children and the title of the poster read: 'Are these yours?' She was just putting the finishing touches to her work of art when Chloe, her mentor, helpfully picked up an indelible pen and added an apostrophe so that the poster now read: 'Are these your's?'

When Alice and Leo were growing up, Mary had, on many occasions, extolled on her children the importance of taking a moment of time when annoyed or frustrated, to avoid saying something that they may later regret. *Do as I say, not as I do…*

Mary's response to Chloe's addition had made her teacher cry. She tried not to think of the exact words that had come out of her mouth but the phrases, 'What the bloody hell do you think you are doing?' and 'Perhaps you need to read up on the use of possessive pronouns', had refused to leave her short-term memory. Worse, almost, than making her mentor cry was the look on Kathryn's face: a look that would stay with Mary for a long time.

And now, just as she was beginning to reassess things and accept that not everyone was as pedantic as she, Grace seemed to be actively encouraging her

42

to look out for the sort of sloppy communication that she was trying so hard to simply ignore. It was all just a little bit too confusing.

Eventually, knowing that she was always going to focus on her bugbear, poor punctuation, she reasoned that, as long as she wasn't rude or sneering, an enlightening conversation may still be possible...

It didn't take her long to find what she was looking for. The market was experiencing a lull and the marketeer was clearly idling away a few minutes on his phone. Mary took a deep breath, determined to handle this conversation better than she'd handled the 'Postergate' one.

'Er, excuse me.'

''Allo darlin'. What can I get you? Those nectarines are as juicy as my missus.'

'No, em, I don't actually want to buy any fruit. It's just I'm a student at the university, and I'm trying to think about the messages that children are getting when they see poor punctuation.'

'The messages that children what? I'm sorry love, you've completely lost me.'

'It's just that you've written the word "tomato's" down there and of course that's a plural.'

'That's a −? What the hell are you on about?'

'A plural. So, of course, it shouldn't have an apostrophe, and I just wondered if children were to see this, especially after they have been taught correctly in school, well, it might just confuse them.'

'Are you taking the piss?'

'No, no, really. Please don't think that...'

'I'll tell you what I think, shall I, lady? Anyone who can read will now know that this box of tomatoes, with or without a fucking apostrophe, costs a pound. And you know what? The day that one of my customers comes up to me and says that she was all ready to buy this lovely fruit but now can't because there's a punctuation fuckin' error on the sign, well that's the day that I give up. Now, will you let me get on with my bloody job − Oh, and incidentally, that's a rhetorical question so it doesn't need a chuffin' question mark.'

Gabriel

Gabriel was really pleased when Callum had spoken to him at the end of Grace's seminar and suggested that they undertook the task together. He hadn't forgotten Callum's kindness during their first Surgery session, when Anna had twisted the knife. For many reasons, not least because they were in separate

43

schools during placement, they had not really spent much time together, and hence Gabriel thoroughly looked forward to their meeting.

They decided that they would simply wander where there was likely to be lots of people and see where that took them. Callum had even suggested surreptitiously recording conversations and then analysing them later, however morally abhorrent that process clearly was.

And so, they spent an enjoyable Saturday afternoon walking, sitting, and listening. They heard examples of both formal and informal communication, and whilst at the fairground, downright inappropriate communication from young men to adolescent girls. Perhaps their favourite, sounding even better when played back later, was the conversation between a grandfather and his toddler granddaughter, concerning the eating of a biscuit. It spoke volumes about the different emphases that people put on communicating effectively or communicating properly.

Girl: Grandpa, can I have a bicca please?

Grandpa: Do you mean a biscuit?

Girl: Yes please. A bicca.

Grandpa: Do you mean '*may I*'?

Girl: What?

Grandpa: Do you mean, *may* I have a biscuit? Of course, you *can* have a biscuit. You are physically able to eat it.

Girl: A bicca.

These last two words, spoken with sheer exasperation from the young girl, were so funny that Gabriel and Callum replayed them several times. They never actually found out whether the unfortunate infant ever received the biscuit. When they moved on, the girl and her grandfather were still partway through the negotiation phase.

Eventually, they decided to take stock over a Chinese meal, and this, in itself, provided a further avenue to explore, given the amount of grammatical and spelling errors that were prevalent on the menu. Both of them readily acknowledged that this was likely to be due to the fact that it would have been written by someone with English as a second language, and with this caveat accepted, they delighted in finding as many errors as they could, and a further hour was spent in merriment, enjoying each other's company. Indeed, it appeared to Gabriel that Callum seemed to be laughing almost too much, especially when Gabriel suggested that they checked their 'egg-flied rice' carefully. Perhaps he simply found grammatical and punctuation errors particularly funny.

Kathryn

Kathryn had always considered herself an expert in body language. She had never felt comfortable talking in large groups, and much preferred to sit and watch, and this had taught her an array of the subtlest of signs, which she could easily use to conjecture, with a high success rate, differing moods and motivations, as well as interpersonal relationships.

One of Kathryn's favourite pastimes, and one which she had never shared with anyone, was creating stories and scenarios based on her observations of the people around her. If she had just a fleeting glance at a stranger, then this would merely take the form of something as straightforward as a perceived profession and likely family setup. But if she saw people for longer periods of time, then her creativity would soar to what she freely admitted as being obsessive levels. For many years, Kathryn would frequent the same coffee-shop after school and, hidden behind the guise of doing her homework, she would watch people. For a while, she deliberately timed her entrance to coincide with a young couple who always seemed to meet there at 4 o'clock on a Wednesday afternoon. Their lives completely fascinated Kathryn and, each week, she would take mental note of their body language and then go home and daydream about their world. If one of them seemed anxious, excited, or upset, then she would work out why, based on the characters and scenarios that she had created.

Therefore, when Grace had told them that they could focus on any aspect of communication for her English task she knew that, for her, it would be non-verbal communication. Indeed, within a few seconds of the task being given, she noted the tiniest of mouth-movement and stiffening of the body that told her categorically that Mary did not want to work with her on this task.

Which was just as well. It certainly didn't take an expert in non-verbal communication to read the signs of stress, agitation, and self-doubt that had been so evident in Mary's demeanour for the last few weeks, and Kathryn didn't want any awkwardness to come in the way of this task.

It was all too easy. Kathryn wandered around the campus for a while, effortlessly working out the social pecking order amongst groups of students; she watched children and their parents, and noted levels of respect or otherwise, and just for the hell of it, she went into a range of shops to seek out the most uninterested shopkeeper that she could find. One guy, astoundingly, did not even look at her for the whole transaction of buying a magazine. His most gracious effort was to flick his hand vaguely in the direction of the card reader, whilst she scanned for payment. Had she had been naked, his response would surely have been the same.

When back in her room, she reflected that, apart from giving her licence to indulge in one of her hobbies, the whole process was really rather disappointing and predictable. She was just wondering what her steer on this would be in the next seminar, when a group WhatsApp message from Anna arrived.

> Hey guys!
> Just wondered if anyone fancied meeting at the bar tomorrow night
> – say 7:30? – for a catch-up and a chance to share all of our
> findings before the next English session? (Thought about asking
> Martin as well, but decided that was too weird!)
> Anyway – see you all there!
> (We need to get a name for our Surgery Set. The A Team?!)

Now, this was really very interesting indeed, for a number of reasons. If there was one member of the Set who had seemed – up until now – most likely to 'go their own way', and focus on different friendship groups, then it was definitely Anna. Kathryn remembered, all too clearly, the night of the programme social and the snub – no, that was not too harsh a word – that Anna had given the rest of them, as well as her fury towards Callum afterwards; not to mention her nastiness towards Gabriel and the sense of dread that she had managed to inflict on Kathryn herself. Anna would never have sent that email a month ago, not with its matey charm and its simple desire to spend time together. What had changed? In their shared house, whilst they still didn't have much to do with each other, Kathryn certainly now felt less wary of her, for reasons that she couldn't quite fathom.

Suddenly, her mission became clear to her. She would go to the pub tomorrow and use the time to really focus on the body language of her Surgery Set and use this to consider how and why people had changed over the last month. She didn't suppose, for a moment, that she would have the nerve to repeat any of this in the English session the following day, but nevertheless, it gave her a strong sense of purpose.

And so, 24 hours later, Kathryn found herself sipping a Coke and looking carefully at the six people around her. Mary had texted her soon after Anna's message to ask whether she would be attending, and Kathryn sensed, in the tone of the text, that Mary hoped that she wouldn't be going, hence giving her more of a reason to decline as well. And this certainly showed in Mary's uneasy body language – an unease brought about by any number of factors, including embarrassment and a simple lack of desire to spend a Sunday evening with young students, rather than with her family. But Mary was not the only one who looked a little uncomfortable. There was a definite awkwardness in Callum's demeanour, and even Anna, who had initiated the evening, seemed unsure how to behave. And then there was Donna. It was entirely reasonable for her to bring her sister with her to the pub. After all, the evening was rather an impromptu event, and Sonia had come up to stay for a few days and it was not as though the meeting was in any way designed to detract the outsider. But when Donna had introduced Sonia, she had displayed, Kathryn was sure of it, a sense of unease. Sonia, on the other hand, seemed both confident and relaxed. Maybe the night would reveal more…

After sharing pleasantries, they started to discuss the task and what they had learnt from it. All agreed that finding 'technically incorrect' communication was easy, and the conversation then moved on to why they thought that this should be. Gabriel suggested a lack of good education, but Anna was adamant that the main issue here was lack of care.

'That's what we've come to in this country, haven't we?' she said. 'I mean, if people can't be arsed to pick up litter, let alone get a job, why should they bother about good communication?'

There were murmurings of agreement, before Sonia pitched in, rather aggressively in Kathryn's view: 'Actually, that's exactly the point. *Why* should we care? What's in it for us? Do you really think any of my friends give a shit if I say, "We was doing this" instead of "We were doing it"? It just doesn't matter. I mean, the things you lot are going to have to teach children. You can imagine the response that Billy might have when he gets home to see his father, high on heroin as usual, and tells him not to feel too worried about life because he can now explain to him that 'heroin' is a noun and 'injecting' is a verb – or whatever. I mean, really.'

Kathryn could see Mary itching to say something. Her face had coloured slightly, and she could even see her hand contort to the 'pointy finger' position, a gesture that she had used on many occasions during placement. But something stopped her from either pointing or offering comment. She had told Kathryn about the incident in the market and how it had really made her think – perhaps a combination of this and the whole school experience had taken some of the fight out of her.

But there was fight in some of the others in what was now a strange dynamic. There was this rather ballsy girl, unknown to all but her sister, effectively telling them not to bother. There was Mary, desperate to speak but being held back, but for Anna, Callum, and Gabriel, Sonia's comments were fuel to the flames, and it sparked off a furious debate. Callum, in particular, was very vocal, arguing that many people do care, but just find effective communication fundamentally difficult. But Kathryn quickly stopped listening to the arguments and focused more on Donna's non-verbal signals. Yes, she had rather an opinionated sister who was very different to her. Whilst Donna was elegant, Sonia was anything but, sporting tattoos and ripped jeans. But it was more than that. There was something about Donna's uneasiness that went beyond having a sister who seemed to come from a very different world.

Donna

It was all a bit too much for Donna and eventually she quietly announced that she was going out for a cigarette, but she was cheered when, a few moments later, Gabriel came to join her.

'Something up?'

Donna sighed. 'Oh, you know, family stuff. Sonia's always enjoyed a good argument − she can be a bit much sometimes, that's all. I'm driving down to Bristol to see my parents next week as it's half term and she kind of reminded me a little about family life.'

Since the infamous incident that resulted in her arrest, Donna had always prided herself in not making rash decisions, of thinking through things carefully, and considering the consequences, hence her following question surprised herself: 'Why don't you come with me? Neither of us have lectures on the Thursday and Friday, and since Sonia moved out, there's a spare room. I'll show you the wild side of Bristol.'

Surgery

'I know that this is what you've all been waiting for, your very first assignment. Two thousand words discussing the importance of effective communication and the barriers that we face as teachers in getting children to want to learn. Now, I know Grace has been through the assignment brief with you, but the idea behind this Surgery meeting is both to get you to understand the importance of writing assignments, before discussing any concerns you might have about your first one. You see, you might view essay writing as just a necessary evil to ensure you get your credits, but it's so much more than that. If you really engage in your work, really try to see how the process will help you to become a better teacher, really enjoy the process, then I promise you that...'

Anna switched off. Martin really could be a boring and annoying little man sometimes. Anna had not paid her £9,000 to enjoy writing essays. They'd get done, of course, but she wasn't going to spend nights in the library creating a work of art and deriving pleasure from the experience. No. Her time at university only had two elements of interest for her: being in school and enjoying herself. She was pretty certain that she was going to be as good a teacher as anyone else on her course, and as for enjoying herself... Well, perhaps the jury was out on that one at the moment. For her to really enjoy herself, she had to have real friends, the sort of friends that she had at school, and, as yet, that hadn't happened. She had spent a long time considering whether to send the WhatsApp message, knowing that everyone would question her motives, but she felt, on balance, that it had been a good idea and that the evening had been a success. Martin was still banging on about grade boundaries or some such rubbish, and opposite her, she saw the same expression on Callum's face that she had seen at school when he had been asked to scribe ideas on the whiteboard. That man, she decided, did not like writing...

The last few days had not been easy for Callum, for a number of reasons, and he now felt a very physical depression as he listened to Martin talk about the importance of clear communication in their own writing.

'It would be a bit ironic, would it not, if I was reading your essays about effective communication, only to have to reread sentences because they don't make sense, or are littered with grammatical and spelling errors? Be warned.'

Be warned. Maybe Callum could hide all of this from the outside world. But he could no longer hide it from himself.

Chapter 6

Donna

She was not quite sure what made her ask; a rush of blood maybe or perhaps just a simple desire to spend more time with a friend. Donna had decided, several weeks ago, that she would drive home to Bristol for a few days during half term, as she had fewer lectures that week. Dominic was away with the boys, and she felt some sort of obligation towards her family, without really wanting to go. But it was only later, after Gabriel had readily accepted her offer and she'd really thought it through, had she thought that maybe this was not such a good idea. Donna had made a huge effort over the last few years to distance herself from her working-class background. She couldn't quite say why, but if pushed, she would probably acknowledge a degree of snobbery, and, fundamentally, both her parents and her sister were just very different people to the young lady that she had become. When she had mentioned to her parents that she was applying to university, the response she had was one of indifference.

'If that's what you want, Donna love, it's just that university – well, it's not really us.'

Her father had not added to this lukewarm response from her mother, and his silence spoke volumes.

But the pride of being the first in her family to attend university was tempered, for whatever reason, by a slight wariness of discussing her roots, which is why she hadn't mentioned her family since starting the course. Sonia's appearance at the pub had been slightly awkward for her, not least because of her forthright views, but it had not been the nightmare that she anticipated that it would be.

And now, on the spur of the moment, she had invited Gabriel down to her family home for the best part of three days. She thought about Gabriel, she thought about her father, and she wondered.

Gabriel

Gabriel wasn't quite sure what to make of things. Whilst he was really chuffed at being invited, he wondered whether there was some sort of ulterior motive involved here. Did she fancy him? Surely not. She was three years older and she had a boyfriend already. But what if she did? It would be awkward in the extreme if she were to make a pass at him.

The journey down to Bristol was uneventful enough, although he could sense something in the air; something that she wanted to say or wanted to ask. Eventually, after a particularly long silence, he felt he needed to fill it.

'Are you okay, Donna? You seem a bit quiet.'

'No, honestly, I'm fine. It's just – well, you don't really know anything about my family.'

'Is that an issue? You don't know anything about mine.'

'I don't think so. It's just – well, my family is very down-to-earth. We're very working class, and I'm the first one of us to go to university – that's all.'

'Surely that's just something to be proud of?'

'Yes, and I am proud, and I love my parents. Only, they can be a bit blunt sometimes.'

Gabriel laughed. 'And you think I might be a bit too sensitive for their fishwife language?'

'No, not at all, Gabriel. I'm sure everything will be fine.'

Another silence fell, and whilst it looked like she was glad to have got this out in the open, there was something else, something she hadn't broached yet. Gabriel was sure of it.

Sonia

At best, it was a cruel trick, and at worse, something akin to nastiness. As she waited now for her sister to arrive, Sonia thought that perhaps she should have told Donna that she was going to be here as well. Anticipating the expression on Donna's face when she realised that there wouldn't, after all, be a spare room, had just seemed like a really good idea at the time. That Gabriel bloke had also seemed like a bit of a wimp, so she wasn't going to miss out on that one.

Donna was always the clever one and Sonia had lived in her shadow all of her life, and when she told her that she had been accepted on to a degree course at university, Sonia's immediate response, without thinking, was, 'Letting the side down there, aren't we sis?'

Not that Sonia had ever had any slight inclination for further education. Working as a semi-skilled administrator in an office had its drawbacks, but it also meant that from five every evening, she didn't have to think about work at all, and that meant a lot.

But sitting here now, with Donna's arrival imminent, Sonia regretted not at least sending a warning text. She hadn't really considered how this act would make her look to Donna and Gabriel, but she now realised that it probably wouldn't be very good…

'Surprise!'

'Sonia – what the bloody hell are you doing here? I thought you were in London.'

'Oh, well, you know. There wasn't much going on, and I had a few days holiday left before Christmas, so I just thought…'

The words hung in the air as Sonia watched Gabriel scan around the tiny lounge area that would now sleep him for the next two nights, and she realised that she simply didn't have anything else to say. As she felt Donna's eyes burning on her, as she saw Gabriel just standing there and, as awkward seconds of silence filled the room, she asked the only question that came to her, 'Er, so Gabriel's bag. Where shall I…?'

'It can go in my room. Don't worry, Gabriel, I'm happy to sleep in here. When Mum and Dad get in, can you tell them that we've gone down the King's Arms?'

And as Donna flounced past her, and Gabriel followed, looking lost and bewildered, she decided, wisely not to ask her sister if she was also invited to the pub.

Donna

'Welcome to my world, Gabriel. That's just Sonia all over. She's always been the same; she thinks of something that she feels might be vaguely funny, just acts on it, and sod the consequences. That little episode, to be honest, was one of her milder ones. Actually – and this may make me look just a little bit hypocritical – I, er, have kind of acted a little bit impulsively myself.'

As she paused, and as her face contorted somewhat, Gabriel realised that this was going to be the moment that explained the vague misgiving that he had had in the car.

'You see, I know, 'cos you told me, that you are single at the moment, and I thought of my friend who lives nearby and I thought that you two would just get on fantastically, and well, I kind of set you up.'

If the moment in the lounge an hour before was horrible, the next three seconds of silence were completely excruciating. What was that about a vow never to do anything impulsively? Donna wanted to crawl somewhere very dark.

'You set me up? What, a sort of date, set me up? Just how much do you not want to sleep on the couch tonight?'

'Oh God, I'm sorry. Look, I'll text and cancel. It shouldn't be too late.'

'No, Donna, don't do that. It's just a bit of a shock, that's all. What's she like?'

'She?'

In the next few seconds, many things happened. Donna's desire to escape to somewhere dark now upgraded to somewhere dark and on the other side of the world. Gabriel, in a moment of clarity, saw everything; from Donna's casual invite to a male friend when her boyfriend was away, to Sonia's rather devilish look when they first entered the house, and to Donna's slight discomfort when talking about her father being blunt. Maybe blunt was the wrong word; try homophobic. And as they just sat there with expressions that would have given Kathryn a once-in-a-lifetime opportunity to invent the most creative of scenarios, the door of the pub opened and they both turned around to the words: 'Hi Donna! It's so lovely to see you.'

The moment simply couldn't get any worse. There was no time for explanations or apologies. Donna realised instantly that unless she could very quickly pull herself together, then there would be three of them wanting to die, as opposed to just the two of them.

'Danny, hi!' she managed, as she forced herself out of her seat and gave him a hug. 'Danny, meet my good friend from university, Gabriel.'

The glance that Donna stole to Gabriel upon introducing Danny was about as pleading as if she were trying to save her baby from abduction. She needn't have worried. Gabriel was simply too numb to do anything other than respond with a neutral, 'Hi, nice to meet you.'

'And you too, Gabriel. Can I get you both a drink?' This was the sort of thing that was said even when you saw that two virtually untouched drinks sat on the table.

'Yes please,' said Donna, without hesitation. 'Same again, please.'

And as a slightly bemused Danny disappeared to the bar to add two more pints to the ones standing there, Donna simply put her head in her hands. 'Oh, my God, Oh, my God, Oh, my God. Please, God, make there be some cyanide in my drink.'

Gabriel, still a little stunned, managed to muster: 'So, you thought I was…'

'Yes of course I bloody thought you were… I mean do you really think I'd set you up with my gay friend if I thought that you were a raging, red-blooded heterosexual?'

'Hmm, I suppose not, but that does leave an obvious question: why? To my knowledge, I can't actually remember snogging too many blokes whilst in your company.'

Why, indeed. Why, indeed. As Donna tried to answer his very reasonable question, she realised, starkly, that she had just made that assumption. Was it the slightly effeminate looks? Was it James Blunt? Was it a look she was sure that he had given Callum on a few occasions? Was it the fact that he had shown absolutely no interest in any girls since he had been there, even with a 7-1 ratio in his favour? Or was it – and here she derided herself for even thinking as much – the fact that he was training to be a primary school teacher?

In the end, feeling nothing but shame and misery, all she could say was, 'I don't know, Gabriel. I just sort of assumed.'

And then Gabriel did something that made Donna vow to herself, there and then, that this man would be her friend for life; he smiled. And within a few seconds, the smile turned to a grin, and then the grin to a laugh, and finally, the laugh to a guffaw. Whether out of sheer relief or a sudden ability to see the situation for what it undoubtedly was, a misunderstanding of the highest order, Donna just let it out and started laughing so hard that soon both had tears rolling down their faces.

'Honestly, Gabriel, I've heard about men "coming out", on many occasions, but you are definitely the first one to "come in"!'

'Can I just say that, as well as liking James Blunt, I also like Iron Maiden, Eminem, and lots and lots of other very macho bands. What the hell are we going to say to Danny? He clearly thinks he's pulled.'

'Oh, don't worry about him. I never actually said anything to him. I just hoped things would emerge – so to speak. Don't worry about him. I'll sort him out.'

Gabriel breathed a sigh of relief, before adding, 'So everything's okay, then. No harm done.'

'Er, sort of.'

'What do you mean, sort of? Oh my God, you haven't said anything to Sonia, have you?'

'Of course not, what do you take me for?'

'Your dad?

'No!'

'Your mum?'

'Well maybe. Just a little bit.' And as she considered this, with all the implications that it held, Danny returned with three more pints, and started speaking easily about himself and asking Gabriel about his life. It was only when Donna gave a surreptitious shake of her head, the meaning of which Danny gleaned instantly, did his tone change and Gabriel could relax, knowing that he was no longer being chatted-up.

Indeed, it all could have all been a lot worse. Danny was actually just a very nice, funny guy, and soon the three of them were enjoying the moment and enjoying each other's company.

They were well into their third pint when the pub door opened once more, and in walked Sonia, together with her parents. Donna surveyed the situation for a moment, before concluding, beyond reasonable doubt, that her mum had mentioned something to both Sonia and her father. Sonia's awkwardness from earlier had clearly changed to one of glorious anticipation. Her mother's eyes were just a little bit shifty, and her father − what was his look? Disgust or just disapproval? So once again, she found herself making introductions that she wished that she didn't have to make. And when she spoke the words, '…and this is my father, Mark; this is Gabriel,' all she could do was wait.

Maybe it was the beer. Maybe it was the whole surreal evening or maybe it was just the fact that Mark looked… well, normal – small, even – that made Gabriel look him in the eye, and say, 'It's very nice to meet you, Mark. My name is Gabriel, and I'm as straight as they come. Now, if you're going to the bar, I'll have a pint of the strongest ale they sell.'

Of all the expressions of incredulity that watched, as Mark meekly walked to the bar, it was perhaps Sonia's that was the most interesting; somewhere between disbelief, astonishment and, it had to be said, slight disappointment.

The stunned silence was only broken by Danny, who, delighting in the parody, shouted out as loudly as possible to Mark, 'And I'll have a snowball, please!'

Gabriel

Gabriel lay down on the couch − he had insisted − and thought back over the evening. Even though the room was spinning just a little, he was still lucid enough to feel a sense of pride, of happiness, and of a massive weight having been lifted from his shoulders. There weren't too many times in his life that he could remember a group of people, especially ones so different to him, who had looked upon him with such unbridled respect. Donna had said to him afterwards that nobody ever spoke to her father with the sort of authority that somehow managed to emit from his mouth, which most likely explained not only his actions, but the looks of astonishment from both his wife and daughters.

All of this, together with the drink, probably explained why he had decided to open up so freely to Donna when they had returned from the pub, whilst sipping a much-needed nip of something very strong. Telling someone, as an adult, that you are still a virgin is a very difficult thing to do.

'The thing is,' Gabriel had said in the intimacy of the moment, 'I – well I've never actually – you know. I had a girlfriend last year – Martha – and she meant the world to me. She said on many occasions that she wanted to wait, wanted to be sure that it was absolutely right and everything, and well, I'm just a very nice guy and I waited. And I waited. I waited for 18 months, all of the time feeling more and more sure that she was the one for me. And then, out of the blue, she told me about Dave from work and that was the end of that. You know the old saying, "First cut is the deepest"? Well for me, that cut was very deep indeed, and now that it has healed a little, I'm just a bit scared about potentially opening it up again. That's probably why you haven't seen me look at any girls since I've been here. I've got you, Donna, and that's enough for me for now.'

And Donna had come and given him the biggest of hugs, and as the room had spun more and more, gradually taking him from his conscious state, his last thought, before deep sleep enveloped him, was that everything was okay.

Sonia

It was not often that Sonia changed her mind about someone. She had always considered herself an excellent judge of character, and she was rarely proved wrong. Gabriel had seemed a bit pathetic at the pub with all of Donna's friends, and her views were only confirmed when he and Donna had arrived at their house. But what she had seen since had completely changed her view of him. By rights, he should have shown nothing but animosity towards her; she had hardly endeared herself to him in their first meeting, she had deliberately set out to embarrass him when they had arrived, and she had clearly delighted in seeing how he would cope with her rather aggressive father.

But in all this time, Gabriel had not once shown any disdain towards her; he had bought her a drink and had simply seemed both humble and grateful at being invited into her family home. In addition, he had shown the depth of quality to stand up to her father, and the two of them had even sat down on the sofa together, beers in hands, discussing the Sunday afternoon football. Neither of them had seemed to notice Sonia, Donna and their mother disappearing out of the house shortly before half-time.

Donna's final words as they had left the house, advising Gabriel not to let her father drink too many beers, 'because I know how he gets', had also seemed to fall upon deaf ears as the two men discussed the merits of the VAR system.

It was not as though Sonia had felt relegated as, together with her sister and mother, she had traipsed out to the shops, but the small part of her that was a little bit peeved that Gabriel and her father were dominating the one television was most certainly tempered by the grudging respect that she now felt towards her sister's friend.

It was Sonia, who first heard the noise upon their return, some 50 yards from their home.

'What the bloody hell is that? It sounds like it's coming from our house.'

Donna stopped, and a grin formed on her lips as the distinctive sound of James Blunt singing 'You're beautiful', emanated loudly from their small house, accompanied by the less dulcet tones of Gabriel, clearly singing his heart out. Just how much had he had to drink over the last couple of hours? But when the harmonies started, unmistakably from the shrill voice of her hitherto middle-of-the-road, pop-hating father – well, that rather finished all three of them off, and it occurred to both sisters, whilst they were doubled up in hysterics, that it had taken this rather lovely young man to bring them closer than they had been in many years.

Chapter 7

Martin

'So then, Martin, ten weeks in, nearing the end of semester A: what's your verdict? Happy with the way the Year 1s have settled?'

Martin took a sip of his beer and thought about this for a moment.

'You know what, Richard, I think I am. I've had very few emails since they've been back from placement, and they seem to have settled into their new modules. A good gauge for me at this time of year is how many students have already left the programme. There are always a few in the first year who realise, especially after being in school for a few weeks, that teaching simply isn't for them. A decent yardstick for success that I always use is: if we've lost fewer than three by Christmas, then that ain't bad.'

'Sounds reasonable. It's only Connor so far, isn't it? Actually, I was going to ask you about that. Didn't you see him last week for some sort of exit interview? How did that go?'

'Do you know, what, Richard, it just astounds me what some of our students experience and don't tell us. If I hadn't asked Connor specifically to talk to me about why he wanted to leave the course, I would have had no idea.'

Martin sighed before relating Connor's tale:

'Thanks for asking to see me before I leave, Martin. I actually really appreciate it. It also gives me an opportunity to rant. You wanted to know why I'm leaving? Well, I can answer that in three words: Ashwood Manor School. I don't know if you've used them before, but don't use them again. My class were an absolute nightmare. There were so many needy children and a teacher, who, quite frankly, wasn't up to the job. They were never fully under control; there was always, at best, low-level disruption, calling out, arguments, and endless excuses not to get on with their work. If I ever hear the phrase, "He's got my pencil" again, I swear I'll need therapy.

'But that I could deal with. I could even deal with a teacher who couldn't control them. But there were three children in there that, ultimately, were just too much for me. I'll change the names. Let's call our first one Joe − well, he simply didn't want to be in school. And when you get a situation when a child

is desperate to be suspended and a head teacher who, rightly, will not pander to him, well that's an explosive situation indeed. He simply knew that he had licence to do whatever he wanted; so, he'd bite, kick, throw things, run away, etc., all the time knowing that this was furthering his cause. His father, a nice but rather inadequate guy, who was trying to bring up two unruly kids on his own, simply couldn't cope, and Joe was now ruling the roost at home as well. I heard thirdhand that he had even threatened his father with scissors. This boy was seven years old.

'And you know what, Martin, I could have coped with that as well − I had nothing but sympathy for the family − who can really blame a seven-year-old for such actions? I could also have coped with the young boy, who decided, for no apparent reason, to go and fart in the face of nice little Jenny. How would you deal with that, Martin? Somehow the words, "Now come on, William, we know we don't fart in little girls' faces, do we?" didn't seem enough. And I could even have coped with the girl who was just so defiant it was unbelievable and who decided, on her birthday, to bring in her BB gun and threaten other children with it. "But it was her main present," her mother said afterwards. "I thought it would be okay."

'But what I really struggled with was the fact that they put me and Janie in there in the first place and the fact that we − in our first ever school experience − were used mainly as child-minders for these children, especially when there was no TA. If the teacher couldn't cope with them, how the hell did they expect us to? It was clear that she didn't really want us there in the first place, and she made no real effort to help us. So that's why I'm going, Martin; I know I should be able to separate one bad experience from the norm, but I can't. Oh, and watch out for Janie. She's clearly made of stronger stuff than I am, but she must be really, really scarred. Give her a nice class in her next placement.'

There was a long silence before Martin spoke again.

'Of course, I tried to talk him out of it, tried to impress on him just how unusual it is to be placed with a weak teacher and reluctant mentor. I tried to assure him that I would personally oversee his and Janie's other placements this year, but I could see that his mind was made up. It does make you realise, though, doesn't it, mate, just how much we are at the mercy of schools. I mean, all the training we do for both head teachers and mentors, all that we impress upon them the importance of good support, and yet we still hear tales like that.'

'Yes, we do, but they are so rare. I know I've only been here just over a year, but that's the first thing like that I've heard. Our partnership schools are fantastic, from my experience.'

'I agree, Richard, but that doesn't help Connor, does it?'

'So, what do we say if anyone asks why he's gone? Just say that he decided teaching wasn't for him?'

Martin thought for a moment. 'You know, I don't think so. I don't want to sugarcoat things. I want all of our students to know the big wide world for what it is and to build up resilience. Talking of which, I think both of our predictions about who would be the one to struggle in my Surgery Set aren't looking good at the moment. Both Donna and Kathryn seem to have settled well. Perhaps, surprisingly, it's the more mature ones who seem to be the ones to watch.'

'Mary and Callum? Mary's seemed okay in my Maths seminars so far, but I'm far from sure about Callum. He seems very wary of Maths somehow.'

'I think he's wary of a few things. Actually, he's asked to see me this afternoon. Maybe I'll find out more then.'

Callum

Callum simply could not articulate why he felt so nervous upon meeting Martin. He knew he had done nothing wrong and that dyslexia was a common enough trait, even in teachers. Yet, if it were as simple as that, he would have disclosed everything months ago. He would have mentioned this from the onset, as he was advised to do; a Study Needs Agreement would have been set up for him, and support would have been available whilst at school. The logical part of him knew this, but however much he tried to tell himself otherwise, he felt a stigma attached to this: a sense that he was in some way stupid and underserving of being a teacher. Indeed, he had dreamt, on more than one occasion, about being hounded out of the profession in shame.

Martin listened quietly as Callum explained, as best as he could, how he had been diagnosed several years before, and how he had managed to get through life struggling to read fluently, whilst finding the spelling of everyday words difficult. He talked about his fear of writing essays and of lesson planning. When he finished, he braced himself for the inevitable question, 'Why on earth didn't you mention this earlier?' but it didn't come.

Instead, Martin gave a rueful, smile and said: 'Let me tell you a story of a good friend of mine. Like you, she was diagnosed with dyslexia from an early age, and like you – and, incidentally, many, many other people – she kept all of this quiet when she started learning how to teach. Eventually, like you, she came to realise that she needed support and decided to speak to her tutor. The main message that she was given was that this is all about spin, and actually you can use this to your advantage. She read up about other teachers who were dyslexic and quickly realised that the most important thing was to be both open and honest, not only with your school but with the children themselves. So, she created a brilliant relationship with all her classes, where they helped each other, where she planned carefully, and became the most creative of teachers by thinking out of the box − by using methods that worked for her and which she shared with her children. You look at this through that lens, Callum, and suddenly things look considerably rosier. Am I saying that all of this will be easy? Of course not − it will mean that you're probably going to have to work harder than most, at least initially, but you wouldn't be here if you weren't prepared to work hard. This woman's name? Grace Peacock, your English teacher. Have a chat with her, Callum, and go on to some of these forums for teachers like you; share your experiences, and you'll soon realise that you're not on your own. I'll also arrange a meeting with Damian, our study needs representative, and we can then create something that will help you with writing essays, creating presentations and the like.'

The phrase 'a weight off your shoulders' was one of those overused clichés, but as Callum left the meeting with Martin, this phrase could not have been more apt, both in a physical and emotional sense. He was well aware that Anna had bailed him out when they were on placement together, and his immediate mission now was to seek her out, buy her a drink, and for the first time in many years, be open with someone about this burden.

Kathryn

Kathryn had always enjoyed Maths, especially when her teachers made the subject interesting and creative, and when she could actually understand what was going on. She'd started a Maths A Level, and gave up very quickly because, in her eyes, she was just being taught a process to get an answer. She had tried, on several occasions, to ask her A Level teacher to try to explain why certain formulae worked or how advanced trigonometry could actually help her in real life, and she never received a satisfactory answer. Indeed, Mrs Patel's responses echoed the levels of frustration that Kathryn felt. They started pleasantly enough, with the soothing words: 'Honestly Kathryn, knowing the *how* is so much more important than knowing the *why*. You're doing really well. Keep listening carefully to the way I am explaining how to get the correct answer, and I have no doubt that you will do brilliantly in your exams. Now, I really am very busy, so if you wouldn't mind...'

Well, Kathryn did mind, and so, after every lesson, she sought out her beleaguered teacher and asked for explanations. She needn't have bothered, because she knew, from Mrs Patel's transparent body language, that she saw this particular student as, quite frankly, a bit of a nuisance. But so determined and conscientious was Kathryn that she persisted until the inevitable happened and her teacher snapped. When Mrs Patel reflected upon her own words that evening, she no doubt regretted her tone and choice of language, but no one is perfect…

'Oh, for God's sake Kathryn, what now? How many more times must I tell you that you don't need to know, at your age, why our formula for differentiation works. Just get the questions right for me and everyone will be happy.'

And so, she'd given up Maths and her sense of disillusionment in the subject was still apparent when she had started her Maths module with Richard. But this concern didn't last long, and she soon realised that Richard's take on the subject was so very similar to her own. His favourite phrase was, 'We need to encourage mathematical thinkers rather than mathematical doers,' and this resonated so much with her. How much she would love to drag Mrs Patel into the seminar room and get her to listen to Richard as he spoke so passionately about his belief that if we could explain concepts in a way that children could really understand − regardless of their age − then this would not only mean that they were less likely to forget, but also that they could see the point in what they were learning.

'So, this is what I want you to do. We've spent lots of time over the last few sessions talking about how resources or simple pictures can help children to explain why something is going on. You have one week. I want you to prepare a microteaching session for about five minutes on any area of Maths you want − fractions, number, algebra − I don't mind. But I want your audience to have a "lightbulb moment" when you have taught them something relatively simple and used any form of representation to get them to understand what is going on, and crucially, *why*. Have fun!'

This task was intriguing to Kathryn but what was more intriguing to her − and old habits die hard − was the look on the faces of those around her when Richard was explaining what they had to do. Mary looked petrified, Callum looked very thoughtful indeed, and Anna − well, Anna was clearly enjoying having a text conversation with someone on her phone, and seemed to have completely switched off.

Anna

Anna couldn't quite put her finger on what it was about Richard that she really didn't like. After all, he was young, good-looking, had an easy manner, and was clearly passionate about Mathematics. But there was something about smarmy young men that just annoyed her. She'd had too many of them try to chat her up in the past and, perhaps unfairly, she now put him in this bracket.

She was also patently aware that it was not in any way his fault that the Maths seminars fell at 9:00 every Thursday morning, but if the university insisted in timetabling Maths the morning after 'Cheeky Wednesday' at the union bar, they couldn't really expect her to engage. At school she'd read about Pavlov's dogs and the whole association lark, and she was now completely convinced that, upon hearing Richard's voice at any time of any day, a Thursday hangover would instantly form, and she would irrationally blame him entirely for it.

And then, of course, there was the actual Maths itself. Anna had loved being on placement, and the only time that she had got slightly irritated, leaving aside Callum's incompetence, was when children needed explaining something in Maths that was just really bloody obvious. The problem, if it was a problem, was that Anna had always excelled at Maths and could quickly and easily work out most questions directed her way. And now here was Richard, actively encouraging them all to take longer than necessary with calculations, to use copious resources, and even to draw bloody pictures. She was rather glad that he wasn't actually looking at her when he asked them, in his do-goody worthy way, to draw different pictures of 2+3, as her face did not even attempt to hide her contempt. And now he was banging on about them teaching something simple to each other the following week.

2+3=5. Next.

Not that she was especially listening because she had just counted a record fifth mention of the old 'Mathematical thinkers and not doers' line, and she was busily texting Tara this exciting nugget of information. Yet another morning of complete predictability was heading to its natural conclusion when Callum sidled over to her, as the session was finishing, and asked if he could buy her a drink. Her first reaction was that here was yet another smarmy bastard trying it on until she looked at his face. This was not someone trying to chat her up; rather, it was someone who looked like he had something important to say. She thought back to their time together in school and her desire to find out about whatever was holding him back, and immediately accepted his offer.

And so, ten minutes later, she listened as he got it all off his chest for the second time in as many days.

'I don't know if you've ever experienced anything, Anna, which just really holds you back in life. It's just so bloody frustrating and there's not a great deal I can do about it apart from, as Martin suggested, simply accepting and trying to use it as a positive. But the main reason I wanted to buy you a drink was really to say thank you. I know you covered for me in school – I suspect you guessed that there was something up – and I'm just really grateful. Oh, and incidentally, if you thought that I was smirking at your "Ulani and the Giant Crap" line, it was honestly just a wry smile. Not only, by rights, should it have been my turn to read to them, but that's exactly the sort of thing that I would have said.'

'Yeah, right. There may have been a bit of a wry smile, but don't try to kid me that you weren't laughing at me as well. If that had been you saying that, I'd have wet my knickers – as I did, by the way, when you told your delightful story about a stripper. But you know what, Callum, this does all sound a bit shit. Happy to help out again any time, as long as you warn me when I'm about to talk about giant craps to children. Deal?'

Callum laughed. 'Yeah, deal. Thanks. What do you think about the Maths module, by the way?'

'Not a lot at the moment. I'm not very good at touchy-feely-wanky stuff with multi-link cubes or Numicon or whatever it's called. What's wrong with just getting the right answer?'

'D'you know what, Anna? I've always hated Maths. I'm pretty sure it's a symptom of the dyslexia, but I just couldn't follow the "rules" that my Maths teachers gave me and whenever it became too wordy then I just glazed over. But what we've been doing with Richard – I dunno – it just feels like the fog is clearing, if that makes any sense? For the first time ever, I'm seeing Maths as a series of patterns rather than a series of rules, and it's starting to make a bit of sense. What are you doing for the microteaching?'

'God knows. I wasn't really listening, to be honest. I expect I'll think of something, but I can't say that I'm especially looking forward to it.'

Mary

'Jesus wept, Mother. Please don't tell me that you're making another one?'

'Well, the thing is, Alice, I just want to get this right, and well, I've experimented with a few ideas and I just haven't been very happy with them so far, that's all.'

'So, let me get this straight, Mum. Last Thursday you were asked to create a microteaching session for tomorrow and – please correct me if I am wrong – the brief was to create something *simple*, to use one *simple* resource and to teach for about five minutes. Let's do the Maths here, so to speak – and, again, correct me if my memory of the timeline of the last week is in any way awry. You decided to focus on comparing fractions: a good choice. On Thursday night, you created some fraction cards, which you insisted on laminating, even though you don't have access to a laminator. But that wasn't good enough to satisfy the *simple* resource criteria, so on Friday night, you decided to create a fraction wall with carefully created fractions strips, resulting in another expensive trip to the laminating shop. On Saturday and Sunday, you opted to have the weekend off so you could read about 30 books, "just to give a bit of background", before starting to write your essay, which has been timetabled for this weekend. On Monday and Tuesday, you surpassed yourself with the creation of your "fraction board game", which I'm fully expecting you to patent, and tonight – well, God knows what you're doing…'

'Well, this is a series of "odd one out" cards, where the learners have to look at a series of different fractions, and, er, spot the odd one out…'

'Just one more question, Mum, before I leave you to yet another masterpiece. Do you now have shares in the laminating shop…?'

Yet again, Mary simply felt confused. She had listened intently to Richard over the last few weeks and found that she agreed with just about everything that he said. It all seemed to make so much sense, and yet it went against everything that she had ever been taught, and every approach that she had ever used herself. Richard had used the term 'instrumental learning', which he described as learning how to do something, such as memorising a formula to work out the area of a circle, but having no idea as to why this formula worked. As he had described it, she realised that this definition summed up her lifetime approach to Mathematics. From that point, she had vowed to herself to change her ways, to embrace these ideas and to be the sort of Maths teacher that she now wished that she'd had.

But changing almost half a century's worth of habits was not easy, and Mary was becoming more and more frustrated, trying to demonstrate how different fractions compared in size. Explaining to someone, using a lowest common denominator, that $3/4$ is greater than $2/3$ was nice and easy, but explaining it using fraction cards, or strips, or board games or odd one out questions – laminated or not – was proving so much harder than it should have been.

And so, Mary tossed and turned in the middle of the night before the allotted day, and finally decided to risk Alice's wrath one more time by making an early-morning trip to Tesco's.

Mary felt a little sorry for Richard. She was as aware as he that a very large proportion of his seminar group invariably turned up to his session with a hangover, so both of them were surprised and gratified to notice a definite buzz in the air when they all converged at 9:00, carrying an array of different resources that they were going to use for their teaching session. As usual, Martin's Surgery Set opted to work together when asked to get into groups of five or six, and Mary quickly offered to go first. She felt a range of emotions as five faces turned her way, varying from pride to anxiety, but the array of laminated resources had been left at home, and there was no going back now.

'Okay. I've decided to teach you all about comparing fractions, and so I've brought along some – er – pizzas to help me to demonstrate.' There was a moment's silence before Gabriel piped up.

'Pepperoni?'

'Er, I'm not terribly sure. I think there might be some meat on them but…'

'Ignore him, Mary,' said Donna, giving Gabriel a kick. 'We're all ears.'

It was only when Mary actually got out the two identical pizzas, still a little warm from her early-morning cooking and already filling the room with pizza aroma, did she begin to wonder, yet again, whether this was a good idea. Feeling a little self-conscious, she delved into her bag again to produce both a chopping board and a pizza-cutter. As she started cutting, she turned to her rather bewildered audience.

'Okay, so the reasons I've brought pizzas are to make it more engaging for you, and to try to put it in context. My question is, "Which is bigger: 2/3 or 3/4?" However, if I said, "Which piece would you prefer?" then this would make it more real for you.'

'Depends whether you like pizza,' said Gabriel, now clearly heckling. 'And incidentally, that third is much bigger than that one and definitely has my name written on it.'

Mary berated herself for not bringing a protractor as she mumbled something about assuming that the pieces were the same size. She then went on to explain that the idea was to pick up the two-thirds of one pizza and place them on the three quarters of the other so that an easy comparison could be made. Unfortunately, as she tried to pick up the first one it sagged pathetically in her hands before collapsing on the table and depositing various bits of meat and vegetable, together with a few dribbles of goo, all over their working space.

'Oh dear, Gabriel,' laughed Donna. 'We all distinctly heard you say that this was your piece. Enjoy.'

It was all too much for Mary, who plonked the sad-looking remains of the pizza on her chopping board, before saying, 'Well, if you're all just going to take the piss…'

'I'm sorry,' said Donna, 'that really wasn't our intention. I actually think this is a brilliant idea, Mary. Maybe, next time, it might be sensible to let the pizza harden in the fridge first? Come on, let's move on. Who's next?'

They all watched quietly as Callum made a tower of 12 Unifix cubes, using six blue, five white and one red.

'My question is this. If I wanted to make another tower of 12 cubes, but this time have an even amount of blue, white, and red, how many of each would there be?'

They all quickly agreed on four. Callum then repeated the exercise with different sized towers and different amounts of coloured cubes, before asking, simply, 'What do you notice?'

It took a few moments of quiet as everyone digested Callum's question, before Anna, with all her usual charm, said, 'Well, fuck me sideways. You've just shown us how to work out the average. That really is quite clever.'

'And I can easily contextualise it as well,' continued Callum, now really warming to his theme. 'Imagine that each colour represented a person and each cube a pound coin. The first tower shows how much each person raised individually for their allotted charity, but they had agreed to share out their total evenly, so the second tower shows how much each charity received.'

As everyone listened and watched and took everything in, Callum realised, for the first time, that he was absolutely going to make it as a teacher.

Mary sat quietly and thoughtfully as she watched how Callum had neatly explained how averages worked, in a way that made complete sense. She thought about his resource, and the fact that it would have taken him a couple of seconds to pick up a pile of cubes from the tray. She thought about all the effort, the angst, and the expense that she engineered for herself in the last week, and she wondered.

Surgery

'Richard asked me last week how I thought things were going with you all, and I answered, honestly, that I felt that the whole year group, in general, had settled in really well and had taken lots on board. So I thought that it would be an interesting task for you today, now that we are nearing the end of term, to have a bit of time for self-reflection, and then to let all of us know what you have learnt about yourself, how your thinking has changed, and how other people, particularly those in this room, have influenced you.'

Everyone was quiet for a while as they digested Martin's words until Anna spoke:

'I don't mind going first. The most important thing that I have learnt is not to always listen to my sister. I was a bit of a cow for the first couple of weeks, and I'm sorry. I know this is going to sound a bit arrogant, but until yesterday, I don't really think I had learnt a great deal. For the most part, it has just felt like everything has really reinforced what I thought, and I was really happy with what I did on placement. But then Callum showed us all something in his microteaching that actually made me think a bit more about how I'm going to teach Maths, so thank you for that, Callum.'

With such an endorsement ringing in his ears, Callum then proceeded, for the third time, to talk openly about his dyslexia and how both placement and the communication exercise had made him realise that this wasn't just going to go away. He spoke of his meeting with Martin, his upcoming one with Grace, and how Richard had inspired him to look at Maths in a different way. He finished by letting them all know that their obvious endorsement of his teaching the previous day had done more for his self-confidence than anything else since he had been at university.

Donna then talked about the importance of not taking things for granted, and while she referred to a story that she had read to the children, where they didn't understand much of the language, Gabriel was very aware that part of her sentiment was aimed at him. He then reciprocated by talking about his growing resilience and how Donna's friendship and belief in him had drastically improved his ability to recover from being knocked back.

Kathryn hated talking in Surgery meetings, and this was, for her, a task made in hell. When Martin asked her about her development, she noticed, straight away, that although everyone looked at her, there were almost imperceptible glances towards Mary, as they were all too aware that Mary had been the only person that she had got remotely close to. But what could she say? An honest response would be that all she had really learnt from Mary was how not to do things. Eventually, she managed to muster:

'I really enjoyed my time in school, and it's made me absolutely clear that I want to teach in the Early Years. I am a little worried about teaching in Key Stage 1, and some of the work we have looked at in Key Stage 2 just isn't me. I just want to say one more thing. I've never been very good at making a lot of new friends, and I am just so grateful to Mary for helping me to settle over the last couple of months. I would have really struggled without her.'

And so, all faces now turned expectantly towards Mary, who seemed to be struggling for words.

'I think that what I have probably learnt over the last few weeks is that I'm not cut out for teaching. That's quite a hard thing to say, as I've always been successful in my career. Maybe I've just left it too late. I need to take a bit of time to think about this and decide whether I want to remain on the course. You lot have all been great, but I just didn't think that I would find things so damned difficult. Perhaps we can have a chat sometime, Martin.'

The silence for the next few moments was palpable, until finally Martin spoke:

'Of course, Mary. Let me just say one thing now, though publicly. I've been in this game for a while and I have become pretty well attuned to spotting students who are not cut out for teaching. You, on the other hand, most certainly have the potential to be a wonderful teacher. Last week, I tried to dissuade Connor Livingstone from leaving but his mind was made up. I really hope we don't lose another one who should be inspiring our children in a couple of years. Have a chat to your family, Mary, and give me a shout when you want to talk.'

Chapter 8

Martin

'So, let me say this starkly, because I can promise you that at least one out of the 80 of you in this room is going to get this wrong. I know that because it happens every year, so don't let it be you. You have been told clearly that your essays need to be handed in at 12:00 noon this Friday at the latest, and if they are late, then they will be capped at a basic pass. Please don't stab your "Martin Summers" voodoo dolls because of this – I'm just the messenger; it's university protocol and we all have to live with it. I can guarantee, however, that at least one of you will be hurtling up those steps at 11:59, desperate to submit your assignment before the allotted hour. And – again – let me remind you that if, perchance, your computer explodes, or if your bus is cancelled, or if a passing Martian has a sudden desire to read all about effective communication and zaps your work from your hands, and if, as a result of any of these everyday occurrences, your essay is handed in late, then it WILL be capped. So please, please, don't view this as a 12:00 deadline, view it as an 11:00 one, to give you that little leeway.'

Martin always felt a little out of breath and a little sweaty after delivering this well-worn speech. He thought he understood students, and he never missed a chance of some good old-fashioned procrastination himself, but this just seemed like such a blatant schoolboy error and he always thought that if he could say these words with heartfelt passion, then maybe one day the inevitable wouldn't happen.

'But let's talk of happier things. As you know, we have booked out the sports hall on Friday afternoon for the end of term inter-Surgery Set "It's a Knockout" competition, and I'm delighted that all 13 sets have entered a team, although, of course, you'll all be playing for second place, as I can now reveal that the lecturers' all-stars will be the 14th team to make it a nice round number, and we've been in full training for the big match. Just a reminder, there will be six events, ranging from Sumo wrestling to egg-and-spoon racing to the perennial favourite and finale, the three-legged race. You need to pick a team name, a team captain, and agree between you who will represent you in each race. Full bragging rights to the winning team.'

Although he had never admitted it out loud, Martin was disappointed that so few of the academic staff had attended the ill-fated programme social at the beginning of term, so he was both delighted and relieved that enough staff members agreed to make up a team for the end of term event. Enlisting Shelley, the RE teacher, as well as Jo and Maggie, who taught History and Music respectively, was quite easy, and of course, Richard was never going to turn down an offer to show off. But he was especially chuffed and a little surprised that Grace also accepted the offer. Perhaps she was mellowing in her old age.

Mary

All in all, Mary was pleased with her assignment. Yes, it had taken her an inordinate amount of time and she had to endure the good-natured jibes from her daughter, but she felt, for the first time in a while, proud of what she had achieved. Meeting with Martin last week had helped to restore a little of the self-confidence that had been recently draining from her. She had changed her opinion of Martin. She still felt that he tried to be a little too matey with the students, but actually, not only was he wise, but he obviously invested a great deal in his charges and was always willing to chat if it would help. And their chat had helped. He had convinced her not to quit, at least at present. If, by the end of the year, she still felt unsure as to whether this was the right second career for her, well, she could move on at that point with very little lost. In addition, he had sounded genuine when he reiterated that he could see a cracking teacher in her, and while she was far from convinced herself, his comments served to chip away at a few of those doubts. And this resurgence of confidence also manifested itself in other ways. When she had told Alice about the upcoming 'It's a Knockout' competition, her daughter's reaction was exactly as she would have predicted.

'Don't tell me, Mum. You really don't want to go, it's absolutely "not you", but you'll endure it for everyone else. You'll take one for the team. Again.'

Mary's response had actually surprised herself, when she replied, with an element of vehemence, that not only was she looking forward to both the competition and the evening's entertainment that they had arranged afterwards, but that she was absolutely determined to win.

Her Surgery Set had agreed to meet at 12 at the essay hand-in point, and then discuss their tactics over lunch. 11:50 and still no sign of Donna, Gabriel or Callum, and Mary began to feel twitchy for them. She looked at Kathryn, who, as usual, was surveying the faces of the steady flow of students as they submitted their essays, and could no doubt articulate the differing emotions that their bodies portrayed. Anna, on the other hand, looked both nonchalant and

71

unconcerned as she engaged in yet another text message with some distant friend.

'So how long did you two spend on this? I'm rather ashamed to say that I spent many, many hours of my time. Anna? How much did you spend?'

'£49.50. Worth every penny.'

'Er, do you mean that you spent all that money on books? That's impressive.'

'No,' continued Anna, still staring at her phone. 'That's what I paid the guy from the internet.'

Mary and Kathryn looked at each other, still trying to comprehend Anna's words.

'What; you mean you paid someone to write it for you? But that's − that's…'

'Resourceful? I thought so. Essay writing is just so long. Ultimately, we don't need to do it anyway, so it's just a waste of time. I just copied the assignment brief, paid him and done! If you score less than 60%, you get half your money back. Less than 50, and you get a full refund. You can't say fairer than that. Do you want me to send you the link?'

Whatever reply that might have come from either Mary or Kathryn to Anna's rather eloquent speech was curtailed by a breathless Donna and Callum as they joined the others after handing in their work with a clear three minutes' leeway.

'God, that was close,' said Donna. 'How hard would it have been to listen to Martin's advice?' She paused as she looked around the room. 'No Gabriel?

Even Anna stopped focusing on her phone as they spent the next three minutes, texting, phoning, watching, and wondering until, with a certain sense of inevitability, the clock struck 12, still without Gabriel. Mary watched as Martin audibly sighed as he sat ticking names off. Not only was there the inevitable late student, but it was one of his own Surgery Set.

At 12:05, a rather wretched-looking Gabriel trudged through the door and passed it to Martin without a word.

'Don't,' he said eventually, as Donna looked at him with concerned eyes. 'Let's just go get some lunch.'

Donna

Gabriel clearly wasn't talking, and Donna wasn't going to press him, at least not at present. She'd prise it out of him eventually. Actually, she wasn't unduly concerned. At first, she'd thought that something serious had happened − missing an important deadline was so unlike him − but as she studied his face whilst they walked for lunch, it wasn't concern or sadness that she read; rather, embarrassment and − maybe − a *soupçon* of coyness.

Donna was delighted and a little embarrassed herself when she was voted in as team leader for the games. Surely Anna or Callum, clearly more athletic than she, would have been the obvious choices. Indeed, upon seeing Anna's slightly pursed lips at the democratic vote, her first words, wisely spoken, quickly healed any potential divide.

'Well, my first decision as team captain is to go with Anna's excellent team name. Go the A Team! Okay, so who's up for which event?'

Such was everyone's good mood at having the burden of essay writing lifted, together with the upcoming holiday, that the 'It's a Knockout!' competition was an instant success. Good-natured banter and a genuine desire to win made for an entertaining afternoon, and Donna was in her element. Before the penultimate event, the 'A Team' were in second place, when Mary, an assumed weak link, stepped up for the Sumo wrestling. Her first opponent, Jackie, who Donna diplomatically described as being 'big-boned', looked like she was going to rip Mary to pieces and indeed began the bout on the front foot. But Mary was no patsy, and a combination of team spirit, pent-up emotion and a sheer desire for success lifted her and belied her diminutive physique, and Donna screamed in delight when a deft piece of footwork and well-timed shove saw the unfortunate Jackie exit the ring. At the end of the event, which saw the 'A Team' catapulted in to first place, the expression on Mary's face was worth the entrance fee alone.

With only the three-legged race to go, and the dream team of Anna and Callum competing in it, victory seemed certain. Donna had never really considered herself to be especially competitive, but with a win in sight and the prospect of her, as team captain, lifting the trophy at the inaugural games, she was beside herself with excitement.

And then the race began.

As it started, it was obvious that they would struggle to win; a few seconds in, and it was obvious that they would lose; after only thirty seconds, it was obvious that they would lose spectacularly. The problem, squarely, was Callum. He appeared to have absolutely no co-ordination whatsoever, and the more he struggled, the more frustrated Anna became, and the spectacle soon looked more like a tug-of-war battle than a three-legged race. Anna clearly decided that they would have more of a chance if she simply tried to pull him along, rather than try to form some sort of rhythm, which just resulted in them both repeatedly falling over. And the more they struggled, the worse Anna's language became. Their final exchanges, as they eventually collapsed over the line a full thirty seconds after everyone else, pretty well summed up their respective moods.

'You completely useless little shit. Never in all my days have I seen anybody so totally lacking rhythm. Are you in some way deformed?'

'You never gave me a chance. I kept telling you to slow down, but you insisted on going ahead and dragging me along. How the hell was that supposed to work?'

During the whole sorry mess of a race, Donna experienced a range of different emotions. Her initial excitement very quickly turned in to frustration and disappointment, and then a childish anger that other people were ruining what was going to be such a wonderful moment. But gradually, this anger turned in to amusement and finally into hilarity as Anna and Callum performed a show that would have made even the most skilful and experienced circus clowns envious. By the time that they finally collapsed over the line, hurling insults at each other, Donna was doubled up in pain from laughing so loudly and needed every ounce of whatever self-control was left in her to avoid wetting herself. When she could finally speak, she turned to Callum.

'Please tell me that you are the twin dyspraxic brother that Callum, rugby player extraordinaire, has enlisted purely to provide us with unbridled entertainment for a sort of early Christmas present?'

Callum would have been better off at this point simply putting his hands in the air in self-deprecation, but such was his indignation at Anna's outburst and Donna's gentle taunt, that he simply couldn't help himself.

'Excuse me, but I'd like to see you playing flanker for Wasps. Do you know what? After my trial, they told me that I was a natural and that I might even get into the Southeast England regional squad. Never once, and I don't think I've remembered incorrectly, did they ever say the words: "You're good, Callum, and we would like to take you on, assuming, of course, that you pass muster in the three-legged race department". **They are totally different things**!'

Maybe it was the indignation, maybe it was the faces on what was now quite a large crowd, or maybe it was just the little bits of spittle that emerged from Callum's mouth during this rant, but upon its completion, Donna had to excuse herself very quickly as she rushed to find the nearest toilet. Perhaps it was for the best, after all, that someone else would now be lifting the trophy; someone, presumably, without a slight wet patch on their shorts.

Kathryn

When Anna had suggested to Kathryn, the previous week, that they should hold a 'pre' at their house before the end of term party, Kathryn could only nod meekly. There were two main reasons for her inability to respond. First, Anna and she had never really spoken to each other in their shared house, beyond pleasantries and necessities. Whilst she didn't feel the same fear of Anna that she had done initially, she was still wary of her and was still very happy to avoid engaging in conversation. The second reason for her silence was that she had absolutely no idea what Anna was on about and certainly didn't want to sound stupid by having to ask. So eventually, after a couple of excruciating seconds, she had managed to reply with a simple: 'Okay.'

It was only afterwards that she began to both wonder and worry. What the hell was a 'Pree' anyway? A Google search didn't particularly help. All she could find was a dictionary definition saying, 'to take notice of something', which simply added to her confusion. All sorts of worrying scenarios began to prey on her mind until she'd eventually texted Mary, whom she could at least rely on to be discreet. When Mary explained, having first consulted her daughter, that Anna meant a 'pre', not a 'Pree', and that this simply meant a party before the main event began, Kathryn had felt a little reassured, although she had very little doubt that there would be vast quantities of alcohol involved...

'Okay, so my game, my rules, and my vodka, but before we start, a very special and generous measure goes to Callum for making a complete arse of himself this afternoon. Down in one, my son.'

'No worries, Anna,' replied Callum, as he smoothly swallowed the vodka in one go. 'Now, where's that stripper?'

'Ha, ha. Now, for those of you who haven't played "Fizz buzz" before, the game is very simple. We simply count up to 200, taking it in turns. However, when it's your go, if your number is a multiple of three, you say "Fizz" instead of the number; if it's a multiple of five, you say "Buzz", and if it's a multiple of both you say, "Fizz buzz". Any questions?'

'Yes,' replied Callum. 'Are we allowed to draw pictures to help us, or maybe cut out pieces of soggy pizza?'

It was Kathryn's worst nightmare. She simply couldn't do it and knew that she would be sick if she tried. It took all her courage, but she eventually spoke.

'I'm really sorry but I − I can't really drink neat vodka.'

Before Anna could reply, Donna quickly stepped in.

'That's fine, Kathryn. I'm sure the rules of the game allow you to have a glug of your wine instead.'

Although she was immensely grateful for Donna's intervention, she still didn't like the sound of the word 'glug'. Some five minutes later Kathryn was saved by the bell; well, technically the horn as their taxi arrived. Whilst everyone else, including Mary, had simply enjoyed and embraced the game,

Kathryn had been a study in fierce concentration, and had only once been subjected to glugging her wine, on a particularly vicious 'Fizz Buzz' for the number 105.

'Our carriages await,' said Anna. 'Time for some serious hot-fussing.'

'Hot what?' replied Donna. 'What the hell does that mean?'

'It means,' replied Anna, taking her by the arm, 'that we are students, and that we are contractually obliged to have a good time.'

Gabriel

Gabriel wasn't jealous. Absolutely not. After all, there had never been, or never would be, any romantic tie with Donna, and it wasn't as if she was even dancing with another guy. It was totally reasonable that she and Anna had hit it off this evening, had laughed and joked like old friends over dinner, and now had spent the last hour dancing together and mildly flirting with other guys from their course. So, he wasn't jealous. Definitely, definitely not. And then of course there was Lily…

Gabriel hated dancing, mainly because he was so bad at it and always felt self-conscious. On the few occasions in his life that he had been frog-marched on to the dance floor, he had always shuffled awkwardly from one foot to another, with all the rhythm and co-ordination that Callum had demonstrated in the three-legged race. He looked now, wistfully, as Donna graced the floor and Anna held centre stage. Callum was laughing and chatting easily to Jamie and Matt from their seminar group − so, no jealousy there either − and even Mary and Kathryn appeared to be enjoying themselves. Mary seemed to be a completely different person today from the one who had struggled over the last few weeks and was currently in her element as '80s music blared out. Kathryn seemed to be in some sort of trance, as she drifted around the dancefloor with a distant yet contented look in her eyes. Gabriel suspected that she had never drunk quite so much wine in all her life.

With a slight shock, he realised that he was now the only person in the room who was not either dancing or engaged in conversation, so he was mightily relieved when Donna came to join him, leaving Anna doing some dance, bordering on the illegal, with a couple of guys.

'Okay, Gabriel. Now if I wasn't pissed, I would be very subtle here, and I would gradually steer the conversation around to what I wanted to find out. But I am pissed, so sod the subtlety. What the bloody hell was this morning all about?'

'Oh, it was nothing, really. I was just on my computer and sort of − you know − lost track of time.'

'Bollocks.'

'No, really, I was. But there might just have been a girl involved…'

Now Donna really started taking an interest.

'You sly little fox. Tell me all.'

'Well, there's not much to tell, really. I met Lily on Tinder and we've sort of chatted a few times, although nothing more, and then suddenly this morning at about 11 she contacts me again and – well – she was a little flirtier. We chatted for a while and then agreed to go out for a drink next week. It was only when we finished that I realised the time.'

'That's just fantastic, Gabriel. So, come on, then. When do I meet her? What's she like? I take it you've checked on the basics, such as that she likes James Blunt?'

'Don't take the piss. At least when I try to set myself up, I manage to choose the right sex.'

'Fair point. But when you meet her, I insist that you phone me up as soon as you get home – assuming you go home – and give me the full lowdown. You know what, Gabriel? I really hope that – woah… shit!'

'What? What's up, Donna?'

'Over there. Kathryn. There's something wrong with Kathryn.'

Kathryn

Kathryn just stared at her phone as if, just by looking, she could make it go away. She barely even noticed when Donna came and put her arm around her, asked her what was wrong, and gently led her off the dance floor. Eventually, still in some sort of stupor, she passed her phone to Donna and showed her the text from her nan's neighbour.

My dearest Kathryn.

I've tried to phone you a few times but haven't been able to get through – I so hope you get this message. My dear I'm so sorry to have to tell you that your nan has suffered a major stroke and has been rushed to hospital. I'm afraid that it doesn't look very good. Please, please get back to me when you pick this up and I can tell you where she is.

Chapter 9

Kathryn

Despite everything, Kathryn's overall sensation, as she held on to her nan's hand, was one of serenity. She had spent much of the last few weeks involved in presentations, games and even partying, and the contrast between that noisy environment and her current peaceful one was vaguely soothing.

She reflected on the other major trauma of her life, when her mum had died of breast cancer when Kathryn was only nine years old, and her mother not yet 40. Of course, she pictured a grieving little girl watching her mother gradually succumb to her illness, but she also pictured a girl secure in the knowledge that there was still someone to look after her. She had never known her father – he had left when she was a baby, and her mother refused to speak of him, even when she was dying – and her nan had been widowed for years, so the three of them had lived as a family in the small terraced house for as long as Kathryn could remember. So even though she knew that she was losing Mum, there was always going to be Nan there to make everything all right. At least, there had been until now.

The doctor had told her that it was unlikely that her nan would pull through, but she was breathing at the moment, her body was still warm, and this was good enough, at least for now, for Kathryn.

Because life with Nan not breathing was just too much to contemplate. For there was no one else; no family and no close friends. No, a nan that was still breathing was enough.

Mary

'No, Mum, absolutely not. Look, I know that the two of you have sort of bonded in a weird sort of way, but this is asking too much.'

'Alice is right, Mum,' said Leo. 'I mean, I've been away all term. I'm only back for two weeks and I want to spend Christmas with my family.'

'Just think about it for a minute, will you, Mum?' continued Alice. 'Do you really want to inflict our family on her? Just think back to last year. Dad was snoring on the couch, you actually produced a tiny bit of vomit when trying too hard at lifting the cornflake box with your teeth, I was called a potty mouth by my effin' brother, for God's sake, who swears like a proverbial, and then of course, there's the Pogues. Why on earth it's become a tradition for Leo to drunkenly sing along to "Fairytale of New York" I do not know, but I do know that his rendition has put many a sane person in the loony bin. One verse of that, and she'll be pining for the relative peace of the hospital ward, with all the jabbering and smells of incontinent old people that that entails. Oh, yes, and then there's Gramps. Last year he nearly ended up getting into bed with me because he was confused. I mean, really?'

With a sigh, Mary looked at her husband, who simply shrugged. He didn't actually say the words, 'I told you so,' but he may as well have done. When Mary had finally managed to speak to Kathryn, some 24 hours after Donna had put her in a taxi, she had been totally moved by Kathryn's words and manner. For here was a frightened little girl who had effectively lost everyone in her life, and who had seemingly lost the ability to speak beyond basic responses to Mary's questions. And when Mary had asked her what her plans were for Christmas, there'd been a pause before she'd replied, in a very thin voice, 'I don't know, really. I suppose I'll stay at the hospital.'

And so, Mary had suggested to Simon, and then to Alice and Leo, that maybe they should ask Kathryn to stay with them over Christmas and their responses, whilst totally fair, had saddened her somewhat.

'Okay, you two. I can see that you're sitting on the fence here... How about – and no strings attached – I ask Kathryn over for tea tomorrow, assuming there's no change with her nan, and let her stay the night? She's only 20 minutes away. I can easily pick her up. There's still nearly a week until Christmas so we've got plenty of time. If you still feel the same afterwards, then I won't mention it again. How does that sound?'

Alice

Alice watched Kathryn sipping her cup of tea and felt both moved and a little selfish. At 21, she was less than three years older than Kathryn. She had completed her degree in finance the previous year and was now living back at home as she started her career in the bank. When Mary had first mooted the idea about going to university, she had seen herself as the one who would guide her mother through the journey – academically, socially and emotionally – but, she now reflected, she didn't think that she had done a particularly good job. The sort of gentle ribbing that she had dished out to her mother throughout the term was in keeping with their relationship, but probably not what Mary needed. Alice had been shocked when Mary had told her that she was considering leaving the programme, and it had only been at that point that she'd realised that the support that she'd promised had not really materialised, and for that she felt guilty.

And here, sitting next to her, was a young girl who had been dealt a poorer deal than Alice in life, who was close to losing everyone dear to her, and yet had been more supportive of Mary than her own daughter. And how had Alice repaid that kindness to her mother? She had selfishly ranted about how Christmas should be a family affair, whilst giving no thought whatsoever to how Kathryn must be feeling.

Kathryn was a plain girl and Alice rather suspected that she would have suffered at the hands of her peers in the past. Yet, despite her outward appearance, and despite the fact that she looked like a frightened and lost little girl, Alice saw something else in her. When she had asked her why she wanted to teach, she'd expected the standardised 'wanting to make a difference' response.

'I think,' Kathryn had replied, 'that I want to be the sort of teacher that I never really had. I don't want my children just to accept things without being able to explain why. It just really annoyed me when my teachers didn't seem to think this was important.'

Alice saw the same shrewd determination that she had always considered one of her own strengths. Perhaps they had more in common than she had initially thought. She looked over at Leo, who seemed to have a similar demeanour to her own, and she resolved, there and then, to speak to her mum as soon as possible so that the offer of staying with the family over Christmas could be made. There was definitely something about Kathryn, and it may just be that she would add to the festivities, rather than simply being there out of charity.

Kathryn

Of course, she'd been pleased and rather moved when Mary had invited her to stay with her family over Christmas, but she wasn't at all sure that it was what she wanted. When she had gone for tea with the Petersons, she felt a little like a potential exhibit in a museum, whom the curator had ordered for inspection. That she had passed that inspection, whilst gratifying, was also horribly awkward. To say 'no' would have been rude and would also have subjected her to spending Christmas Day in a hospital ward. But saying 'yes' also brought with it all sorts of burdens and worries. Did Mary's family really want her there or were they just being nice? Kathryn sensed during the inspection tea visit that, ultimately, they all just felt sorry for her and were prepared to compromise their family Christmas for this reason. And then there were other worries. Should she get presents, and if so, what on earth would this affluent family want that she could afford? The thought of Leo opening his gift of a cheap bottle of wine and saying, 'That's lovely Kathryn, thank you,' whilst his body language screamed, 'That's disgusting and won't even make it into the stew,' was just too horrible to contemplate.

And then, four days before Christmas, Nan had died. The doctor told Kathryn gently that she slipped peacefully away in her sleep, and suddenly there were no more warm hands to hold. It had taken her an hour to come out of the stupor that had enveloped her before she rang Mary. It occurred to her, whilst Mary and Alice were helping her with funeral arrangements, that, had her nan died six months previously, she would have had no one to turn to; no one to help shoulder the burden and no one she could lean on and cry. She had known Alice for less than a week, but she couldn't think of another person of a similar age, with the possible exception of Donna, who she could cry openly in front of.

So now, sitting here playing cards on Christmas Eve with Alice, Mary and Leo, whilst Simon was out collecting his father, a lot of that awkwardness had gone, and she simply felt an immense gratitude towards Mary's family.

'Gramps!' shouted Leo as the front door shut. 'Who the hell let you out of your home? Don't worry, Kathryn, he'll have forgotten that sentence by now.'

'Dad, let me introduce you to Kathryn, Mary's friend from university. You remember that I mentioned to you on the way down that she was staying with us over Christmas?'

'Kathryn. Kathryn… Yes, I remember. You're the one whose Nan's just kicked the bucket. That's right isn't it?'

Despite everyone in the room knowing about her father-in-law's dementia, Mary simply couldn't help herself: 'Oh, Albert, please.'

Later, when Kathryn and Alice would share a drink together, Kathryn would describe those few seconds as if she had been living in a glass bubble for nine years, which had just shattered.

Kathryn looked around her in the stillness which followed Albert's comment. She saw shock and embarrassment on Mary's face, exasperation on Simon's, stunned stillness on Leo's and – yes, she was sure of it – something akin to amusement on Alice's.

And then the bubble smashed. Her nan had clearly loved her, had brought her up and had tried to do what was best for her granddaughter. But this had produced a young lady without any friends, with little humour and with limited ambition. Kathryn had never really understood the comedy which her nan had loved and which had been bestowed upon her on many a Saturday night when

81

other girls of her age were at parties. She watched Monty Python with a nonplussed and slightly confused air as her nan guffawed at jokes that she had heard many a time before. She had never really got it.

But she got it now. As the bubble exploded a certain gallows humour emerged where it would never have been before, and she found herself replying to the old man: 'Yes, Albert. She kicked the bucket. This… is an ex-grandmother.'

And as the full Dead-Parrot sketch got replayed by Alice, Leo and Kathryn, as Mary and Simon watched on open-mouthed, and as Albert scratched himself absent-mindedly, Kathryn found herself being able to accept her nan's death and being able to look forward to the future, however uncertain that future was.

Mary

As she prepared the beef for the New Year's Eve party, Mary thought back over the previous week with great satisfaction. She had known that inviting Kathryn for Christmas was ultimately the right thing to do, but she had been pleasantly surprised at how well she had been received by the family. To see her daughter and her friend from university bond as well as they had was immensely satisfying, and the laughter had flowed as freely as the wine during the festivities. Even Albert had seemed to brighten up simply from Kathryn's presence, and when he had openly flirted with her after one too many sherries, Mary couldn't suppress a few giggles herself. This was, she now concluded, just what she needed. It was only when she could step back from the unrelenting pressure that she had inflicted upon herself during term time that she could fully appreciate just how important a complete break was for her. She was still far from sure that teaching was for her or whether she could survive the rigours of the three years, but she was pretty convinced now that she would, at the very least, see out the year. Indeed…

Mary was awoken from her reverie by the familiar buzzing of her phone, signifying a WhatsApp conversation taking place. She had initially agreed to join the WhatsApp group as she thought that it was the right thing to do and that it would help with communication. What nobody had told her was that it was primarily used, especially by Anna, Callum and Donna, as a means for inane conversation.

Assuming this would be the case now, and that Callum would somehow think that she would actually want to see a video clip of him downing pints with his rugby mates, Mary, with a degree of reluctance, clicked on the WhatsApp icon. Her interest, however, was suddenly piqued upon seeing the current thread:

Anna Mills

75%!!! Oh, ye of little faith. My mystery internet guy is definitely getting a tip for his work. Roll on the next essay. LOL. How did the rest of you do?

Donna Martindale

You jammy cow! I didn't tell you this at the time but apparently a friend of a friend did what you did and failed with 24%! The comment from the lecturer was: 'if you don't answer the question how can you expect to pass?' Apparently, the idiot hadn't even read the script that he got back and his mystery internet man had, seemingly, picked out some random essay vaguely matching the chosen title from his batch and returned it to him totally unedited. Luckily for you, I got 78% or you would have seriously been dobbed in...

Anna Mills

Shit, nobody told me that I had to actually read it!!!

Callum Williams

Ha ha! Would have seriously served you right. 56% and very happy! Also, a great message from Grace about saying I'd done her proud. Might even have half a shandy tonight to celebrate.

And so it went on. Mary vaguely flicked through the rest of the thread, noticed that Gabriel would have scored a very creditable 82, if it weren't for his capped grade, before deciding, perhaps wisely, to abandon reading halfway through Anna's description of what she was going to wear and what she planned to do at her fancy dress New Year's Eve party that evening.

With everything that had gone on, Mary had completely forgotten that Martin had promised to email his Surgery Set their essay marks before the start of term. With a slight flutter in her stomach, she quickly switched on her laptop to check her emails.

Simon

Simon looked on as his wife opened yet another bottle of wine. Well, it was New Year's Eve after all. He tried to decide whether her getting more drunk than he had ever witnessed was a good or a bad thing. On the one hand, Mary

83

was clearly in need of letting her hair down and of freeing her mind from all of her worries. Yet, he had seen lesser hangovers in his wife than the one that was surely awaiting her in the morning and had witnessed how incredibly downcast they had made her. Simon had always been immensely proud of his wife, and he had only ever viewed her dogged determination to master everything that life threw at her as one of her great strengths. But lately, this strength was also becoming a weakness. Perhaps it was her age; perhaps she subconsciously felt that, because she was twice as old as most of her cohort, she needed to work twice as hard and be twice as good. Anyone else in the world would have been seriously pleased about achieving 72% in their first essay; a grade − indeed − classified officially as 'excellent'. But Mary, being Mary, could not see the 72 bit, but had to focus on the 28 bit. Mary's mind would naturally assume that she had got 28% wrong. He rather pitied the tutor who would be subjected to the inevitable debriefing that Mary would insist upon.

He watched now as she talked with Kathryn and Alice. Alice had spoken to him earlier in the week and confided that she felt that she needed to be more supportive of her mother, but old habits die hard and here she was giving her mother tips about how to cut corners in essays.

'You really don't need to read all of those books, Mum, especially in your first year. The secret is to open the book at a vaguely relevant page, find a vaguely relevant quote and shove it in. Saves you hours, you won't be so stressed due to overworking and you'll then write better. Job done.'

Alice had never had any problems making friends, but since starting a very demanding job in the bank, Simon had become a little concerned about his daughter. She'd barely been out over the last few months and seemed to have accepted − perhaps reasonably enough − that she needed to devote a year of her life to establishing herself in a demanding environment. Hence for her to bond so well with Kathryn over the last week was wonderful to see. He watched Kathryn now as she chatted easily with his family and realised what a humbling experience it had been for all of them having her there. She had told him about the 'bubble-bursting' experience, and whilst he was happy for her that she had actively embraced the last week, he wondered what would happen when she returned to the normality of life, without a surrogate family to cushion the massive blow that had befallen her.

Kathryn

However much she had pushed it to the back of her mind, Kathryn always knew that saying goodbye to the Petersons on New Year's Day was going to be a very difficult thing to do. Her plan had been to go back to her family home for a week, try to sort some things out and then be ready to return to university for a week before the funeral. Indeed, she had found the email that she had written to Martin explaining this quite easy to write. It was only upon receiving his reply, as well as her imminent departure from a noisy and cosy environment, that the full enormity of her situation really started to dawn upon her. She was more determined than ever to make it as a teacher, but she now realised, starkly, that making friends was going to be just as important. The kindness shown to her by Alice over the last week, and from Donna over the last few months, was warming, but she still viewed it as kindness rather than as true friendship. Both Alice and Donna were so different from her that socialising with either in the way that good friends do just seemed very unlikely. And then there were living arrangements. Kathryn gave a wry grin at the fact that she was actively looking forward to going back to university and not living on her own. The irony of this did not escape her. She had already overheard students discussing living in a shared house together in their second year, but nobody had spoken to her about it, and this now also became a source of concern.

Kathryn took a deep breath as she said her goodbyes and thanks to the Peterson family. The hugs she received from both Alice and Mary were clearly genuine, and both Leo and Simon also seemed genuine when they spoke about how much they had enjoyed her staying with them.

'You must come back and stay with us again sometime, Kathryn,' said Simon, 'if only to keep Dad happy. He seems to have taken a shine to you.'

'Thank you. And goodbye, Albert. I'm sure you won't be aware of how you made me see life in such a different way.'

'I'm sorry,' said Albert. 'Who are you again?'

Surgery

Dear Kathryn

Thank you for your email. I am very sorry to hear about your nan. It must be such a huge loss for you. I've heard you speak so fondly of her in the past and she has clearly been a massive influence on your life.

I totally understand your view that you intend to return to university for a week before the funeral, and of course you can do this if you want to. But I would say this: give yourself time to grieve, Kathryn. If you need a couple of weeks to yourself without having to concentrate on the demands of university, that is absolutely fine. You can always come to see me afterwards and I can help you catch up with your new module. I note that you've chosen Geography for your option this term. I can easily chat to

85

Frank, your tutor, and I'm sure he'll be happy to give you some extra support if you decide to stay away for a while.

Keep in touch − I hope everything goes well for you over what will be such a difficult week.

Martin

Chapter 10

Anna

How's it going?

Donna

We're 10 minutes in to our first session – it's not really going yet at all. Text me again in an hour – I might have some sort of update for you.

Anna

Sod that. I'm already bored. At least tell me how Martin looks in his PE gear. Is he wearing shorts? Has he got nice legs?

Donna

Yes, he's wearing shorts but no to the legs! Not really a sight you'd want with a hangover. His shorts are just a little bit short and clingy. Not looking forward to when he – OMG he's now bouncing on the spot. That's horrible! How's your bloke? Frank is it?

Anna

LOL! Yes – Frank. Looks a bit of an arse to me. He must be all of 65. At least he's unlikely to don shorts, a thong or whatever. Never seen any of that sort of dress in any Geography lesson I've been in before.

Donna

Always a first time? What's he like?

Anna

Annoying! You know me – never judgmental, but I can already see that three weeks with this guy is going to piss me off. He's that really worthy sort – you know – the type that likes to tell you how wonderful they are. We've been here ten minutes, and he's already mentioned the word 'sustainability' twice, and one each for 'climate change' and 'carbon footprint'. Callum looks as bored as I am.

Donna

But is he fit?

Anna

Very! Assuming, that is, that you like bald, fat men in their sixties, who have something like scabies at the corner of their bottom lip. Tell you what, as I'm in a good mood, I'll resist him and leave him for you.

Donna

And who said you didn't have a heart of gold?! Okay now Martin's starting to sweat a little and he's just about to get us running round the hall. Talk soon.

Anna

When Martin had told them, shortly before Christmas, that they would be able to choose a foundation subject to focus on for the first three weeks of the new semester, Anna's immediate thought was that she would opt for PE. After all, that was her strength, and whilst all lecturers were slightly annoying, Martin fell on the okay side of things and she was intrigued to see how he would fare at teaching them PE. But then he had banged on about not going for the obvious choice, about coming out of your comfort zone and about increasing your subject knowledge in one of your weaker subjects. Indeed, he had drawn a representation of this 'comfort zone', arguing that outside of this was 'where the magic happens'. In any case, he had argued, they would major on one foundation subject every year so there would be plenty of time to also focus on building on strengths.

There weren't too many times in her life that Anna could reasonably say that she had done the 'sensible' thing, but in a moment of weakness, both she and Callum, as well as Kathryn, had decided to opt for Geography.

'In fairness,' she'd said, 'I don't know one end of a map from the other, so it might not be too bad an idea.'

But a bad idea, quite definitely, it had turned out to be. She knew from the outset that she and Frank weren't going to hit it off for so many reasons. One of these, on day one of three very long weeks, was when he told her, loudly, to put her phone away if she wanted to stay in his class. Now Frank didn't know Anna at that point, but everyone else in the room did, and there was an expectant hush after he'd said those words. A few of the more timid members of the group visibly grimaced at the prospect of Anna's response, and there was a mixture of surprise, relief, and − certainly, in some cases − disappointment when she silently did what was asked. Had Kathryn been in the room at that moment and seen Anna's face however she, for one, would have read Anna's body language for what it was. This was no meek subservience; this was the face of a girl biding her time…

'I genuinely thought you were going to hit him,' said Callum, during a coffee break a few minutes later. 'After all, you attacked me for simply leaning back in my seat at the programme social. This guy gave you a public bollocking.'

'I attacked you for being a knob, if you remember. But you know me, Callum, never one to hold a grudge, even when some baldy virtually shouts at me in front of everyone. I didn't like to say that the only reason that I was texting Donna at the time was to relieve the monotony. Are we gonna survive three weeks of this?'

'We'll find a way, Anna.'

'Too right we will. Fancy a burger?'

Frank was just itching to say something upon their return to the seminar room. Anna could see it in his face. The eating of food, especially hot food, during seminars had always been a bit of a grey area. There were some lecturers who were really strict about it − Grace had politely but firmly asked Jamie and Matt to finish their hot breakfast before joining her English lesson − and there were some who were a little more lenient; perhaps taking the view that on very full days, their only opportunity to grab something to eat was in a 15-minute break. Anna was completely certain that Frank was in the former category, particularly with all the plastic packaging in view. But something held him back. Perhaps he was beginning to get the measure of Anna, perhaps he regretted the rather public shaming and perhaps he simply didn't want a potential stand-off in their first seminar. But he twitched. He twitched when Anna noisily opened the packaging, he twitched when her coffee drinking teetered on the brink of slurping, and he twitched as she slowly and deliberately ate her food, whilst giving the outward impression of listening attentively to every word he said.

Donna

It took her a full half an hour, but eventually she did it. Donna had never even picked up a cricket ball before, let alone attempted to bowl one, and when her first few attempts at bowling started to interest the health and safety inspector, Gabriel had loudly and joyously commented that she certainly bowled like a girl. Such casual misogyny, Donna knew, was designed purely to add to her determination and it certainly had its desired effect. When Donna finally got a decent length and trajectory, her delight was evident. When, a few balls later, that decent trajectory turned out to be an unintentional 'wrongun', which bowled Gabriel all ends up through the gate, her delight was audible several hundred yards away. After appealing unsuccessfully to Martin that it was perhaps a 'no ball', Gabriel did the right thing, smiled broadly, and gave Donna a kiss.

'You're not going to forget this, Donna,' said Martin, as Gabriel hurled down his pads theatrically. 'I want everyone here to remember Donna's reaction when she learnt a new skill and put Gabriel in his place, and I want you to remember it for two reasons. First, part of the reason why you are doing this course is to build up your skillset, so it is easier for you to teach, and now, of course, you can teach the subtle differences between various spin options. But far more importantly than that, you are going to get moments like that with your children. You'll be teaching a child something who is certain they can't succeed, with or without Gabriel's heckling, and eventually, through your teaching, your encouragement and your persistence, they will succeed. And I promise you, when you hear a child's reaction which echoes that of Donna a minute ago, all those long days and all those stresses − well, they'll be worth it.'

'Great. I'm so glad you're having a nice day,' said Anna bitterly over lunch, after hearing Donna relate her morning's exploits. 'I'm so glad that Martin is really inspiring you all, and I'm so glad that I listened to him and chose bloody Geography. Do you want to know what we have done this morning? We've done exactly the same as we've done all week − we've listened to Baldy banging on about the environment. You know Molly in our group? Molly, who has returned early against her doctor's advice after having her appendix out and who is walking around in pain? Well, she now knows, as do we all, that her taking the lift up to our seminar room today was economically inefficient as she was the only person in it. But it's not even about him just transmitting useless facts; it's about little victories. The only way to describe the look on his face when he gave that little speech was smug. I tell you, Donna, one of us isn't going to see these three weeks out…'

Frank

Frank had worked at the School of Education for nearly a quarter of a century, having spent five unsatisfactory years as a primary school teacher prior to that. He had no doubt at all that education had been the wrong career choice for him – he had spent several years after completing his Geography degree in dead-end jobs until someone had suggested a post-graduation in teacher training, which he completed almost for want of something better to do. His five years in a tough inner-city school had been long years indeed. There had always been a shared animosity between himself and the children, so he jumped at the chance to join the university, where his prime focus would be teaching Geography. From here, he could bend the rules a little to preach his passion: the importance of caring for the environment, with all that this entails.

And now, at 62, he wondered how long left he had in him. He could reasonably take his pension at any time now and live relatively comfortably for the rest of his life, especially as he had no dependants or mortgage. Part of him was greatly tempted by this. He knew that neither the Dean nor his colleagues would try to stop him; he had had many an argument about his methods and teaching content, and had managed largely to get away with his approaches. But he really didn't like how the university had become, with its growing mantra of 'student experience is king', and he really didn't like how several of the students were these days. That arrogant girl in Year 1 – Anna somebody – was trying her hardest to wind him up, when all he was doing was trying to teach her and get across his passion for the subject. But of course, student experience is king so she could bring in her array of plastic and deliberately discard it in the wrong bin, she could eat unhealthy food and stink out his lessons, and she could openly text her friends in his sessions, even when he had asked her not to. Twenty years ago, students weren't like this; they used to respect him. But, maybe it was the increased fees and hence a sense of entitlement, maybe it was a societal change in attitude towards education, or maybe it was just that student bloody experience is now king, but respect for him seemed to have largely gone. They sauntered in when they felt like it, and many of them just didn't bother attending. If there was one thing that riled him more than any other, it was when students couldn't be bothered to turn up and then expected him to give up his time to speak to them, because after all, student experience is king.

So maybe it was time to go. But what then? He had no close family or friends to share a retirement with; at least at present, his passion might get through to some students, which may in turn get through to some children. It wasn't a great choice, really, gritting his teeth through seminars with undeserving students, or living a life very much on his own.

Anna

I don't think he's going to do it. I really thought today might be the day. A full six hours, on a Friday, and I've given it my best shot. I spent the first ten minutes this morning with my earphones on and even started humming to Ed Sheeran singing 'I don't care', for God's sake. Yes, he bristles. Yes, the corner of his mouth trembles, and yes, he looks at me with hatred, but I just don't think he's going to crack. What do I do?

Donna

Maybe you're focusing on the wrong person. Your mission, if you choose to accept it, is to make Callum lose it. You know what he's like when he starts laughing. He's loud and uncontrollable. I'm not sure that Frank could cope with that.

Anna

And I didn't think that you had a sneaky bone in your body. Definitely worth a try. How's things at your end?

Donna

Sorry, Anna – still good! In fact – hilarious. We've had double prizes today. You know I said that we were having Gary, a specialist swimming coach, in today to teach us basic life-saving skills? Not only is he drop-dead gorgeous and a really good coach but – you're not going to believe this. One of the best things about these last two weeks has been watching Hannah from Richard's Surgery Set in action. Every day she comes in dressed totally inappropriately. Martin's face when she came in with high heels on the first day was a sight to behold. Since then, she's sported a ridiculously tight skirt, bangle-sized earrings, makeup that runs when she sweats, and a bra that, quite frankly, isn't up to the job. Anyway, I thought she looked a bit sheepish today, and it turns out that she only went and pulled this Gary at Cheeky Wednesday this week!!! We've already had the mouth-to-mouth jokes. You've got a disgusting mind: let me know if you've got anything a bit filthier that

I can rib her with. Just about to go back in the pool. Make Callum
lose it! Speak soon.

Callum

Callum had mixed feelings about everything. He'd never been in any doubt that
he wanted to choose Geography for his foundation option – he'd enjoyed the
subject at A Level and was genuinely interested in the whole sustainability
thing. He knew he'd have to put up with Donna's inevitable teasing about not
being allowed on the PE course due to his three-legged blah-di-blah-blah, and
he'd accepted this in good enough spirits. But now here he was, at the end of
the second of three weeks, being left frustrated that he hadn't actually learnt
very much. Of course, Frank meant well and spoke passionately, but he really
wasn't a very good lecturer and he repeated himself to the nth degree. But
whether he deserved the vitriol that he was receiving from Anna… Well, that
was an interesting one. At least it had been an interesting one until Anna played
her trump card on the Friday afternoon, her *coup de grâce,* if you like.
Reflecting back on it in the pub with the gang later, he did feel slightly guilty
and a tad ashamed, but they do say that laughter is an involuntary action, so
perhaps there was no blame to be laid at his door after all…

She arrived back after their final coffee break of the week, sporting a
baseball cap with the words 'speed merchant' emblazoned on the front. She sat
down meekly enough and looked at Frank with doughy and attentive eyes as
he started, perhaps unsurprisingly, talking about the environment. And then he
looked over and saw her subservient smile, he saw the blatant meaning of her
baseball cap and he twitched. This twitch seemed to go on for longer than usual
and there was some sort of evidence of apoplectic rage emblazoning inside of
him. But, yet again and to his utmost credit, he didn't say anything. Callum was
confident that he was going to be able to hold the laughter in, despite Frank's
reaction, until Anna finally broke him.

'I'm sorry Frank. You seem to be looking at my cap. I wondered if you
wanted to borrow it. It's cold today and maybe your need is greater than mine.'

In the seconds of silence that followed, Callum felt himself going. His chest
began to rise and fall as Frank gave the mother of all twitches, bursts of loud
air emitted from his mouth as Anna took off the cap and proffered it to Frank,
and finally huge snorting guffaws erupted from him as Anna calmly put the cap
back on backwards and gently uttered the words 'broom broom' under her
breath.

Callum had no idea what followed as he only lasted a couple more seconds before diving out of the door and surrendering to the kind of laughter that would kill one with a lesser heart.

Martin

'It's a really difficult one, Richard. What the hell am I supposed to do?'

'God knows. I think this is a classic case of damned if you do and damned if you don't. What did he actually say to you?'

Martin sighed. 'It's difficult to remember the exact words. He just banged on about never before experiencing such insolence and demanding what I, as programme leader, was going to do about it. The problem is, Rich, that whilst Anna's behaviour was completely unacceptable, I do have an element of sympathy. A couple of the more studious members of Frank's group had already spoken to me this week and complained that they weren't learning anything and that the sessions were boring. How the hell am I supposed to deal with that? I'm on the same pay grade as him, for God's sake, but Ranch has told me I have to deal with it because it's a programme issue. Well thanks, William, for that show of support. Was Anna like that in Maths?'

'Not really. I mean, I wouldn't want to get on the wrong side of her, but she was basically okay.'

'As she is in Surgery and she excelled in school. So, what's the common denominator here then, eh? Bloody Frank. The problem is, Rich, he just knows how to rub people up the wrong way. Have I told you the story about when we went to Africa? No? It was about five years ago and Frank organised a couple of trips to Sierra Leone with the students so that they could see first-hand the poverty there and what we, as privileged first-world citizens, could do for them. It was a brilliant idea and the students got the most amazing experience from it. Full credit to Frank. Anyway, during our first visit, I got talking to some of the local boys who played together in a football team, and their "kit" was whatever they could find on the day. Now, I have loads of spare kits in the PE cupboard that are simply never going to be used again. When we got back from our first visit, I suggested to Frank that, when we next went, I could surprise these boys by gifting them a complete kit for their team. Frank thought about it for a moment before speaking those immortal words: *"I don't think so, Martin. You see, the idea of sustainability is to help these people to help themselves. If we give them this kit, then we will be depriving the local tailor of potential business."* I kid you not, those words actually came out of his mouth. You know me, Richard, I don't like to swear, but the only suitable word to describe him when he said this was "wanker". Of course, I ignored him, and

I took the kit with me the next time we went. I promise you, Rich, you simply cannot know the meaning of the word happiness unless you were there to see the expressions of pure joy on the faces of those boys when I presented the bag to them. If it wasn't for the subsequent suicide of the local tailor due to a lack of business, it would have been such a good thing to do.'

'I think the worst thing about that story, Martin, is that nothing about it surprises me – apart from maybe your generosity. But you're still left with your problem. What the hell are you going to do?'

'I'll have to talk to her, won't I? I can't not. But it ain't gonna be very pretty…'

Kathryn

In the end, Kathryn was glad that she'd taken Martin's advice and stayed away from the university until after the funeral. Whilst the first week of the New Year was uneventful and gave her much time to ponder and worry about her future, it felt, in hindsight, better than the alternative of being in lectures and having to talk to people about the impending burial of her nan. The funeral itself was a quiet affair, in which she rather went through the motions in a state of numbness. She had expected Mary to show solidarity and miss her music session to be there, but she was astounded and quite overwhelmed to see the whole Peterson family join the small congregation and pay their respects to a lady that they had never met. The sight of Leo, in particular, whom she barely knew and who would have had to travel for a couple of hours each way to attend, was one of the most moving things that she had ever encountered.

And now, with just one week to go before their second placement experience, she had returned, to gain as much as she could from just five days' worth of Geography input. When she arrived in the seminar room, she rather hoped that her tutor would acknowledge her in some way, and perhaps give her some sort of gentle reassurance that what she had missed was not insurmountable. But Frank ignored her as she entered and seemed both tense and abrupt as he addressed the group. She noticed a rather battle-weary demeanour throughout the class, and a glassy-eyed stare as he began talking about the imminent irreversible effects of global warming. Now Kathryn was not one to be especially vocal in seminars, but as he repeatedly made reference to conversations from the previous week, she felt that she had little choice.

'Er, I'm sorry but I haven't been here for the last couple of weeks and I wonder if you wouldn't mind recapping a little for me?'

Frank's reaction was as shocking as it was sudden. Some bubble of pent-up emotion finally burst as he strode up to Kathryn and shouted: 'And whose fault is that, eh? I've been here teaching for the last two weeks and now you saunter in and ask me to recap? How about just being here in the first place?'

As he turned from her and walked forcefully away, as Kathryn felt the eyes of 20 students burn on her and as the full impact of the last few weeks finally hit her, all she could do was to burst into tears and run from the room.

Anna

When she had been summoned in to talk to Martin at 5:00 on the previous Friday afternoon, Anna's initial reaction had been one of both annoyance and indignation, and her opening gambit, much as Martin expected, was to rant about value for money, about repetitive content and about uninspiring teaching. But as Martin started talking calmly to her, she had quickly realised that, despite justifiable provocation, her behaviour towards a member of the teaching team had been wholly unacceptable. Indeed, as the weekend had worn on, the nice side of Anna, which had tried so hard to surface over the previous few months, briefly shone through and made her feel slightly guilty, and in her weaker moments, even a little sorry for Frank, despite everything. By the Monday morning, she had resolved to keep her head down for the final week, and to simply accept whatever came her way.

But this resolve was shot to pieces within a few minutes when Kathryn asked a reasonable question, when Frank exploded and when Kathryn ran from the room, distraught. Because in those few seconds, two things struck Anna with distinct clarity. The first was the realisation that Frank was, ultimately, a coward. He had refused to rise to her bait throughout the module, presumably because he was concerned about her reaction. Yet, when someone who may as well have had the label 'underdog' attached to her spoke out timidly, he took this opportunity to unleash all that had been bottled up. The second thing to hit Anna was that this poor girl — a girl that she shared a house with, for God's sake — had recently lost her only meaningful relative, and Anna had not sent a card, and if truth be told, had not really thought about her welfare since the Christmas party. And this made her feel just a little sick. With the words 'Fuck this!' echoing loudly across the stunned room, Anna picked up her things, walked to the door and began the process of finding Kathryn.

Surgery

Sometimes, Martin regretted advertising the agenda for Surgery in advance. Had he simply said, 'Looking forward to seeing you all at Surgery this Friday,' instead of, 'Looking forward to seeing you all at Surgery this Friday, when we

96

can discuss how your foundation option went, and then look forward to School Experience Two,' he could have reasonably avoided dredging up what had happened. After all, by the time that his Surgery Set arrived on the Friday afternoon, things had more or less been resolved. When an apoplectic Anna had virtually stormed into his office on the Monday morning, with a disorientated Kathryn in her wake, Martin had finally decided that enough was enough, and told William Ranch that sorting this out was well outside of his pay grade. So, William had listened as Anna had detailed the morning's exchanges, and eventually, he had decided that he had no choice but to get Frank to apologise to Kathryn. Any argument that Frank may have had was blown away by evidence of an email that Martin had sent him at the beginning of the module, informing him of the reason for Kathryn's likely absence. He could hardly blame anyone else for not reading that email. Such was Frank's anger, embarrassment, and humiliation when he left William's office after apologising unreservedly to Kathryn, that any doubts about whether this would be his last year at the university completely evaporated. For the rest of the week, all parties had a tacit and unspoken agreement that they would just let time go by as painlessly as possible.

'Er, so I know that you've all been studying for your foundation choice this week' began Martin, 'and, em, I wondered if any of you wanted to discuss it at all, maybe.'

Mary, who had been made aware of the week's events, quickly chimed in, and talked freely about her Music option, and how inspired she had been by its content. For several reasons, not least because they were talking directly to the person teaching them, Gabriel and Donna gave a rather muted account of their experiences in PE.

'Er, anybody else?' The next few seconds were as excruciating as Martin could remember, as Kathryn stared at the ground, Callum looked uncomfortable and Anna folded her arms and stared at Martin.

'No? Er, okay, let's talk about other things. As you know, you are to start your second placement experience on Monday, for the next four weeks. Now, you all know your schools, and, as before, you'll be with the same partner as last time, but there will be a few differences. The main one of these of course is that this is your first assessed placement, where you will be formally judged on your teaching. I know that may sound a little scary, but we all know that this is your first go, so nobody will be expecting miracles. The other big change is that, this time, whilst you'll be in the same school as each other, the two of you will be in different classes. We feel that this is important as you begin to stand on your own two feet.'

Gabriel had not been especially looking forward to this placement. He had found things tough the first time around, and the only real saving grace for him was that Donna had always been there and had helped him to believe in himself. The thought of his friend being behind closed doors in a different part of the school made him physically shudder. Everyone in the room could see his awkwardness and could also read the reason for it. Donna tried to lighten the mood by saying that it was good that she wouldn't be shown up by him, but it didn't help. Martin decided not to speak to him directly as this would only heighten his anxiety.

'And the last main change from last time,' he said, looking at Gabriel, 'is that you'll be having a visiting tutor to oversee your progress and to make sure everything is okay. Not sure if this is good news or bad, but the visiting tutor for all of you over the next four weeks will be me. I'm sure that everything will go swimmingly...'

Chapter 11

Gabriel

It had all begun so well. On Martin's advice, Gabriel had phoned the school on the Friday afternoon to touch base with his mentor. Denise had been lovely. In the ten minutes that they had chatted on the phone, she had given the air of one who would be supportive whilst trying to develop his skills, and she seemed to be genuinely looking forward to having him in her class.

But the call to the headteacher's office first thing on Monday morning, the explanation that Denise had been granted indefinite compassionate leave due to a sudden bereavement at the weekend and the announcement that he would now be mentored by Joe instead, had sent alarm bells ringing. Gabriel had spoken to Joe on occasions during School Experience One and had not really taken to him. Yes, he was suave; yes, the children ate out of his hand; and yes, he clearly had a natural talent, but there was an undefined arrogance about him and the sort of casual approach to teaching that made Gabriel concerned that maybe he was not going to be the ideal mentor. Indeed, Donna had told him that not only did Joe once boast to her that the writing of lesson plans was completely unnecessary 'unless you're a crap teacher', but, in the same conversation, had asked for her phone number and had suggested that the two of them might share a meal together.

'Good to meet you, mate,' said Joe, as he smiled and shook Gabriel's hand. 'I hope you know what the bloody hell you're supposed to do over the next four weeks as I most certainly don't. Being told you're gonna be a mentor one hour before the placement starts is a bit much if you ask me, but hey, I'm sure we'll wing it together. So, you're teaching Maths in twenty minutes, yeah? Sorry, mate, couldn't resist that. The look on your face! Just watch me today, yeah, and then we'll have a chat at the end of the day.'

So, Gabriel watched. He watched with an excruciating expression for the first ten minutes before a cocky-looking boy said, 'Who's that man, Mr Wilson?'

He watched as Joe then laughed, and replied; 'Oh, yeah, sorry, this is Mr, er, Mr, sorry, Gabriel, what's your surname again?'

He watched as the class sniggered at his discomfort, and he watched as Joe joked his way through the day with his Year 4 class, who all clearly loved him.

At the end of the day, Gabriel got out his folder and showed Joe all that he needed to do over the four weeks. He handed Joe a piece of paper and explained that these were the milestones, a sort of checklist of what they both needed to do from week to week. Joe studied these for a moment before stating: 'Jesus; that seems like a hell of a lot of paperwork on your part. Rather you than me, mate. Okay, so you need to teach at least one lesson this week, yeah? What do you fancy?'

Gabriel didn't really know what to say. In truth, he didn't particularly fancy teaching anything at the moment and so just shrugged. 'Er, I don't know. Anything?'

'Tell you what, mate why don't we start with something easy, eh? Don't want you worrying all week about some complex algebra lesson. How about some PSHE? You know, circle time and all that malarkey. Bullying. That's a good one. Do a lesson about bullying.'

'Er, okay, have you got a plan for me or something?'

'Not really. To tell the truth, Gabriel, you'll feel far more comfortable delivering something that you've planned yourself. Happy to have a chat beforehand, but give it a go, eh? Bullying. One hour on Thursday afternoon. What can go wrong?'

Donna

'Honestly, Donna, he's all smiles and jokes and everything, but I can't actually see him really mentoring me. What the hell am I going to do on Thursday, eh? He's given me absolutely nothing to go on.'

'You should be so lucky. When I found out that Year 2 were studying the Romans and that I'd be teaching them a session on the subject this week, it sounded great. I could just see Grace telling me to be really creative. And then Jean gave me the script.'

'Script?'

'Yes, Gabriel, script. Not a lesson plan, not a few ideas, but a bloody script. And, actually, not just a script. A script with stage directions on it, for God's same. Read it, Gabriel. I promise you that, in a minute, you'll be pining for a free rein session on bullying.'

Dear Donna

Please find below details of the lesson that I'd like you to teach on Friday. As it's your first go, I thought that it would be useful for me to let you know what to say as well as what to do. Please don't stray from the following:

'Good afternoon, Year 2. I hope you had a lovely break for lunch. (Pause for three seconds.) Now, this afternoon, we are going to learn more about the Romans. In a minute I'm going to read you a piece about how they used to live and then you are going to write a "Cloze procedure" about it. Now, you all know what this is as you've done it several times before. I'll give you a piece of writing with some gaps in it, and you need to fill in the gaps from the word bank below. I'd like you to do this in silence, and if you finish in time, then you can draw a picture from one of the books.' (Pause again for a few seconds in case any of them have any questions.)

I'd then like you to give out the worksheets which I've prepared for you, and then go around and help anyone who is stuck. After twenty minutes you can…

But Gabriel could read no more as he was laughing so much. 'If you need to sneeze, Donna,' he said, 'take a handkerchief out of your pocket, turn a full 90 degrees away from the children and then make sure you blow your nose.'

'Ha, ha, bloody hilarious. Is it me or is that the most shite lesson in the world? And talk about a control freak. Jean actually said to me in our meeting after school that if I wanted to go to the toilet in a lesson, I needed to ask her permission. Perhaps she can come and wipe my arse.'

They both looked at each other over their much-needed beer. Both were feeling the same; that the next four weeks could be very long indeed.

'Let's give it a few days, Gabriel. Things might settle. Maybe we're being too harsh. After all, both Joe and Jean seem to think that they are helping us − albeit at totally different ends of the spectrum. Who knows, Jean might relax and let me fart without her permission and Joe might actually give you some semblance of support. Remember, Martin's coming in at the end of the week. We can always speak to him if we're not happy.'

Gabriel

'Okay, Year 4, let's start by listing all of the types of bullying that you can think of, and then we'll have a chat about them.'

'Hitting people.'

'Yes, good. Well, I don't mean good as in − well, you know. Er, anything else?'

'Being nasty to people.'

'Yes, Jenny, well done.'

'What about cyberbullying, Mr Morgan?'

'Yes, Sanjay, very good. Anything else?'

The moment the cocky-looking kid from day one − Billy by name − put his hand up Gabriel felt a slight misgiving. Something in Billy's expression concerned him.

'Sexual bullying. That's definitely one I know, 'cos my sister told me.'

There was only about a second's pause before Gabriel replied, but within that second, the whole class and Billy, in particular, noted his unease. What had possessed him to start the lesson this way, throwing himself open to awkward moments and completely inappropriate content for eight-year-old children?

'Well, yes, Billy, you're right, but I think we'll stay away from that one today, if you don't mind.'

Gabriel was pretty sure that Billy did mind, and he saw Billy glance at Joe questioningly. Thankfully, Joe's face clearly discouraged further comment and the moment passed.

'So then,' continued Gabriel, as smoothly as he could muster, 'how do you think people feel when they're being bullied?' He was happy with this question and was pleased with the inevitable responses that he received. 'Sad', 'unhappy', and 'alone' were nice safe responses, and he even got a 'powerless', which was a fantastic reply.

His confidence grew: 'So why do you think people bully other people?'

Another nugget, though he said so himself, and again the thought-provoking answers, including, 'Because they're just nasty', 'Maybe they are sad too', and the quite inspired response of the day, 'I think that bullies are often insecure' even received a nod from God himself, or Joe, as he was sometimes known. As he started leading the conversation on, Gabriel felt a tangible and physical sensation as his confidence grew and he realised that this was what it was all about − this ability to inspire children and provoke thoughtful discussion and Joe was clearly impressed.

But emotional highs can quickly change to depressive lows, as Gabriel was about to find out. An experienced teacher would have noted a change of demeanour as the conversation veered from the generic to the specific, and as individual children started talking about how they had been bullied, there was an awkwardness emerging from some of the class and some surreptitious glances around the room, suggesting that something was about to happen. It was all just about okay until Michael, a small and sensitive child, but one unafraid to air his views, suddenly piped up in a slightly quivering voice: 'I just hate bullies, and I hate you, Billy Robinson.'

'I'm not a bully − you're just a wimp.'

And in the moments that followed, Michael's high-pitched indignation pierced the room, Billy sneered back at him and the faces of the other children alternated between concern, embarrassment, solidarity, and amusement. And in the centre of it all, Gabriel looked pleadingly at Joe for intervention − intervention that surely must come, but Joe's expression said clearly that he was expecting Gabriel to rescue the situation.

And so, he did − in a way. He shouted loudly for everyone to stop and he ended the session a full twenty minutes before it was due to finish. Eventually, when it was clear that Gabriel had no more to say, Joe calmly took over, and asked them all to continue with ongoing topic work.

Gabriel was still shaking when Joe spoke to him immediately after the children left for home.

'That may have seemed harsh, Gabriel, but it is important that you learn to stand on your own two feet from the outset. How would it have looked if I had bailed you out?'

Gabriel said nothing and just stared at the floor. That was his first ever go at teaching a proper lesson, and his mentor hadn't helped him when he was so clearly ill-equipped to deal with a powder keg of a situation. And that was simply wrong. Of that, he had absolutely no doubt.

Miriam

Miriam had been married to Martin for long enough to know when something was really troubling her husband. As a teacher herself of a particularly challenging Year 6 class, she was very conscious that, on most days, it would be he who listened as she ranted, often for a full 30 minutes, about her daily woes. She was also very conscious that, after this rant, she could completely forget to ask after his day, especially as he tended not to bring his stresses home with him. But as she opened the mandatory Friday bottle of wine, she could see from his expression that he was concerned about something.

'There you go. Looks like you need that. So, what's going on?'

Martin sighed. 'Oh, mentor issues − potentially serious ones this time.'

'You've dealt with dodgy mentors before, Martin, what's so wrong about this one?'

'Two − potentially, but for very different reasons. I went to visit two of my Surgery Set after school tonight, Gabriel and Donna − both lovely and able students − and I rather hoped it would be a quick, easy-going chat between us and their mentors to rubberstamp that all was going well, but I could see instantly from their expressions that this wasn't going to be the case. Donna is potentially an outstanding student and I had to listen to her vent her frustration

103

about the lesson that she'd just delivered. It seemed like she had been treated like some sort of incapable helper, rather than as a trainee teacher and the lesson that she described having to teach would have sent even the most conscientious of pupils to sleep. "But swings and roundabouts," Donna had said bitterly. "Apparently I did very well − for a first go. Maybe I just need a little more practice reading aloud her scripts."

'So, I had to have a really awkward exchange with Jean, her mentor, and ask her to perhaps give Donna a bit more licence to plan and teach with a semblance of independence. Such was her prickliness at this that I stopped short of questioning the nature of the lesson itself, which would have sat nicely in the 1950s curriculum. We reached a sort of uneasy truce, but I'm far from certain that Donna is going to be happy moving forwards. And then there's Gabriel.'

After taking a particularly large glug of Malbec, Martin went on to describe how Gabriel, holding back the tears, had talked through his first experience of teaching, 'Gabriel was just upset, but Donna was furious that this had happened to her friend, and made it very clear that she expected me to tell this Mr Wilson that his actions, or lack of them, were wholly unacceptable. So that conversation, as you can imagine, was lots of fun.'

'Oh dear. What happened?'

'Not a lot, to be honest. He was completely charming and explained his rationale. His firmly held view is that teachers learn on the job, and they learn from making mistakes. I tried to argue that the incident with the bullying was less of a mistake and more of an impossible situation for a novice to cope with, but he was unrepentant. He said, with a wide smile, that he was happy for Gabriel to stay in his class and learn from him, but if this didn't suit the university, maybe they needed to find a different school for Gabriel.'

'Bloody hell. How did you deal with that one?'

'I said, trying to smile as widely as he did, that by agreeing to have a student, the school agreed to offer the sort of support that we expect, especially for first year students. His reply was that he wasn't actually sure whether he had agreed to have a student in the first place, given that Gabriel was thrust upon him at 8:00 on Monday morning.'

'Ah, the reluctant mentor. Therein lies the rub.'

'Exactly. So, I went to speak to the head, who assured me he'd have words but − God knows. The placement is only for four weeks. How long do I leave it before making the call to pull Gabriel out? The thing is that, despite everything, I rather liked this Joe guy. He's clearly an excellent teacher and Gabriel could learn a lot from him. Let's hope that the head can influence him more than I clearly could.'

Miriam poured another large glass of wine. 'Hmmm. Good luck with that one.'

Jean

Jean had worked at Willow Fields School for many years and had been in Year 2 for the last five. She understood that children had tests at the end of the year, and that, if she were to do her job properly, then she needed to cover the curriculum fully. In order to do that, she often had to get through things quickly so that another box could be ticked. Both Donna and Martin were pleasant and polite, but she could see, very clearly, that they did not like her methods, and that Donna, in particular, wanted to be given more of a free rein with things. Okay, maybe giving her a complete script was unnecessary, but it was her first go, and with a class that she was unfamiliar with. Donna was clearly one of these idealistic young students who believed that a creative approach was the way to go, but maybe Donna didn't live in the real world. It was all very well for her tutors to espouse the benefits of original and imaginative teaching methods, but these, from Jean's experience, often took an inordinate amount of time, and generally didn't allow for the mandatory curriculum to be completely covered. But Martin had asked her specifically to let Donna try things out a little differently, and so Jean had agreed, with an element of reluctance, to listen to Donna's ideas. Give someone an inch…

Jean tried not to shudder when Donna talked enthusiastically about arranging an 'Ancient Roman day', where the children would dress up and be in role for the complete day. Yes, it might be an enjoyable experience for them, but would they cover all of the objectives? How was Donna planning to organise everything and how would it be resourced?

'I'll give them a homework task to make a Roman shield for the day,' said Donna enthusiastically. 'Honestly, it will be fantastic…'

Donna

'You did what?' wrote Mary in their group chat. 'You really aren't a parent, are you? Have you any idea how annoying it is, when you've just sat down and put your feet up on a Friday night, to be handed a note from your offspring demanding the creation of a Roman shield over the weekend? We had this several times when our kids were young, and it completely ruins your weekend. The thing is that you simply can't produce any old tat. Whether anybody actually says so or not, it becomes a competition, not just for the poor children, who have to bring the bloody things in on the Monday morning, but for the parents, who quite clearly push the children out of the way and make the damn things themselves. Have you thought about what little Johnny will feel like on Monday when he comes in with his badly cut out piece of cardboard, crudely adorned with felt tip, because his parents couldn't be arsed to help him? That feeling will be magnified when he stands it next to the museum piece created by the local carpenter.'

No, Donna hadn't thought of that and she'd spent most of the weekend worrying about it. Her second week in Jean's class had gone better than her first and she was being given greater licence, but she was also learning very fast that veering off a carefully-designed lesson plan, as a fledgling teacher, was actually a very difficult thing to do, and Jean had needed to step in when the children got completely lost whilst trying to do a Maths investigation. Jean could easily have made it obvious that she'd warned Donna about this, but to her great credit, she didn't, and for this, Donna's respect for her had risen dramatically. But now the highly anticipated Roman day was approaching like a speeding chariot threatening to overturn, and Donna's initial enthusiasm and confidence was starting to waiver.

Joe

Joe was torn. Five years ago, he had completed the 'School Direct' programme, a sort of 'learn while you teach' approach, and whilst his weekly days at the university were not wasted, he learnt considerably more 'on the job' and it was his fully held belief that this was the best way to learn how to teach. Indeed, his mentor at the time had constantly told him that the best way to improve was by making mistakes, and he had quickly developed a hardened edge because of this.

But now he wondered. Gabriel had been visibly upset by his first teaching experience. Martin had spoken eloquently about the need for support, particularly for young and inexperienced students and now Sally Wells, his headteacher, had gently but firmly suggested that, for the rest of his placement, Gabriel needed more guidance from his mentor. Joe was still a little bit miffed about becoming a last-minute mentor, but he also realised that this was hardly Gabriel's fault. Maybe it was time to change his mantra so that his fully held belief was that learning 'on the job' was the best way to learn how to teach *for him*, but maybe not for everyone.

'So then, Gabriel, a bit more hand-holding this week, eh? Let's plan a lesson together, and you can deliver either some or all of it, whatever you fancy.'

Gabriel

'Cheers!'

'Cheers, Gabriel!'

'You know what? When I first thought about going in to teaching, people warned me about the workload, the pay, challenging children, and the like, but no one ever said that you're likely to triple your alcohol intake. I tell you, I thought that I was drinking a lot as a normal student, but since placement began, I've started enquiring about buying shares in my off-licence.'

'Oh dear. Gabriel the wino. That has a certain ring to it. So how did it go today?'

'It's ironic, it really is. There's me banging on about not being supported enough, but if it weren't for Joe's suggestion, it wouldn't have happened.'

'What wouldn't?'

'Okay, so we are currently reading *Boy* by Roald Dahl, and we've got them to write all about his adventures as a boy from different perspectives and we've talked about the difference between a biography and an autobiography − all the usual chestnuts. Anyway, Joe suggested getting them to write an extract from their own autobiography. They had a couple of days to think about it, and then today they got to write it, using all of the features that we'd discussed. Well, they were full of it and the lesson passed swimmingly. I got a few of them to read theirs out to the class at the end of the day before I sent them home. Everyone happy. And then I started marking them. All I can say is that the Gods must have been smiling on me, because I didn't choose Chloe to read out hers even though she put her hand up. I've told you about her before, I think. Lovely girl, supportive parents − the works. And then I read what she'd written. Chloe, in her wisdom, decided that she wanted to write about her father's girlfriend, and how this woman is spoiling things for her. No great surprise there − wicked stepparents and stuff; but then I read the words, and I quote: "*And mummy is really cross*!" It turns out that Mummy and Daddy are still together, but Daddy has a girlfriend, and Mummy has the gall to be slightly pissed off about it! But the best part about the writing? Chloe had clearly read this somewhere else, and so decided to leave a cliff-hanger with the wonderful phrase: "To be continued…" And now I have to mark this. I mean what the bloody hell do I put? "*What a lovely story, Chloe. Looking forward to hearing what happens next*". This work is in her English book, for God's sake. I can't rip it out. Sooner or later Mummy or Daddy, or quite possibly Daddy's bit of stuff, will read this and realise that their intricate little love triangle is now the subject of discussion around the school.'

Lily touched his arm affectionately. 'That is absolutely hilarious. What did Joe say?'

'Typical Joe. He thought it was as funny as you did. Ever the professional, he then went on to muse about the possibility of asking Mummy out on a date to redress the balance. He doesn't have to mark the bloody thing. He didn't deliver the lesson.'

'Yes, but he'll have to deal with them at parents' evening. You'll be well gone by then. You must get him to promise to let you know how that little bombshell explodes.'

'Definitely. D'you know what? I'm so tired. I can't believe just how exhausting these few weeks have been. I am so looking forward to the weekend.'

'So am I Gabriel, so am I. First time away together, eh? We'll have a wonderful time, and I'll make sure I knead all of those stresses out of you.'

'Sounds fantastic, Lily. I'll hold you to that.'

Donna

With one last defiant glare at Donna, Mrs Nobbs stood up and walked out of the room. Donna could feel the tears starting to well as she spoke.

'Thank you, Jean, thank you so much.'

'Don't worry about it, Donna, I've had several parents come storming into my class, who were so much worse than her. And ultimately, Donna, it was an accident. By the time that she left, I think that she understood that. She'll have calmed down by the morning. Tell you what, why don't you fill in your daily journal, and I'll go and get you a strong cup of tea.'

So, Donna picked up her pen, took a couple of deep breaths, and began to write.

I was so looking forward to this. I'd spent ages planning it, the kids were all excited, and I think even Jean was at least curious as to how the children would respond. By now, the embarrassment created by the different standards of Roman shields seemed to have disappeared (I won't do that again!!), and everyone was all smiles as they compared togas and tunics when they came in. It was so nice to see them happily stay in role as I made the first hour deliberately boring, getting them to recite tables and learn the Roman numerals by heart. Separating the boys and girls after break, and getting the boys to understand about devotion to the state and the girls to appreciate devotion to family is something I don't think they'll forget, and it will be good to have a discussion about this tomorrow. They even seemed happy enough to eat their lunch of fish, cold meat, bread, and vegetables as it meant they could continue to 'be Romans' throughout their lunch hour.

Maybe they were simply too excited about the Roman marching in the afternoon, or maybe I simply hadn't thought it through. They loved marching around the playground and there was many a jealous glance from other children, looking out of classroom windows. I still maintain that getting them to form the famous 'tortoise' formation was an important part of the day, so that they could see for themselves how this Testudo worked. (They loved the idea of being able to teach their parents a new word!)

But the whole health and safety thing is just a little new to me. Had I have mentioned this to Jean beforehand, then she would have straightaway looked at the risk assessment, but I just wanted to surprise her, as well as the children. (Another thing I won't be doing again!) I swear the scream that came out of Daisy's mouth as they bent down into the formation and she was caught just below her eye will stay with me for a long time. Stanley had been justifiably proud of his shield, and I'm sure that his father didn't think about tortoise formations when he reinforced the corners with metal. But the blood. It was horrible. Thank goodness it missed her eye.

Jean came back into the room with the tea and read Donna's diary entry.

'At the end of the day, Donna, there are only two things that are important here. The doctor has said that there won't be a permanent scar and you have learnt the importance of risk assessment.'

'I know, but I just can't stop thinking about the "what ifs". I will never forget how you spoke to Mrs Nobbs then. How you talked about the importance of active learning and basically took the blame for everything. I know this isn't the sort of thing that you do with your class. I know that you only let me because Martin asked, and I'll never forget how you stood up for me back then. Thank you.'

Jean pursed her lips. 'Well, Donna, I'm the class teacher, so the ultimate responsibility lies with me. I know that you're very keen to teach a creative curriculum, and I'm sure there's merit to that, but don't forget the basics, Donna. They are our bread and butter.'

Surgery

'I just want to start by saying "well done" to both of you. Though I don't suppose you had any cause for doubt, let me qualify, officially, that you've both passed your School Experience Two. Now, have you had any thoughts about your presentations on Wednesday? I'm looking forward to hearing them.'

'Perhaps unsurprisingly, Martin,' said Donna, 'the theme of my presentation is going to be about understanding just how much I have to learn. I might also mention that I now appreciate that someone with twenty years of experience probably knows more than I do. I shall be humble.'

'That's fine, Donna. But don't forget that different teachers have different styles, which is how it should be. I don't want this chastening experience to stifle your creativity. What about you, Gabriel?'

'I'm going to call my presentation: "Why a three-year B.Ed degree is the right route for me", and I'm going to talk about how all that I'm learning in my modules is linking with all that I learnt in school.'

'Sounds good. Maybe you could invite Joe along to that one. As you know, you've got Monday and Tuesday to prepare these, so that should give you plenty of time. I hope you've both got something nice planned for the weekend?'

'Oh yes,' replied Donna quickly. 'I've told Dominic that if he ever wants to see me again after Sunday, he is going to be my slave for the weekend. If I click my left fingers, I want chocolate, and if I click my right fingers, I want alcohol. Simples. Mind you, I think Gabriel's weekend sounds far more interesting than mine. Oh, and incidentally Gabriel, when we meet on Sunday night, I want a full blow-by-blow account − so to speak.'

Chapter 12

Kathryn

'Angela's story'

I've decided to just focus on one child for my presentation and use this case study to show what I have learnt through getting to know her. I was a little nervous anyway being in Year 1 – all my previous experience has been in the Early Years, so suddenly having to work from the National Curriculum was a little out of my comfort zone.

I knew as soon as I set eyes on Angela that she was going to be a challenge, and so it proved. Mrs Franks, my mentor, had just told me to observe for the first few days, and I was intrigued by this little girl straightaway, and her relationship with her teacher. Angela couldn't keep still. She spent the whole time, when the children were on the carpet, crawling under tables, making rude sounds, and fiddling with anything in her way. I just couldn't understand why Mrs Franks allowed it. She seemed oblivious to the child and never told her to be quiet. She had other difficult children who she made sit close to her or the teaching assistant, yet Angela was allowed to run wild. When they started independent work, she would often walk out the classroom and just sit in the corridor. Mrs Franks would calmly go out and say to her that when she was ready to start working, she should come back in. Angela could often just sit there for several minutes before coming back in and joining in with the work, as though nothing had happened.

When we had our first meeting on Wednesday, Mrs Franks asked me what I thought about the class. I didn't really know what to say because I didn't want to sound like I was being critical, so I just murmured something about them seeming fine. She just smiled and asked me directly what I thought about Angela, and all I could say was that I thought she was a bit naughty.

'You're dying to ask me why I let her get away with so much, aren't you?' she said. 'Tell you what; you see if you can answer that question in a few days' time.'

Mrs Franks was a really good mentor. She would support me when I needed it but would let me try out things myself if I asked. And so, when I taught my first lesson a few days in, I asked Angela to come and sit by me on the carpet.

I just – I just find it really difficult not doing anything proactive in this sort of situation. I knew that Mrs Franks was a good teacher, and therefore would have thought through her dealings with Angela, but I just couldn't stop myself and was pleased when Angela did as she was told and sat next to me as I started teaching, and after a couple of minutes, I relaxed and could then concentrate on the lesson, rather than on her.

At first, I thought it was a spider and yelped, and all the children laughed as Angela slowly pulled her little hand out from where it was tickling my thigh under my dress. I was so shocked I didn't know what to say, and then she got bored of sitting and started her usual antics. You know sometimes that words just come out of your mouth, even when you know they shouldn't? I just couldn't stop myself shouting at her to sit back down and then she blew a raspberry at me, laughed and ran out of the room. Mrs Franks calmly went out to talk to her – I don't know what she said – and I tried to carry on with the lesson. Later, when Angela had agreed to come back in the room and was concentrating hard on her work, I decided to go up to her to see if she wanted any help.

'No thank you,' she replied calmly. She turned her attention back to her work, but I didn't move away immediately. She then looked back at me and stared at me – through me, even.

'Are you okay, Miss Wood, you look very sad?' It was just all so confusing. This little girl, for all her bad behaviour and rudeness, now showed a maturity far beyond her young years. Given how I had treated her, I'm not sure that I deserved the genuine empathy that was now radiating from her.

I hadn't really had a chance to speak with my mentor when, at the end of the day, she told me that Angela's mum wanted to see her and it would be a good idea if I was there as well. I was terrified. I'd shouted at this little girl who had obviously run straight to her mum in the playground to tell her, and I was going to cop for it.

I was thrown even more when a smiling, attractive and well-dressed woman came through the door.

'So, you must be Miss Wood,' she said, offering her hand for me to shake. 'Angela's told me all about you.'

It seemed that Mum just wanted to talk about a PTA event. Towards the end of the conversation, she asked casually how her daughter was getting on. Mrs Franks smiled and said she was doing really well and was happy, especially in the playground where she had lots of friends. Then, to my horror, she mentioned the hand up the skirt incident and Mum just laughed!

'That's Angela for you. You won't do that again!'

112

'So then, Kathryn,' said Mrs Franks after Mum had gone. 'Tell me what you've learnt about Angela and the way that we deal with her.' I thought carefully before answering because I was still so confused. I'd always been under the impression that we should treat all children equally as teachers, but this simply wasn't what was happening. It was especially odd because she is an intelligent girl with a lot of friends. She doesn't have any condition such as ADHD – she just behaves oddly. By the end of the conversation, I was still confused but I did try afterwards to use the strategies that my mentor used and I was really pleased the first time that Angela came to ask for my help.

I looked at this presentation brief carefully before starting to prepare it and I really tried to focus on the words, '… and make sure that you explain what you have learnt from your experience'. It took a while – probably two or three weeks, before I could articulate what I was learning from both Mrs Franks and from teaching Angela, and this is what I concluded: each child is different and learns in their own way and in their own time. We can and should have rules in the classroom, but sometimes if you try too hard to enforce those rules with every child, things can backfire on you and the situation can just get worse. Get to know your class as individuals and get to know what makes them tick and what not to do. This is very separate to having general class rules that we expect most of the children to follow. Angela, for whatever reason, isn't ready yet to sit still and to be micromanaged. She will be, in her own time. When I could eventually articulate that to Mrs Franks shortly before the end of my placement, she smiled, nodded, and told me how much more I'd learnt from working that out for myself. I will certainly remember Angela.

Mary

'Why I know I'm doing a good thing'.

As you all know, I nearly gave up this programme shortly before Christmas. There were many reasons for that – trying to cut up a soggy pizza was a low moment and trying not to be so much of a perfectionist was even harder. But my main problem was on placement. I'm 50 years old and really, really struggled trying to learn from a much younger teacher. You were all wonderful and supportive, and my meeting with Martin helped a lot, but in early January, we had some friends round to dinner and I made the mistake, after a few glasses of wine, of telling them that I thought that teaching wasn't for me. I've known Peter and Sue for many years. Like us, they are successful in business, and I know that Sue, in particular, struggled with the idea of me retraining. She's a hardened lawyer with pots of money, and the whole notion was just completely foreign to her. Her reaction, though, when I said I was probably going to quit, really threw me.

'Oh, Mary. Thank God for that. I didn't like to say anything but…'

And then it all came out – all the reasons why I shouldn't teach and why the profession was apparently so beneath me. So, I decided, there and then, to use this placement to not only test her views against what I really think, but to use her 'reasons not to teach' as a basis for this presentation. I'll go through her arguments one by one.

Her first point – and you may need to grip something quite hard here – was that children only really start learning anything of value at secondary school. She said this without any irony, and went on to explain that her memories from primary school were 'writing a few stories, learning my times tables, and finding out useless facts about Ancient Greece'. I didn't rise to the bait. For this placement, as many of you will know, I was in a Year 5 class, and I had a brilliant mentor who was one of the most inspiring teachers I have ever seen. Everything that Grace, Richard, and Martin have been saying to us all year was reflected in Katy's teaching and the children lapped it up. But more than this, the quality of their learning was breathtaking at times. Katy's real passion was creative writing and drama. We were reading *The Hobbit*, and she got them to invent their own mythical creature that Bilbo and co might meet on their journey. She got them to effortlessly use personification and metaphors in their character descriptions, and then visualisation techniques and hot-seating to add to their personalities. They made masks of their creations, before sharing these in the most imaginative class assembly you could think of. The whole school was gobsmacked, and I would have loved it if Sue could have been there. It also completely made up my mind that this is what I want to do. That sort of inspiration doesn't come with too many jobs, and it certainly didn't come with the work I've done for most of my career.

But of course, none of this comes without sustained effort and hard work, as you know, which leads on to Sue's next point, which was about teaching being a 9 to 3 job, with outrageously lengthy holidays.

'We used to meet for lunch at three, if you remember, before starting the second half of our day. Surely you don't want to take such a backwards step when you're in your prime?'

Katy gave a really nice analogy about this misconception. She spoke about the 9 to 3 bit as being the 'front of house': the polished play that you pay your money to see. What you don't see of course are the rehearsals, line-learning and other backstage shenanigans that go into that production, in the same way as nobody else sees all the planning and angst that goes in to making lessons exciting. Sue also intimated here that being a teacher is a waste of talent. When

I first started this programme, I thought that maybe this was the case – that all I would be doing is transmitting knowledge to children. But everything I've learnt at university and particularly from Katy has taught me just how skilled you need to be in this job. It's all very well making lessons exciting, but the skilful bit is how you model, question, support, and scaffold, and how you use resources to demonstrate so that all of the children can learn. I'm a million miles away from really getting that yet, but it's a great thing to aspire to. I've often heard the phrase: 'Those who can, do; those that can't, teach' bandied about. I always felt that a little unfair and unnecessarily antagonistic. I must say that I'm looking forward to the next time someone says that. I have my response ready.

And then of course, there's the holidays – all those weeks every year, that, as Sue delighted in saying, makes teaching a part-time job. I knew I wanted to mention this in my presentation, so I asked all of the teachers how they spent their holidays. The most common answer was 'recovering' or 'recharging batteries', followed closely by 'planning for the next term', and in a few cases, 'time to be ill'. Several of them also mentioned that it was time to go on the most expensive and busiest holidays of the year.

I'm seeing Sue for lunch next week and I'm going to talk to her about this presentation, and about how it was inspired by her views. It will be really interesting to see her response. She's an intelligent, caring person and a long-time friend. I'll let you know how that goes.

I said at the beginning of this talk that one of the biggest problems that I've had with this process is trying to accept the fact that I am going to learn from people younger than me. Katy is 22 years old and in her second year of teaching. She really is an inspiration.

Anna

'Where has all the music gone?'

You may remember me saying, during our Maths module, that I'm not very good with the whole touchy-feely-wank aspects of teaching. I always found learning quite easy, especially in Maths. I could get the right answers, do well in exams, and that was absolutely fine for me. And so, I was really pleased when I found out that I was to be in Year 6 for this placement, knowing that they would be focusing largely on preparing for SATs. Moira Cox, the Year 6 teacher, told me frankly at the beginning of the process that our job at the moment is to train the children to be able to cope with their SATs in May, and that they had a right to achieve expected standards wherever possible. Not surprisingly, her lessons were very formal and focused largely on looking at previous exam papers in both English and Mathematics.

At first, this suited me fine because it allowed me to teach in a way that was very familiar for me. We explained procedures and the children listened carefully – there were no behaviour issues – and then they practised techniques and skills and they were clearly making progress. To see a child not understand something at the beginning of a lesson, but then be able to get correct answers in the end was very satisfying, and I got some really positive feedback from Moira.

Because I was living this scene day in and day out, it became the norm and I somewhat disregarded the messages that I've been receiving at uni all year. It was only when I knew that Martin was coming in to observe me teach Maths in a few days' time that I began to think. Now, I say this grudgingly, but Richard's mantra of developing 'Mathematical thinkers rather than Mathematical doers' was just about getting through to me by the end of his module, especially when we watched Callum, and I say this even more grudgingly, do something really rather impressive with some Unifix cubes. I knew, beyond any doubt, that Martin would have something to say about it if I taught a totally procedural lesson without any opportunities for reasoning, justifying or all those other words that Richard used to bang on about.

So, I took a risk. We were doing fractions, so I borrowed trays of dominoes from Adrian and asked them to turn them vertically and order them in terms of value and then to use them to show each other how to change a mixed number into an improper fraction. Their reaction, to be honest, shocked me. At first, they moaned about having to manipulate 'things that we used to use when we were infants', and then they simply didn't know what to do, especially with the improper fractions activity. You see, I didn't tell them what to do; I wanted them to work it out themselves. At one point, one of them, who was actually a really nice kid, turned to me and asked me why they were using kids' stuff, when they weren't allowed them in SATs. I could also see that Moira was twitching a bit by now while Martin looked on impassively. So, I kind of lost my nerve, explained exactly what they needed to do and quickly put the resources away. The feedback that I received from Moira and then Martin was really very different, and it got me thinking. When I looked back at the lesson and I pictured their faces when they were playing with the dominoes, I pictured confusion, pointlessness, and a certain amount of derision. But I pictured something else as well. It was there, definitely, on several of the faces – longing. Longing to be able to explore Maths and explain things as they must have done at some point in their distant past.

I didn't ask Moira if I could use the resources again because I knew what she would say, but from that moment on, I started looking at the children in a slightly different light. Initially, I had seen well-behaved kids who were keen to get the right answer but now I saw soulless robots. It suddenly hit me just how seldom anyone laughed in the classroom. Yes, they'd go out to play, kick a football, or kick each other, but as soon they got back into class, the programmed robot took over. It was really quite scary. I was aware that the curriculum was getting more and more narrow, as extra bits of time were created for English and Maths activities. They went through the motions of topic work, they had sports coaches teaching them twice a week, and they even did an occasional experiment in Science, but this was now early March, not early May, and it seemed an awfully long time ahead of them to just focus on SATs preparation.

But then Moira unleashed the big bombshell, the thing that made me think that, after all, the world really has gone mad. I asked her about how things would change after SATs. I remember at my primary school we virtually stopped doing formal lessons – the focus became on extended topics, residential trips, and putting on a big production. I've tried to remember the exact words that she replied – it was something along the lines of:

'Not much will change at all, Anna. We mustn't forget that we are preparing them for the Key Stage 3 curriculum. The secondary schools won't thank us if they've forgotten how to read, write, and add up, but can now sing a range of songs from the musicals, and have had a bit more practice swinging a rounders bat. They're just not interested in that.'

Now you know me. I'm really shy. I never speak out unless, maybe, Callum makes an arse out of himself, and so I just murmured something and shut up. But I wanted to say so much. Moira talked all the way through my placement about children's right to be prepared for the secondary school curriculum, but she never once spoke about their right to a broad and balanced curriculum, and their right to enjoy their final year at primary school. So that's why I've called this presentation: 'Where has all the music gone?' I always thought that I wanted to be a Year 6 teacher and you might think that after this experience, I've changed my mind. Well, I haven't. I'm now even more determined to teach children in their final year, to prepare them for their exams, but also to allow them to look back at Year 6 with real fondness. Here endeth my party-political broadcast for the '*right to let children be children*' party.

Callum

'A day out at the zoo'

Well, I may as well get it over with straight away just to stop Anna saying it all the way through my presentation. I'm learning; I'm definitely learning, but I know I can still make an arse out of myself sometimes. Being in Year 3 this time has been a really good thing for me. I know that I was too familiar with the kids last time, but this lot just seemed so young, and even if I hadn't made a few slight misjudgements last time, I really don't think even I would have thought that blokey and slightly adult humour was appropriate for these little children. I quite liked my mentor. Ms Jones was obviously a good teacher, and she supported me a lot when I was planning my lessons, but I never quite thought that she really saw me as a proper teacher in the making. I'm certain that Mr Gray would have told her about me, and I know that on at least one occasion she was inwardly smirking about the stripper story. She was also clearly very good friends with her TA, Mrs Cole. They were both in their late thirties, ten years or so older than me, and I often saw little surreptitious glances between them when I was talking to the children. Maybe I'm just paranoid, but I'm sure that they used to have a good laugh at my expense on the phone every evening.

Anyway, we were doing a topic about animals and habitats and so Ms Jones organised a trip to the zoo. Again, maybe this was not her intention, but she didn't want to seem to trust me with any of the organisation. 'Just watch this time, Callum,' she'd say. 'You'll learn a lot that way.' On reflection, I think that one of the reasons that I didn't learn too much at the time, and one of the reasons why I made so many mistakes, was that I wasn't given responsibility, so I just kind of went with the flow, and didn't pay too much attention to things.

It's rather ironic that it was actually I who gave out the letters at the end of the day, it was I who mentioned the importance of ensuring that they gave these to their parents and it was I who said that, now they are in Key Stage 2, they should perhaps take a little responsibility for themselves and not just let Mummy pack everything for them. If you ask me why I didn't actually read that letter myself and why I didn't follow its instructions, I'm not really sure that I could give you a very good answer. As I said, I'm learning.

The day of the trip dawned to bright early spring sunshine, so I put on a T-shirt and rugby top, confident that this combination would be warm enough. When we arrived at the zoo, it was absolutely pissing it down, and all of the children and all of the other adults dutifully took out their waterproofs which, I later found out, were not only top of the 'things to bring' checklist on the letter that I had given out, but were also underlined and in bold.

118

'You not got a waterproof, Mr Williams?' chirped Sophie. 'You're going to get soaked!'

Neither Ms Jones nor Mrs Cole said anything; they didn't need to. The look that they gave each other said everything, and I was actually really grateful to Kara Cole for sharing an umbrella with me until the shower had passed.

So, the sun came out again as we started our walk around the zoo and my confidence returned somewhat. I'd been given a group of six children to look after, and we all got on very well and were having a great time. Ms Jones had asked me, the previous day, to think about all the learning that was going on during the visit and to tell her, at the end of the day, why it was important to actually visit the zoo, rather than just look at pictures and videos. It soon became obvious that many of the children had no real idea about the nature of a zoo, or indeed, the nature of the animals inside it. When Millie asked me when we would be seeing the sheep and cows, I assumed at first that she was joking. But she was deadly serious. This child had clearly no concept about the difference between a farm and a zoo – they were both just places that animals lived.

And then we came to the lions' enclosure and we were fortunate enough to have a lion come really close to us. I'm afraid the next part of this story will make the stripper tale seem like one of my more inspired moments, but I'm going to tell you anyway. My psychiatrist has told me that I need to talk about it if I'm ever going to get over it. All I can say is that my sole intention was to teach Naomi in a way that she would remember. Practical experience and all that.

'Mr Williams,' she said, without any trace of irony as the lion came even closer, 'can I go in and stroke it?' Here was a beautiful large cat that would purr contentedly as she rubbed his majestic mane. People have told me over and over in my life that I need to think about my actions before I do them, but in the spur of the moment, I thought the best way to teach Naomi about lions was for her to see them in action. And so, I went up to the cage, rattled it loudly and yelled even more loudly. Well, in fairness, Naomi will never again ask to stroke a lion, and a large crowd got to see something really rather exciting, but the looks on the faces of all around me as the zookeepers spent the next ten minutes calming the bloody thing down will live with me forever. Fortunately, after this little episode, I wasn't very hungry. Guess who was the only person in our party not to have brought a packed lunch?

The afternoon passed without too many embarrassing moments as I got more and more of a sense of how much a 'real life' trip adds to children's learning, and by the time we got back into the bus for the return journey, with the sun still shining, I was in a really good mood, but, like everyone else, was very tired. With just ten minutes to go before the sanctuary of the staff room and a hot cup of tea, up stepped a small child and said that Naomi was feeling sick. Now, rightly or wrongly, I've always assumed that sick duty was a woman's job, and hence I was slightly surprised at the reaction of the five female adults when I said, with a touch of humour, I thought: 'And which one of you *ladies* is going to deal with that one?'

'Now let me see,' said Ms Jones, through gritted teeth, 'how about the arse who frightened her to death this morning?'

I really don't know what it is with me and that word, but I did think it rather unprofessional in front of such impressionable youngsters. So, armed with just a bucket and a sick bag, I strode reluctantly down to the end of a bus, where a very pale-looking Naomi looked like she had just seen a ferocious lion. I handed her the sick bag – well that's what you do, don't you – and she promptly hurled something chunky and orange into the cheap bag, which promptly split. So in between the screams, the smell, and the mass exodus from Naomi's seat, I stood there limply holding my bucket as little bits of sick started dropping from her lap on to the floor. Without thinking – yes, I know there's a theme developing here – I went over to her and started scooping bits of sick from said lap to said bucket until, a good minute into the process, Mrs Cox tapped me on the shoulder and offered me some rubber gloves. I swear I can still smell Naomi's vomit on my hands.

You may be wondering why I have chosen to talk about this day out for my presentation – watching your faces while I was telling it, I'm starting to wonder myself. You see, I could have talked about some of my teaching, especially when Martin observed my Maths lesson and said that it was excellent. Or I could have talked about some of the self-help strategies that I used to cope with my dyslexia, how I tried to turn it into a positive, and how Grace came in specially to see how I was getting on. But I didn't. I decided to give the likes of Anna and Donna even more ammunition to take the piss. Part of me feels that there should always be funny stories in a presentation and that's one of the reasons, but the main one is that I know that if I want to make it as a teacher, then I just need to stop doing really stupid things, and if I talk about these rather than brush them under the carpet, then maybe – just maybe – it might act as some sort of warning system before I wind up another wild animal. Anyway, that's my presentation. I hope you enjoyed it.

Surgery

There was a moment's hush before Gabriel started applauding and everyone else joined in, but there was something about Callum's last point that made

Donna rather subdued as she stood up for her presentation and it took her a moment or two to regain her composure. But Donna was a good orator and she quickly found her feet, and then Gabriel concluded the session with an excellent and heartfelt account of why the three-year B.Ed route was right for him. When the applause for his talk died away, Martin stood up to speak.

'We thought long and hard about whether to conduct these presentations in your seminar groups or as an extended Surgery meeting, and I'm really glad that we went for the latter, as it made for a much more intimate atmosphere. First, I'd like to say thank you; it's been a real privilege listening to these and seeing just how far you've come in your first six months here. It was also great to come and see you all teach and to know that there is a good teacher in all of you. I don't want to talk for long as I want you to go and enjoy your extended weekend, but we had a few aims for this session:

'Being open and honest – check.

'Being highly reflective – check.

'Presenting with confidence – check.

'Making an arse of yourself – check.

'Okay, maybe one of them wasn't on the original list. As you know, next week you start your Professional Studies module and one of the themes we'll cover is working with other adults. As this is something all of you have mentioned in one form or another it might make for some interesting discussions. See you next week.'

Chapter 13

Jo

'It's so lovely to finally meet you all. I've seen a few of you around and remember you from the Christmas "It's a Knockout" competition. I'm Jo – you may know that I'm a seconded teacher from a local primary school. I'm only supposed to be here for a year, but between you and me, if anything more permanent comes up, I'd love to stay. I hadn't realised just how satisfying teaching adults would be. It's really powerful to think that if I can inspire all 25 of you to all inspire another 30 children – well, I'm no good at Maths, but you get my point. I may not be the best person to ask about university procedures and the like – I'm certainly still learning there – but hopefully, what I can offer is someone who has a very current view of education. I really hope we all get on, as I'm teaching you for both your Professional Studies modules, one now and one in the summer. Over the next couple of weeks, we're going to look closely at one of the most important things for you to think about as a teacher – your involvement with different adults. It's all very well for us to build a great relationship with the children, but that's only half the battle. You've got to know how to deal with parents, with teaching assistants, and with all other stakeholders. Get on well with the school cook, and you'll be served a bigger portion at lunch. Ingratiate yourself with parents – especially initially – and the conversations that they will have about you at the school gates will make your life that little bit easier.

'We're going to start by thinking about relationships with teaching assistants – TAs – and how these relationships can severely impact on your wellbeing as a teacher. Good TAs are like gold dust and you've got to know how to work well with them. I want you all to log in to the Padlet address on the board and start typing anything at all about your views or experiences of working with TAs. Your comments will show on the board in real time, so that you can all contribute to the session. We'll then go from there.'

Kathryn

Kathryn, like the rest of her group, was pleased when she found out that Jo was to be their Professional Studies tutor. Jo brought with her a youthful enthusiasm, as well as the kudos of being straight from the chalk face, and it was clear from the vibes around the course that she was a good tutor. Kathryn hadn't used Padlet before, but she rather liked it. It allowed her views to be seen and discussed by everyone, but due to the anonymity of the comments, without the sense that she was being judged. But even with this screen of anonymity, Kathryn preferred to watch first, as other comments appeared on the screen in front of them. She read as her seminar group described tales of TAs thinking that they were clearly more of an authority than the student, or of them demeaning the students in front of the class. She instinctively glanced at Mary when she read the phrase, 'My TA really wasn't that smart but I think she meant well,' and it was very obvious by her facial expression that Mary had written these words and was clearly now embarrassed about her behaviour in School Experience One. Perhaps the biggest gasp followed the words, 'My TA used to do my observations when my mentor had a better offer. She once told me that my teaching wasn't good enough.' At this point, Matt was happy to expand on this, opting not to hide behind the anonymity of the Padlet.

'I kid you not, this bloody woman thought she knew it all, just because she'd worked at the school for ages and was twice as old as me. I was teaching Music, for God's sake, and was trying to get my Year 2 children to create sounds from the rainforest using a range of instruments. You know what she said to me during her pompous feedback session? *This class always works quietly, and they were much too noisy for my liking.* For her liking? I mean, is she even allowed to do a formal observation on me, given that she's a bloody TA and that she has over-delicate ears?'

Kathryn was really impressed over the next few minutes as Jo used Matt's outburst to pose probing questions to the seminar group about appropriate and inappropriate behaviour, about what to do if they feel that the TA has overstepped the mark or undermined them, and about techniques to get TAs on your side in the first place. The statements were still appearing on the Padlet, and Kathryn now felt the confidence not only to write, but to speak up as well.

'Working with a TA has always been one of the things that I've been most worried about since starting this course. I've no problem with the relationship with my mentor, because she is the authority and I'm learning from her. But I don't think I'm very good at asking adults to do things and to ensure that they are done. My TA in my last placement was a qualified teacher who had decided that she wanted a few years as a TA before taking up a teaching post. As you can imagine, this made me feel even worse – I had to somehow be the authority for a trained teacher. But I quickly learned that Miss Smith was actually really glad when I went through things with her before my lessons. I'm not sure that I've ever been in a situation in my life that an adult has been pleased about me telling them what to do. I don't know whether Miss Jones knew how much her responses helped me to develop my confidence. As I've already said, Mrs Franks was a brilliant mentor, so it may well have had something to do with it. It seems that most of the conversation so far has been about negative comments towards TAs, so I felt I wanted to say something positive.'

'What an amazing thing to say. I wish I could be that honest.'

These words, uttered by Anna, added more fuel to the feeling Kathryn had that Anna was actually beginning to like her. It may have been a sympathy vote, but since Anna had stuck up for her in Geography, she had been pleasant rather than dismissive. Despite this, Kathryn had no illusions about Anna suddenly losing that acerbic streak that had reared its head several times, and she was to be reminded of that before the end of the seminar. Jo was summing up an interesting and thoughtful session, and commented that the most important thing, right from the onset, was to develop a positive relationship with your TA.

Whether she meant to say it as loudly as it came out was questionable, but everyone distinctly heard Anna say, with a sidewise glance at Callum, 'Not a problem for you, was it, Callum? Developing a positive relationship with your TA?'

Callum

Callum had been really pleased with his presentation, as well as the responses that he had received, especially from Martin. He had felt that he had turned a corner and was distinctly moving away from 'cocky rugby player' and towards 'professional teacher-to-be'. And that felt good. But now all that good work had been undone by one snide remark from Anna. Yes, her line had been perfectly set up for her; yes, he supposed he deserved it; and yes, he probably wouldn't have missed an open goal from five yards either if it were Anna, and not he, who hadn't returned home alone last night.

This was the first public unveiling of Lily, and Callum had no hesitation in accepting Gabriel's invitation to meet at the pub, along with Anna and Donna. He genuinely didn't know, when he arrived, that Lily would be bringing her friend, Jackie, in tow, hence there could be no accusation of malice aforethought. So, okay, he did assess the situation as soon as he walked in, he did take in the fact that there was a space next to Donna, which was clearly the nearest available space, he did take in that the decidedly-pretty Jackie also had a space next to her, which would involve a small element of clambering and he did − indeed − clamber. It was only when he had sat down that he realised that the patently obvious ploy had been noted by all, and this was amplified when Donna made a show of sniffing her armpits, but needs must.

'Hi, I'm Callum, nice to meet you.'

'I'm Jackie, nice to meet you too.'

'Oh, and this is Lily,' said Gabriel, with a definite lilt in his voice, 'in case you are interested.'

So, it wasn't an auspicious start to the evening, but Callum had figured that it was worth it for the few hours or so that he could now work his magic. The awkwardness of the moment quickly dissipated as Callum offered to buy a round of drinks, and after a bit more clambering, he had sat back down next to the decidedly gorgeous Jackie. He was fully aware that his token effort of speaking to Lily was seen by all as exactly that, and after a few stilted pleasantries, he turned his attention back to Jackie.

Fortunately, she was aware, from Lily, that everyone present was training with Gabriel, hence the conversation quickly turned towards his training and why he wanted to be a teacher. Okay, so maybe he over-emphasised the 'making a difference' and 'children needing a male role model' gambit, but it seemed to do the trick. Even Anna's glance at him mid-flow which said, unequivocally, 'lecherous git', didn't put him off, and soon, as he had hoped, Jackie was eating out of his hand. There was a definite flick of the eyelids when he talked about his trials for the Southeast of England, and eventually, he realised that, even by his standards, he was talking about himself rather a lot.

'So, what do you do, Jackie?'

'I'm a teaching assistant at a primary school.'

Even now, as he reflected back on this conversation, Callum could not really put his finger on why he had felt slightly blindsided by this revelation. Maybe, given the conversation that they had just had with Jo, his unease might have stemmed from the potentially awkward relationship between student teachers and TAs, or maybe it was his own experience of feeling slightly outnumbered by a teacher and TA, who were clearly good friends.

'Oh, right, that's nice. Are you planning to always do that, or maybe, well, you know?'

It was all very well Callum having these grand ideas to grow up, but he had to acknowledge that there were times, as Anna so eloquently put it, that he behaved like an arse. What a stupid question, with all its veiled implications. Fortunately for him, Jackie was a very down-to-earth sort, laughed at his awkwardness and made a joke about this being a stopgap to her long-time ambition of being an astrophysicist.

And so the evening went on, and Callum was delighted when Jackie had asked him if he would like to come back for a nightcap. Whilst nothing had happened, he was deliberately coy when Donna and Anna had grilled him the next day. But now, as he felt the gaze of the whole seminar group upon him, he rather wished that he had made it clear that the evening had ended with a simple peck on the cheek.

Martin

Martin didn't really know what to say. Jo was beside herself and blatantly suggesting that she was not up to working with young adults. His words, however true, felt hollow even to him.

'Jo, it wasn't your fault. You did absolutely the right thing by coming to speak to me, even if it was all a misunderstanding. To be honest, if anyone is to blame here it's Anna, not you.'

'But I'm supposed to be leading a module about working effectively with other adults. How the hell am I going to face him, let alone the rest of them, when I see them again tomorrow?'

Martin knew that there was no easy response to this. Jo had agonised for ages before speaking to him about what she had heard Anna say. The meaning of her words was crystal-clear; Callum had been having an affair with his teaching assistant, presumably on his last placement. Martin had then felt that he had no option but to broach this with Callum when the misunderstanding had been sorted out. Unfortunately for Jo, however, Callum did not take kindly to being accused of such gross unprofessionalism, despite his wandering eyes at anyone female and attractive when he had first arrived at the school or, indeed, anywhere else.

'Don't you think it would have been a good idea for her to have talked to me first, so that I could explain before my name is smeared in front of my programme leader? I wonder if this would have happened had it been, say, Gabriel, rather than me.'

Martin had to agree that this probably wouldn't have been the case, and stopped himself, perhaps wisely, from commenting that Gabriel wasn't a womaniser. Instead, he had tried to defend Jo as much as he could and state that it was university policy for any suggestion of gross unprofessionalism to be followed up. Whilst this was probably true, he was also pretty sure that he would have dealt with it differently and defused the situation before it got to this stage. However he tried to dress it up, it was obvious to both him and Jo that tomorrow's session was going to be awkward.

Anna

Anna worked out what was going on straightaway and she found it really rather funny. Jo was a different person to the confident young lady who had taught them before; indeed, she looked like she didn't want to be there, standing and talking to her students about working with adults. And when Anna saw Callum's face everything fit into place. One way or the other, Jo must have got the wrong end of the stick after Anna's gentle jibe the other day, and had either spoken to Callum directly or, even worse, spoken to Martin or the Dean. And when the truth of the matter had come out, Jo had been devastated by her false accusation, and Callum had been apoplectic with the injustice of it all. Oh, joy of joys. Not that Anna had anything against Jo – this was hardly Frank standing there – and also, she had come to rather like Callum; but Callum-baiting was still one of her most enjoyable of hobbies. She was so going to make this last.

As the session got going, some of the awkwardness in the air began to lift as the students were asked to give scenarios where they had witnessed tension or animosity between a teacher and one of the parents, and this was to be followed by some roleplay exercises, exploring different responses. Many of these scenarios were highly entertaining, not least when Gabriel described a scene towards the end of his last placement.

'It was at the end of the day, and Joe and I had just sat down to go over my lesson. You all remember Joe, yeah? From my presentation? Mr Cool Dude who everybody loves. Well, not Mrs Patterson, apparently. She stormed through the door dragging a rather sheepish-looking offspring with her and demanded words with Joe. She then spent the next two minutes ranting at him for telling darling Jamie off the previous day because he had apparently flicked a dirty paintbrush onto another child's uniform. This couldn't possibly have happened, according to the venerable Mrs Patterson, because Jamie said it didn't, and he always tells the truth. Joe, as calm and smiling as ever, turned nonchalantly towards the unfortunate Jamie, and said, lightly, "But Jamie, I saw you do that. Are you suggesting that I am lying?" Jamie's response, after a few moments of unease, as he weighed up his options, was priceless, "Er, oh yeah, I did. That's right. Er, I forgot." During the next five seconds of silence, Mrs Patterson's face went from indignation, to confusion, to embarrassment, to gradual realisation, and then finally to undiluted fury. As she spun away from Joe and hurled vitriol at her son, I stood there unsure whether to laugh or call

Social Services. I am certain, had we not have been there, that she would have murdered him.'

By now, everyone was laughing as Gabriel embellished his anecdote, and Anna found herself laughing as well. She reflected, whilst endorsing Gabriel's words, that she might not have done this when she initially started the course. There was a part of her, she knew, that got slightly irritated if someone else had the best stories rather than her, and if someone else was the centre of attention. But that part of her was definitely beginning to dissipate, as she led an impromptu round of applause for Gabriel. Nevertheless, she was still keen to have attention diverted her way and she took centre stage as she told the tale of meeting the father of one of her class in Sainsbury's, and of wanting the earth to swallow her up because she hadn't put any makeup on. 'I can't leave the house without makeup. Yes, call me insecure if you will, but here was Amy's dad right behind me in a long queue. There was nothing I could do, especially when he recognised me and started engaging in conversation. The fact that he clearly fancied me and had been mildly flirty at parents' evening didn't help. I'd just got this massive spot on the right of my chin, so tried to talk to him without fully turning around. It was horrible. I'm sure he thought that I was playing hard to get. Mind you, with that spot, he would have kept well away anyway.'

As more and more students chipped in with their stories and observations, Anna watched as Jo relaxed back into her role, and Callum started to thaw a little. When Jo then announced that they would begin by exploring these scenarios with roleplay activities in threes, Anna was just a little peeved not to be put with Callum, as there was just so much potential for teasing. However, if she thought that the drama of the last couple of days had ended, she was soon to see that things had barely begun.

Donna

Donna could see, from the outset, that she was going to have her work cut out here. It was patently obvious that Kathryn did not want to engage in roleplay and Callum continued to look surly. Someone was going to have to take the lead here.

'Tell you what. Let's go for Jamie's one, where he was pretty sure that Ms Cooper was coming on to him, and he didn't know what to do. I'll play Ms Cooper, Callum can be Callum, and Kathryn, why don't you be the observer, and tell us what you think? I know you're a bit of an expert on the whole body language stuff, so you can also comment on that. Okay?'

128

Despite the shrugs that she received from both Callum and Kathryn, Donna was in the mood for this, and determined to make it work.

'Excuse me, Mr Williams? My name is Jane Cooper – call me Janie – and I'm Pippa's mum. I wonder if I could have a word with you in private? I'd really value your advice on something.'

Despite himself, and as Donna had predicted, Callum simply couldn't resist turning on the charm, especially when Donna, fluttering her eyelids, said that she couldn't say this to Pippa's dad, as she didn't quite trust his response, 'It's a bit personal, you see. I hope you don't mind me being so open with you. It's just that Pippa speaks so highly of you and...'

'Of course, Janie. I only hope that I can be of help.'

So, Donna shamelessly turned on the charm, confided that things weren't going too well at home – all the usual chestnuts – and Callum reverted to type like the proverbial duck to water. When, eventually, the inevitable happened, and Callum suggested that maybe they could discuss this further over a drink, Donna burst out laughing, and said, casually, 'You know what, Callum, that was so convincing, it almost looks like you've done this before.'

Callum's response was one of sheer indignance, 'What do you mean, I've done this before? Don't be so bloody ridiculous.'

Reflecting on this later, Donna was unsure exactly how the next few seconds panned out. The only thing that she was sure of was that a bomb exploded. After Callum's response, Donna turned to Kathryn to ask for her take on the scenario, but Kathryn was unable to talk. Donna looked at Kathryn, and then at Callum, and then at Jo, and finally at Anna, who had given up any pretence of working with her group. Kathryn's expression said it all. Callum's outburst meant one thing and one thing only, such a scenario had really taken place, and Callum had been at the heart of it. It seemed to Donna, in the moments of silence that followed, that everybody was computing this all at once. It was left to Anna to say the words that really hit home.

'It seems to me, Callum, that thou doth protest too much. Oh my God. Miss Draper. Mia's mum. That's it, isn't it? I saw you talking to her a few times and I definitely thought that there might be something between you. You slept with...'

'Fuck you. Fuck you all.'

Callum, red in the face and close to tears, picked up his bag, ran out the door, and slammed it behind him. Again, Donna's sharp mind quickly assessed the situation. Kathryn continued to look horrified, Anna looked somewhere between amused and shocked, and Jo – well, Donna could not really describe Jo's expression. If Jo looked awkward at the beginning of the session, she looked – frankly – out of her depth now.

Jo

There is something about mulling things over in the middle of the night that is so much worse than doing so in the cold light of day. At three o'clock in the morning, with both the silence and the darkness absolute, Jo started reliving the horrors of the last few days, and of the bad decisions that she had made. She saw now that she had made a mistake in going straight to Martin initially, when Anna spoke of Callum's involvement with a teaching assistant. A quiet word with him would have sufficed, and they might even have ended the conversation with a mutual laugh at the misunderstanding. But if she had made a mistake in speaking to Martin about the initial incident, she had made an appalling lack of judgement by not speaking to him after Callum stormed out of the subsequent seminar, leaving no one in any doubt that he had, indeed, had some sort of relationship with one of the parents in his class.

Even now, as the silence of the small hours screamed at her, she found it hard to articulate why, when Martin had asked her how the session went, her response had been, 'Fine, thanks. I think everything will be okay.'

As soon as she had uttered these words, she had regretted them. What had possessed her to say this? Was it the fact she had had been so spectacularly wrong once that she was terrified about making a further accusation, or was it simply that she hoped that the whole sorry incident would just go away, and that her silence was the most likely way for this to happen? But then Martin had smiled, said that he was glad to hear it, and disappeared to another engagement.

As each hour had passed since then, telling the real story had simply got harder, but as it did, it tore Jo up more and more. She had been almost relieved therefore when today, some 48 hours after Callum's dramatic exit, Martin had asked if he could speak to her. Someone, and she hadn't even asked who, had gone directly to Martin and explained what had happened, and explained that Callum hadn't been seen since. As Martin had looked at her with enquiring eyes, she had felt like a naughty schoolgirl who had just been caught smoking behind the bike sheds. Martin had always been very even and approachable and had always adopted the 'we all make mistakes from which we can learn' approach. But as he'd asked her why she had said that all had been well, it was very clear from his demeanour that he was mightily pissed off, and that he now had an extremely delicate situation to deal with. Jo had always prided herself at her ability to be able to cope with awkward or demanding situations − God knows this had happened enough at school − but this had just been too much, and she'd had to fight back the tears as she'd murmured something incomprehensible to Martin. He'd squeezed her arm, and said that everything would be okay, but at three o'clock in the morning, feeling very alone, it felt anything but okay.

Surgery

There had been several awkward moments in Surgery over the year, but there had always been all of them there, and this, somehow, had helped to make things okay. The absence of Callum at this session was so palpable that the overriding emotion amongst the whole of the Set was one of concern. It had now been three days since Callum had left the seminar so dramatically, and he had not been in contact with any of his fellow students since. When Martin entered the room, everyone was surprised to see Jo with him. This was another first − it was an unwritten rule that Surgery would consist of Martin and his six personal tutees.

'I suppose there is no point in beating about the bush here,' he began. 'We all know what everyone is thinking about. I have to say now that I finally managed to talk to Callum about half an hour ago. The nature of this discussion is, of course, confidential, but suffice it to say that, at present, no further action is needed. We have had no complaint from the school, and therefore he has no official case to answer. However, he has made a grave mistake, and has potentially embarrassed the university, and his indignation about being falsely accused earlier this week has not helped him. The reason that none of us have seen him for the last few days is that he is simply too ashamed and embarrassed to show his face. It was only when I left a voicemail saying that not talking was not an option that he finally got in contact. One can only guess how he must be feeling. So, this is what I want you to do. I want you to be his friend. Don't engage in mild banter − that's not what he needs. Just be his friend and invite him for a drink. Callum will be okay.'

There was a lengthy silence after Martin finished speaking before Jo spoke. Kathryn noticed how she held her head up high and talked about how much she had learnt from this experience, 'Perhaps you look at your lecturers the way that the children in your class will look at you; as people who always know the right thing to do and who don't make mistakes, but of course, that isn't the case. The main reason that I wanted to speak to you directly today is because I want all of you to learn, first-hand, that there are going to be times as a teacher where you feel that you have made such a colossal mistake that there is no way back. Well there is, and sometimes that might mean you having to apologise to children, in the same way as I want to apologise to you now. Let's move on. I hope you all have a great weekend, and as Martin says, be nice to Callum. I'm looking forward to seeing you all on Monday, when I'll talk you through your next assignment…'

Chapter 14

Mary

'You're really not getting the hang of this, are you Mum? I thought that your New Year's resolution was to be more decisive and to spend less time reading around a variety of topics, before deciding which one to write about.'

'I have done, Alice. I know that I'm going to write about either working with teaching assistants or working with parents. It's just – well, you know.'

'Yes, I do know, Mum. I know that you are struggling to decide whether to go for the safe option and write about dealing with parents, or whether to confront your demons and write about working with TAs, with all the uncomfortable reflection that that would bring. But the fact remains the same: you were given this task three weeks ago now, and you've spent ages reading up on both, knowing that half of all your work will be discarded. Just be decisive for once on this course. I'll toss a coin for it, if you want.'

Mary knew that Alice spoke the truth and the rational side of her also knew that time was marching on – there were only three weeks before the hand-in date – and she hadn't started writing yet. She'd asked Grace after their last assignment how she could improve on her grade of 72. Grace had told her that really high grades in Year One analysed subjects in even more depth, and of course Mary interpreted that as doing even more reading.

'Okay,' she sighed. 'Heads it's parents, and tails it's TAs…'

Anna

Anna took another sip of her piña colada. She'd been looking forward to Leah's long hen weekend all year, and four days in Corfu was just what she needed. Yes, it meant missing a couple of sessions at uni, but this was more than made up for not only with the alcohol and partying, but also with the highly creative and entertaining discussions that she had largely initiated. She was very much aware that her sister had been judging her for most of her life, and it only took a moment of weakness, such as when she told Molly, Leah's chief bridesmaid, that she thought that university was maturing her, for her to feel the sneer in

Leah's voice, 'You're not turning in to one of those boring students who don't know how to have a good time, I hope?'

Maybe it was overcompensating, but Anna then delighted in embellishing stories about how she had put Frank in his place, or how she had been the chief cause of such embarrassment for Callum. When asked what excuse she had used for missing sessions this week, Anna had replied, with a certain degree of pride, that her sister was ill, and she had to look after her, 'Okay, so what I meant to say was that Leah is *going* to be ill due to the vast quantities of vodka that she'll be downing over the next few days, but hey, no one's perfect.'

This then developed into a sort of 'truth or dare' scenario, where all Leah's friends had to agree on Anna's next excuse for being absent for a seminar. Warming to the theme and taking delight in being the centre of attention, Anna stated that so far, she'd been absent through illness three times, bereavement twice, and once for the old 'car not starting' routine, 'But my personal favourite was when I told Frank that I wouldn't be learning about the environment that day due to women's problems. That shut him up.'

'But they're all dull,' said Molly, between swigs of something decidedly blue. 'Let's find something really daring for Anna when she next fancies a day in bed.'

Such was her mood, and such was the whole hypothetical nature of the discussion, that Anna was more than happy chipping in, and even said, 'That's *so* going to happen,' when 'religious observance' narrowly beat 'initial consultation about plastic surgery' as the allotted excuse.

It was only when Leah gave her one of her looks that Anna began to have vague misgivings.

'So, let's get this straight. You told this Jo woman that you wouldn't be in today because you were kindly looking after me. Is that right? So then there's the weekend and then of course there's Monday… Didn't you say that you had a different lecturer on Monday? Richard someone?'

Anna went pale. 'Er, yes, it's just a one-off lecture about cyberbullying. I'm not even sure that we need to…'

'Excellent. So that's a different lecturer, and therefore a different excuse. We're waiting.'

And so, Anna sat there dumbfounded as eight slightly drunken women watched her and waited. She thought about saying that she'd copied in Richard to the initial email, but such was the look on Leah's face, she knew that this would be pointless. There was only one thing to do, balls it out. She wasn't entirely sure whether she was pleased or concerned that it would be Richard at the other end of her email. She had absolutely no doubt that he'd know that she was taking the piss, but on the other hand, he did fancy himself as a bit of a joker…

Dear Anna

Thank you so much for your kind email, letting me know that you'd be absent from the lecture on Monday due to religious observance. As I am sure you are aware, the university has full tolerance for any absence due to religious or cultural reasons, and of course I am very happy to put this down as authorised absence. You may be aware that we are keen to celebrate diversity of any kind on our programme. To that end, I'd like to invite you to have a chat with me on Tuesday afternoon when you can discuss your beliefs with me. In fact, it would be fantastic if you could also chat to the year group about this — I can easily give you ten minutes during Wednesday's lecture. If you could just discuss your beliefs and how these may impact on your chosen career, I'm sure that everyone will be fascinated. See you Tuesday. We'll talk it through then.

Richard

There had hardly been a moment in her life that Anna hadn't craved her sister's approval or to be the centre of attention. Well, now she had both, and she felt sick. All she could do was to meet up with Richard on Tuesday and tell the truth. Turning up with a rosary and a few Hail Marys on Wednesday simply wasn't an option. So, she could either sweat on this or milk it for all it was worth. There was absolutely no point in the former, so she laughed along with everyone as they read and reread the email, and even wrote one back in full view of the girls, stating how delighted she'd be to meet up. In for a penny…

And as the weekend wore on, she tried to sink into the sort of forgetful blur that alcohol induces, but the nagging thoughts that kept seeping into her mind were only exacerbated when Molly said, towards the end of the weekend, 'Didn't you also say that you had an essay due soon? How's that going?'

Kathryn

It was no good. However hard she tried, nothing would go in. The longer Kathryn tried to focus on background reading and on structuring her forthcoming assignment, the more frustrated she became, and the more the fog swirled around her brain. Her grief counsellor had told her that there were likely to be moments when she would struggle to concentrate, and Martin had been happy to allow her an extension for the essay, but she knew that any extension would simply exacerbate the problem. This fog wasn't going to lift any time soon.

Mary

So, it was to be teaching assistants. When Alice had tossed the coin, she'd said, before revealing it, 'What are you hoping for?' and at that moment, Mary had realised that she knew what she had to do, and that the process of reflecting on her awful behaviour towards her TA in school placement one would be both cathartic and would also serve as a timely reminder to her that, however much it went against the grain, she was the one learning here, and that learning extended to her TA, as well as her teacher. But that didn't make writing it any easier. Whilst she now had a wealth of background reading at her disposal, trying to analyse and reflect on her own attitudes, whilst extolling the virtues of a good teaching assistant was proving to be a very difficult thing to do. She wasn't sure whether the constant texts between herself and Kathryn, where they both bemoaned their inability to write, was a help or a hindrance. Mary did not take kindly to failing to do something well. The breakthrough would come.

Anna

Anna knew, the moment that she walked through the door, that things were going to be okay. Richard's eyes sparkled with something akin to amusement and a definite wry grin emerged on his face as Anna risked her opening gambit of crossing herself, and saying, 'May the peace of God be with you, Richard.'

She then explained, openly and honestly, what had happened and how she had felt that she'd had no choice but to send the email.

'Remind me never to cross your sister, Anna. Sounds like she would eat me alive. You see, the reason that I've got a smile on my face at present is that you had 100% attendance for my Maths seminars, your placement reports have been excellent, and everyone says that you are going to make a great teacher. You don't need me to tell you to be careful and that sometimes practical jokes – or lies as they may be interpreted by some – can come back to haunt you. You have so much potential to thrive at this university, Anna. There are a lot of us on the staff who have made it our mission to ensure that you take the right path. Anyway, enough preaching – so to speak. Two weeks to go until your assignment is due in. How's that going? I don't suppose you gave up too many parties in Corfu to read. All done, or are you relying on divine intervention?'

Anna's respect for Richard rose considerably after their meeting. Here was a lecturer – albeit one who was a bit of a cocky lech – who understood students, and who could separate an important family occasion – with all that entailed – from someone's overall achievements at uni. She could only imagine how this

136

conversation would have gone had it been Frank, rather than Richard, who had delivered the lecture on cyberbullying.

But the relief felt from this most satisfactory of meetings was more than tempered by the ongoing nagging inside of her about the imminent due date for their assignment. As she walked into their shared house, she saw Kathryn sitting at the kitchen table, staring blankly ahead of her. With something akin to empathy, Anna approached Kathryn and spoke to her.

'How's it going, Kathryn. Finished your assignment yet?'

'It's just not going to happen. I've spent over three weeks trying to make sense of this and write something down, but I just can't. There's just too much other stuff.'

'Have you tried talking it through with anyone? Mary?'

'Many times. We've met for coffee and both bemoaned our lot although I do think Mary's problems are a little more self-inflicted. I don't know what to do.'

Anna pulled up a chair and sat down next to Kathryn.

'You, know, there is an alternative.' She waited for some sort of reaction on Kathryn's face, but none appeared. 'For our last essay I – well – I kind of ran out of time so I sort of thought outside the box a bit.'

'I know what you're going to say. I remember you telling us all that you'd cheated and paid someone on the internet to write it for you.'

Anna sighed. 'I don't really consider it as cheating. I did all the work on the module; I went to all the seminars and always joined in with conversations. At the end of it all, I still felt like I understood more about the importance of good communication. I just – well – I just didn't write about it. To be honest, it made no difference whatsoever to my ability to teach. The thing is, Kathryn, you've just said yourself that this is not going to get done. What's the alternative? Leaving the course? We both know that unless you get all your credits, you won't progress to Year 2.'

Kathryn bit her lower lip and stared somewhere a long way away. 'How much – how much would it cost?'

'That depends,' said Anna, edging a little closer, 'on what sort of grade you want. The place that I found on the internet offered different services and different guarantees. At the end of the day, when you get it back, you can edit it as much as you want. One of the services guarantees a first, or your money back.'

There was a long pause as Kathryn mulled this over. In the end, she glanced briefly at Anna, before saying: 'A first. Mum would have been so proud if I got a first…'

Kathryn

There were times, thought Kathryn, that she really didn't like Mary that much. Here she was banging on about having finally 'broken through the wall', how her essay was now flowing smoothly and how she secretly hoped for something in the mid-80s this time. Of course, she asked Kathryn how hers was coming on and Kathryn replied, a little stiffly, 'It will be done.'

Now had it been the other way around, and had Mary uttered those words with that rather stiff and clearly uncomfortable tone, Kathryn was certain that she would have noticed, and she was equally certain that she wouldn't then have quickly changed the subject back to herself, and back to how much of a relief it was that she had now broken the back of it.

'To be honest, Kathryn, I've never been in a situation where I haven't completely finished something with a week to go. But I'm nearly there now. You're welcome to look at it if that would help?'

But it wouldn't help. Indeed, it would be less than helpful. Indeed, it would just be plain annoying and frustrating to read Mary's perfect essay. She knew that Mary's heart was in the right place and that she was genuinely trying to help, but right now Anna's sort of help seemed more attractive than Mary's. One week to go. It simply wasn't going to get written. Kathryn tried to block out the vision of both her mum and her nan shaking their heads as she finally made her decision.

Gabriel

They really weren't being that loud. They were simply doing what anyone else does in a pub, enjoying themselves and sharing stories. Gabriel realised that, whilst he knew that Lily was an A&E ward receptionist, he had never really asked her too much about her role and experiences in the hospital, and so he resolved, this evening, to mainly listen as she embellished tales about her time at the emergency ward, involving drunken and irate young men, embarrassing injuries due to a rather creative sex life or grisly tales of sawn-off fingers. Gabriel laughed heartily as she told him about 'Needy Neil', who came into the ward every day presumably to get out of the cold and to have a little company, and how his entrance always brought much-needed entertainment to beleaguered nurses, who ran a daily sweepstake, trying to guess the day's chosen ailment.

'Drinks are definitely on me tonight, Gabriel,' said Lily, waving some fivers casually. 'I only went and guessed today that he was going to complain of a touch of cholera. How fantastic is that?'

Gabriel was genuinely glad that Lily phoned and texted him so much. He had never been out with a girl who paid him such attention, and it was really rather flattering. Even the last few days, when there had seemed to be a slight tension in the air, were forgotten now as she relaxed into her dialogue. He had stated candidly to her that he wouldn't be around this week as he had to get his assignment completed – he wasn't going to hand anything in late ever again – and whilst she 'totally understood', she had contacted him every night this week to see if he could meet for a swift drink. So, there was genuine relief – in more sense than one – when, after duly handing in his assignment, he could enjoy the evening in her company. The guffaw that he gave on hearing the cholera story was, admittedly, noteworthy for its decibel content, but they were both a little shocked when a rather stern middle-aged woman, who had been standing at the bar in silence with a stern middle-aged man, strode briskly towards them, and told them, in no uncertain terms, to shut up.

Gabriel's immediate response was to hold up his hands ready to apologise, but Lily got in before him. 'What's your problem?' she said, staring the woman out. 'Why should we be quiet?'

When the woman replied that she didn't want to hear them banging on about their jobs and unprofessional bets, Lily replied in kind, 'Just because you two have nothing to talk about. We're minding our own business in a pub and will talk about anything we want.'

The bar was rather empty at the time, and there was an eerie silence as the woman, clearly slightly wrongfooted by Lily's assertive riposte, scowled at them both and returned to her bar stool.

'Wow,' said Gabriel eventually. 'Remind me to let you do the talking when we meet an axe-murderer on our way home.'

Alice

Alice watched carefully as Kathryn gripped on to her coffee cup, clearly unsure what to say. They'd already done the pleasantries, and both had agreed that they made nice coffee here and that it was warm for this time of year. But it had been Kathryn who had initiated this meeting, so Alice thought that she would wait until Kathryn obliged. There was clearly something troubling her and Alice was happy to let her broach whatever this may be in her own time.

'Thanks for seeing me, Alice. I wasn't really sure who to – well, I didn't really want to – you know – with your mum and I couldn't really with Anna and certainly not with one of my lecturers and there wasn't really anyone else that I could think of so I, well I thought, maybe…'

'I'm very flattered that you wanted to confide in me, Kathryn. What are you worried about?'

And so, Kathryn spoke. She blurted out things that she had held back from her grief counsellor about how she was failing to cope, she spoke about her writer's block and of her conversation with Anna, and how she had felt when she'd submitted an assignment in her name that she had not written.

'But the worst part was after I'd handed it in, and I asked Anna which service she'd bought. She replied that she had written her own assignment this time; that she suddenly had some inspiration and had written it all the night before it was due in. I know that I made my own choice, but this felt like betrayal. She'd got me to use this dodgy site and then didn't even use it herself. I'm not sure why I feel so awful about that.'

Alice had been aware, primarily from Mary, that Kathryn had been struggling all term, except during placement two, when she had appeared to thrive.

'I just don't know what to say to her, Alice,' Mary had said. 'She can spend the whole of a two-hour seminar just staring into space, and then the next day appear absolutely fine. I know she's seeing someone, but I'm not entirely sure that's doing any good.'

'So, what are you going to do about it, Kathryn?' asked Alice. 'Are you going to speak to your lecturers?'

'Oh no, I don't think so. You see, the essays are marked anonymously so there's little chance that anyone will notice it's not my style of writing. I don't suppose I'll get caught.'

Alice wasn't quite sure what made her snap upon hearing these words. Maybe it was the girl in her own seminar group, who always scrounged notes from everyone and ended up with better grades than she, or maybe it was the fact that Kathryn had gone from guilt to connivance in an instant, and was now almost boasting about getting away with it. Either way, Alice saw, in a moment of clarity, what she needed to do. The slam of her hand on the table was so sudden and loud that several customers in the coffee shop turned their heads, and Kathryn physically jumped.

'Is that what this is about, Kathryn, not getting caught? Is that what would make your nan happy? And if you are caught, what then? Are you going to hide behind your grief? I'm sorry if this sounds harsh, Kathryn, but she's gone, and she would have wanted you to get on with your life. It seems to me as though your life is on hold at the moment. You can't go on like this.'

And as the tears started to flow, and as Kathryn opened up more, Alice had the distinct sense that Kathryn's state of limbo was beginning to wash out of her. Whether this would end up being a defining moment for her, only time would tell.

'Right, Kathryn, first thing tomorrow, you need to go and talk to Martin. You'll have your grade capped but it will work in your favour that you are admitting your mistake. You also need to let Anna know that you are going to do this, and perhaps, at the same time, suggest that she doesn't give you any further duff advice. There will be plenty of people to help you to write this essay for yourself, assuming you're given that opportunity. And then next Saturday this will hopefully all be over, and you can get on that coach to the Peak District.'

'Oh, no, Alice. I can't go. I never wanted to in the first place and now what with everything I'll tell Martin that I'm sorry, but…'

'You are going to get on that bloody coach, Kathryn, if, for no other reason, the only way that we could persuade Mum to go was so that you'd have each other. I promise you, if you're not there with your backpack first thing on Saturday, I'll personally come and pull you out of bed.'

Surgery

'First of all, congratulations all of you for getting your assignments in on time. I know how much of a stress this can be for you, and if truth be told, it's a bit of a stress for us as well, especially when there is an issue of some sort.'

Kathryn watched everyone's faces carefully as Martin spoke these words. Fortunately, Gabriel put two self-deprecating hands in the air, which sufficiently drew the attention of Gabriel, Martin, Donna, and Callum away from her. In the couple of seconds that this gesture took, she focused carefully on Anna and Mary to try to gauge their reactions. Both shared a mixture of emotions. Kathryn was quite sure that Alice would not have told Mary her secret and would have respected her confidentiality, but Mary's face was not impassive or relaxed like the other members of the Set. She was aware that something was awry, and Kathryn had to make a call of what, if anything, to say to her. And then there was Anna. What did her face say? Kathryn spotted an element of relief but – most certainly – there was concern there as well. But what was the nature of that concern? Was it concern for Kathryn's welfare or concern that her part in this affair might come to light? Was there a small element of threat there, as well, as their eyes met for the most fleeting of seconds? Kathryn wasn't sure; in the same way that she wasn't sure exactly what she would say to Martin in the meeting that she had arranged with him immediately after Surgery. She would, most certainly, admit to what she had done, but would she mention Anna's involvement, and even if she didn't, would Martin work it out and tease it from her? Martin wasn't stupid. He was unlikely to imagine that Kathryn would have done this off her own back, and he would very quickly narrow down the suspects, and force it out of her. Yes, she was sure of it; there was definitely a hint of threat in Anna's gaze. It was all a bit too much for Kathryn.

'So, I hope you have all been in training for next week. The weather's set to be mixed, so please, everyone, can you all check Callum's bag to see if he's packed his raincoat? I'm so pleased that all of you are coming. It's unusual for a complete Surgery Set to volunteer for this trip. Eight is a great number for this, and to have four boys and four girls is even better. I'm sure you'll all make Matt and Jamie feel like part of our Set. I look forward to seeing you all at 8:00 sharp on Saturday. Until then, have a great few days. Now, Kathryn, did you say that you wanted a quick word?'

Chapter 15

Callum

'We're all going to the Moors.
  (We're all going to the Moors.)
We're gonna tame the great outdoors.
  (We're gonna tame the great outdoors.)
We're gonna do some stupid stunts.
  (We're gonna do some stupid stunts.)
We don't care if they call us –'

'Yes, thank you, Callum. Whilst we may not have children with us at the moment, we do have ladies present, and I know that Anna in particular can get easily offended at some of the more uncouth of your rugby songs.'

Callum felt good. Martin's words were met by all with good cheer, and Anna played along with the succinct, yet elegant riposte of, 'Yeah, I fuckin' hate rude rugby songs, me.'

Callum had been looking forward to this trip all year, ever since Martin had mentioned, back in September, that there would be an opportunity to have three days at an outdoor residential centre in the Peak District. Indeed, it was he who had managed to persuade all of them to go along, arguing that the experience would be a fantastic bond-builder for the Surgery Set. He hadn't expected Mary and Kathryn to sign up and felt rather proud of himself when he had finally talked them into it. That Jamie and Matt had also agreed to come was, on the one hand, a bonus. They were largely revered as being the 'jocks' of the year group, to use American parlance, and he very much wanted to become friends with them. However, as well as their reputation as being 'jocks', they also had a reputation for practical jokes, and it has to be said, rather immature behaviour at times. Callum knew that things had to change if he was going to make it through these three years. Somehow, he had to separate blokey-rugby banter and blokey-rugby behaviour, from the professionalism that was non-negotiable as a trainee teacher. Part of him was ready to pack it all in after his public humiliation, and his subsequent meeting with Martin and then the rest of his peers had been excruciating. Yet, instead of being lectured at by Martin and instead of being teased or isolated by his peers, he had sensed that everyone wanted to support him and see him through such a wretched time. Astoundingly, Anna had verged on the apologetic for her part in his shame, and then there was Mary. Callum had never really had a lengthy conversation with her before, and he'd thought that she, more than anyone, would have been unforgiving of his behaviour. Yet, she had made an effort to seek him out and to say that she knew how he must be feeling and that they were all on his side. Quite where her empathy originated from, he couldn't imagine – somehow, he hardly saw her as a man-eater in her day, but even so, he was most grateful for the sentiment.

Yet, he had still, undeniably, behaved like an arse. Yes, the parent in question had most certainly been the instigator of things, and yes, it was only one night, but even so; he simply had to curb things. And here he was instigating rude rugby songs on the coach to the outdoor centre. Yes, he felt good, as everyone was in high spirits and joining in gamely, but he knew how quickly he could slip into the inappropriate, he knew how much easier that would be with Jamie and Matt egging him on, and he knew that he was now running out of both sympathy and empathy from his peers.

Martin

'Welcome, everyone to Whitestone Cottage, in the heart of rural Derbyshire. As some of you may know, I am a trustee of this educational centre, due to links with my previous school. I trust that you will also be trustworthy trustees for the next three days. Let me just remind you of the main reason that you are here. As primary school teachers, you will, at some point or another, experience a residential visit with your children, and these can be incredibly memorable. You will also soon understand the importance of careful planning, safeguarding, and risk assessment when organising such trips. I want you to experience this first-hand, with both your "teacher hat" and your "learner hat" on, and at the end of our stay, I'll get you to reflect on what you have learnt.

'But I also want you to enjoy your time here, and I'm sure you'll get even more out of this if you do. In a minute, I'm going to split you into two random teams, and for each exercise and activity that you do, there will be points given for enterprise, endeavour, creativity, and showing initiative. Who knows, there may even be a few bonus points available for anyone who can make us all laugh. The scoring system will be made up on the spot by me and will be completely unfair. Clearly, I am open to bribes. The winning team will have full bragging rights and will enjoy ordering the losing team around on the last night when they will be our slaves. In a moment, we'll start on our first task, which is to make a fire and cook these tins of beans and sausages, which I will then judge on taste and creativity of presentation. Any questions? Anna?'

'Yeah, I don't seem to be getting a phone signal, and I can't get online. What's the Wi-Fi code here?'

'Oh, didn't I tell you? Modern technology's not going to work here. Too far out in the sticks. A few days without your phones aren't going to hurt you, are they? They are? Oh well, never mind, eh?'

Donna

Donna looked enviously at the other group. Mary and Anna had taken charge, and there was clearly an element of careful planning going on, with Kathryn and Gabriel listening attentively. Already an impressive structure had been assembled, in which to support their fire. When the teams had been drawn an hour before, Donna's initial thought was to ask for a recount, as she had landed with all of the class clowns. Matt was okay, at least when he was on his own, but Jamie was just a bit of an idiot, if truth were told. So, he was tall, strong, and handsome, and this, in his view, seemed to give him full licence to do whatever he pleased and to assume that everyone else clearly thought he was hilarious. Well, he wasn't, and when he and Matt started playing off each other, they were, quite frankly, a couple of overgrown schoolboys. Martin had said that this long weekend was all about understanding how to interact with children. Perhaps that's why they had been invited. And then there was Callum. As perceptive as ever, Donna could see that Callum wanted to befriend Jamie and Matt, and the immature side of him was desperate to escape. But she could also see that there was an element of contrition about him, and a need to prove himself and gain a shot at redemption. Indeed, he was trying to help her now, as the boys had gone in search of wood. Someone had to be the mature one here, and Donna had suggested that the four of them sat down to carefully plan things through, but Jamie, in particular, was having none of it.

'Me Tarzan. Me go fetch wood. No wood, no sausages.' And then he was off, followed, rather pathetically in Donna's view, by his sidekick.

When she was eight years old, Donna had asked her parents if she could join the Brownies, as many of her friends had recently started. She remembered her mother's response, word for word: 'Dib, dib, effin' dob. Really, Donna?'

And that had been the end of that. So, Donna never went to Brownies, in the same way that she never went to ballet classes or swimming lessons. But these setbacks at the hands of her family, she was sure, had made her the self-determined young lady that she was today. She hadn't rued a lack of Brownie

145

experience many times in her life, but she did at this moment. Making a campfire, and cooking beans and sausages on it is high up on the agenda of any self-respecting Brownie unit, and Donna had absolutely no idea what to do. Nor, it seemed, did Callum, who decided that their best course of action was to creep, commando-style, as close as possible to the other group and to closely examine their structure, with the view of emulating its design. So, Donna sat there, on her own, twiddling with some twigs, whilst the boys were out on their various expeditions. When Callum returned, a few minutes later, there was genuine excitement in his voice: 'It's okay, Donna. I think I've worked it out. The first thing we need to do is to create a base. What they've done is to…

'I'm a Lumberjack and I'm okay.
I sleep all night and I work all day.
I cut down trees, I wear high heels, suspenders, and a bra.
I wish I were a girlie, just like me dear papa.'

Donna and Callum watched with mouths agape as Matt and Jamie appeared, carrying between them a log the size of a small pig, and jauntily singing the famous Monty Python song. Without another word, they dropped the monstrosity squarely in the place where Donna and Callum had started to work, to an explosion of cracked twigs and flying dust.

'There we go, Donna,' said Jamie proudly. 'Don't say we never do anything. Now, where's that match?'

In the end, things weren't quite as bad as Donna had anticipated at this particularly low moment. They managed to get a fire going and even managed, more or less, to cook the food to the point where it was vaguely edible. This was due, in no small amount, to Matt having had the brilliant idea of bringing his lighter fuel with him; a ploy not lost on Anna, who muttered something about checking the rulebook when they returned to base and of bringing in her legal team, if necessary. But she wasn't too upset. Donna's team managed a fairly respectable five marks out of ten, whilst Anna and co, upon completion of their Michelin star quality sausage and beans, received a whopping nine out of ten for both quality and presentation. It was very obvious to Donna that this was thanks largely to the practical skills of Mary, who, yet again, was showing an array of hidden talents. They were all very aware that Mary needed more persuasion than anybody to venture on this trip, but her look of sheer pride on completion of the task totally belied these initial concerns.

Mary

Had it not been for the fact that they were completely cut off from civilisation, Mary would have happily phoned Simon and demanded that he drove out to pick her up and take her home. They had been assured that there were two dormitories, and whilst the prospect of sleeping in bunk beds alongside Kathryn, Donna and Anna seemed abhorrent, it was just about acceptable for three nights. But the 'partition' between these dormitories was no more than an inadequate and translucent curtain. This, in itself, would have been bad enough, but the curtain's existence merely served to bring out the adolescent side of most of the party. When Alice had teased Mary at the start of the course about immature behaviour, she had, not unreasonably, been a little concerned, but she was pleasantly surprised by the lack of silliness, especially when in seminars or during Surgery. But this confidence in the behaviour of a group of young people, many of whom were still teenagers, rapidly started to dissipate. First, Anna had the wonderful idea of stripping off down to her underwear right next to the curtain, so that the backlight silhouetted her as she danced, and as the boys hummed along to some sleazy number that Mary had never heard of. This then seemed to give the boys licence to respond in kind, staging a silhouetted version of some sort of axe murder. This would have just about been okay until someone – presumably Jamie – had the great idea of throwing some tomato ketchup at the curtain – Heavens only knew why he had ketchup with him in the first place – and they all had to watch as it slowly worked its way to the floor.

How could she tell them to grow up; to quieten down and let her sleep? Nobody apart from her and Kathryn seemed to want to sleep, even though they must all have been tired. She wasn't their mother, after all. The elation that Mary felt after showing off her campfire skills earlier in the evening had well and truly gone, and this now felt like it was going to be a very long three days indeed.

Anna

Anna and Gabriel marched on. Both were hot; Gabriel concerned and Anna palpably annoyed.

'We must have passed it by now, Gabriel. The map shows that it's 200 yards or so along this path, and we've been trudging along here for bloody ages.'

'I agree, but it might be just round this corner. How annoyed will we be if we turn back now and admit defeat, only to find out we were really close? Besides, the buckets are big enough, we can't possibly have missed it.'

'Unless we're on the wrong path, but I don't see how we can be. Okay, one more corner, and then I'm turning back. You can turn round as many corners as you like. I hate bloody orienteering. Did I mention that?'

Gabriel laughed. 'Only about eight times. One more corner it is. Tell you what; I'll run up there to save your legs. If I can't see it, I'll come back.'

So, Gabriel ran, and Anna stood waiting with increasing frustration, especially when she saw him shake his head, and start to walk slowly back. Anna had enjoyed things well enough up until now, and the distractions had eased her vague concerns that still lingered. When Kathryn had told her that she was going to confess to Martin, Anna had tried her best to talk her out of it, citing a whole range of reasons from a waste of money, to a potential horrendous backlash, and finally, to what would happen if Anna's part in the tale had ever got out. Kathryn had assured her that she wouldn't bring her into it, but Anna was far from convinced. When Kathryn had returned to their shared house, she'd simply said, 'Don't worry, I didn't say anything,' and she'd gone to her room.

Anna felt it best to leave it there, but an uneasiness still lingered, especially as Kathryn had been virtually silent for the whole of the trip so far.

Today was a particularly hot April day, and this did not help Anna's mood. The instructions from Martin had been clear; there were eight large buckets that they needed to find using their compasses and maps, and upon reaching each of them, the pairs needed to collect the envelope with their name inside, and return back to base when all envelopes were collected. They were to go out in pairs and score points for their team, according to how quickly they returned. They'd all started at different points and Anna and Gabriel had raced around, collecting the first seven quickly, and reading the map well. But now, admitting defeat, they trudged back to base and their frustrations were only heightened when they saw the other six students, clearly refreshed, and rested.

'What happened?' said Jamie, with a smirk on his face. 'Get lost?'

And suddenly everything became clear. Matt and Jamie had started one base ahead of them; hence Anna and Gabriel had been following them around the whole way.

'You useless piece of shit!' yelled Anna through gritted teeth. 'You hid that fucking bucket, didn't you?'

Anna, along with the rest of their seminar group, had always seen Matt and Jamie not only as an inseparable pair, but also as a pair who thought and acted alike. Yet the reactions on the two boys' faces after Anna's accusation were markedly different. Matt looked both contrite and ashamed, whereas Jamie continued to smirk. 'As if we'd do anything like that. Although, I do remember Martin saying something about getting extra points for showing initiative or

148

making us all laugh. If we *had* done what you're suggesting, I reckon our team would be in the lead right now, and you'd…'

There were many times in her life when a red mist descended suddenly upon Anna. A psychiatrist could probably have explained her anger bouts and related them to her relationship with her siblings, but she simply knew that, on occasions, she felt a sudden and uncontrollable desire for violence. The speed at which she marched across the floor towards Jamie stopped him in his tracks, and had it not been for Donna's anticipation and her firm hands when moving Anna away, there would have been blood. Whilst she didn't attempt to shake Donna off, she still had time to vent her anger once more at Jamie.

'You stupid, immature little arsehole. Why the hell did you two have to come on this trip? How the hell can you claim to be teachers? I've seen five-year-olds with more about them than you.'

And as she stormed out of the room, she left behind her a silence which spoke volumes about how everyone was feeling at that moment.

Matt

Matt had always been 'kingpin' at school. A combination of athleticism, good looks, and a seemingly effortless ability to do well academically had been a highly desirable combination, and he'd been popular amongst boys and girls alike. When he began his teacher-training course, he quickly became friends with Jamie, and they both shared the mantle of continued popularity, with no shortage of potential girlfriends or invitations to parties. When Anna had accused them of sabotaging the orienteering exercise, and he'd seen the faces of the rest of the students, he'd felt, perhaps for the first time in his life, his popularity waning. Whilst it had been Jamie's idea to hide the bucket, Matt had gone along with the ruse willingly enough. His initial sense of shame at Anna's outburst changed somewhat when he and Jamie shared a beer later that evening.

'Anna completely flipped earlier. I don't get what her problem is, honestly, Matt, I really don't. She overreacted massively. Anyone would think that they'd been left starving and alone for hours. It was only a joke, for God's sake. Someone needs to explain to her what a bloody sense of humour is.'

By the time he'd crashed out, Matt had just about persuaded himself that they hadn't really done anything wrong, but now, as they all began the day's hike, he felt a distinct sense that he and Jamie were being ostracised by the rest of the group. Neither of them had ever felt any particular affinity with their Surgery Set − they shared this with two quiet young women, who kept themselves to themselves, and two other women, both in their mid to late twenties, who both lived away from campus and seemed intent on attending

149

university purely to work. He had rather assumed that this Surgery Set would also have little affinity, given the disparate nature of the group, therefore he felt both surprised and more than a little frustrated when they appeared to close ranks on the two outsiders. Well, if that's how they wanted to play it, so be it.

It seemed to Matt, from the beginning of the hike, that there was a different and more serious air about Martin today. Up until now, Martin had been very relaxed and had happily joined in with banter and evening games. Everything about him today, though, was focusing on health and safety.

'You all have to understand how potentially dangerous this hike is. If we don't stay on the paths, if we're not very careful when climbing the peaks, or if we go too close to the edge, there is a real possibility of serious injury, especially with the gusts of wind that we will experience at the tops of these hills. Also, it is your responsibility to keep up with the group. There are only nine of us, but people have got lost in smaller groups. Remember, there will be no mobile signal out here.'

Matt and Jamie looked at each other, and Jamie rolled his eyes at the looks of earnest expressions on the faces of Martin's Surgery Set. Sometimes, people seemed to forget that this was a group of adults, rather than a group of children.

So, they started walking, and no harm came to either of them, when Jamie hid behind a bush until the group wondered where he was, when they raced each other up a hill that Martin had told them to climb slowly, or when they pretended to teeter on the edge of a precipice. At lunch, they sat on their own, feeling more ostracised than ever, and as they continued on a path, leading through tall ferns and bracken, they kept their distance behind the main group. When, eventually, they all stopped for a drink, the silence was broken when Mary said, 'Where's Gabriel?'

There was a pause before Anna explained that he'd nipped off to the loo several minutes ago, and told her that he'd catch them up.

'Has he got a map?' said Martin.

Matt distinctly heard the slight catch in Donna's voice as she lifted her map in the air. 'No, he hasn't. It was my turn to use it.'

'Okay, there's no need to panic,' said Martin. 'We'll retrace our steps for a while and keep calling to him. The problem is that it will be difficult to see him with all these bushes, and it's possible that he's taken the wrong fork back there.'

Matt carefully looked at the faces of everyone as they retraced their steps and called out for Gabriel. He also noted how these faces gradually changed as the minutes passed and there was still no sign of him. Donna, in particular, seemed to be verging on the hysterical as she continued to call out his name.

'We're bloody miles from anywhere and he's got no phone or map. What the hell are we going to do?'

In truth nobody, including Martin, really knew what the best thing to do was. As well as the look of concern on all faces, Anna also looked guilty, as if it were somehow her fault that Gabriel had nipped off to the loo. It suddenly occurred to Matt that Martin had been in serious mode this morning for a very good reason, and that Gabriel might actually be in trouble, especially if he had fallen and potentially twisted his ankle, or worse. He thought about the morning's antics, and how he'd felt just a little smug as he'd reached the top of the hill without harming himself, despite Martin's remonstrations; or the look on Kathryn's face when he had pretended to teeter over that precipice. He also thought back to the vitriol which Anna hurled at him and Jamie the previous day, and how they had simply made themselves unpopular. He could almost hear the inevitable thoughts of his fellow students, 'Why couldn't it have been one of the arseholes who got lost?' These thoughts, plus the very real sense of danger echoing between them, made Matt feel very uncomfortable indeed.

'I think we have no choice but to go on,' said Martin eventually. 'We can be back at base in an hour or so, where we will be able to put out an alert, if necessary. Please don't panic, look at this rationally. There are many hours of light left, Gabriel has water with him, and if necessary, the emergency services will have equipment with them that will help to find him. Gabriel is a sensible lad. Things will be okay.'

But things were anything but okay as they headed back to base as quickly as they could, with images of helicopters scouring the wilds of the Peak District, and Gabriel, possibly injured, waiting, and hoping. Seeing Jamie looking both surly and unrepentant made Matt think, for the first time, that perhaps he needed to widen his circle of friends. At the very least, he thought, he would be buying Gabriel a drink, assuming he was all right. Surely, he'd be all right…

It was a sombre party indeed that eventually found its way back to base, with Mary comforting a now inconsolable Donna. As they finally sat down at their original starting point, a figure emerged from behind an ice-cream van, holding a carton containing a tray of 99s.

'Gabriel?' said Matt incredulously. 'What the…?'

And then, as seven faces turned to look at Matt and Jamie, everything suddenly sank in.

'I'm sorry, boys,' said Martin, 'but I'm afraid you asked for that. If you are going to become teachers, then it's my job to ensure that you are ready to do so. At the moment, you're not.'

And for the second time in as many days, Matt felt guilt and shame as seven pairs of eyes bore down on him. As with last time, his reaction was different to

Jamie's, who swore, muttered something about a stupid bloody trick and stormed off back to the minibus.

'I'm sorry,' said Matt. 'Lesson learnt. And I'm glad you're okay, Gabriel.'

Donna

Donna sat at the bar with Gabriel, chatting easily and enjoying the sight of Matt and Jamie, dressed elegantly as housemaids, collecting a procession of drinks and answering to individual whims.

'Oy, slave,' shouted Anna to Matt, 'my shoes need cleaning.' After yesterday's ruse, dreamt up by Donna and Gabriel over their packed lunch, and eventually supported by Martin, Donna had noticed a complete change in Matt. On the journey home in the minibus, he had pointedly sat with Callum, rather than Jamie, and had gone out of his way to be both polite and helpful. It had taken Jamie considerably longer. During the day's kayaking and cycling, he had still appeared petulant, although he did not attempt to retaliate when Anna had soaked him with a well-directed splash of her oar. By the evening, though, when Martin had declared the competition a draw, Jamie had begun to thaw slightly.

'It's a bit of a dilemma,' said Martin. 'Now it's a draw we don't have anyone to be our slaves at the pub tonight. Any volunteers?'

It had taken Jamie all of one second to volunteer himself and Matt, and they had been more than happy to be dressed up by the girls and to ham it up all evening.

It was Mary's suggestion that they all switched their phones off before entering the pub, when they would finally be able to communicate once again with the real world.

'I'm going to make you all an offer,' she said. 'If everyone can avoid turning their phones back on until 9:30, then I shall buy two bottles of champagne. As I have two children of your sort of age, my guess is that my money's safe. What do you reckon?'

Like drug addicts having to wait for their next fix, the younger members of the group then spent the next ninety minutes or so trying their hardest to prove Mary wrong, and there were several hands that were visibly shaking as Mary counted down the last ten seconds before ordering the drinks. Donna was keen to see her messages, and had missed Dominic like mad, but even she marvelled at how strong the desire was amongst everyone to finally have their fix. She was also rather surprised at just how agitated Gabriel was when he saw that his phone was out of charge. As he plugged it in and nipped to the loo, whilst it regained life, Donna reflected on the week, and indeed, the year so far, and

152

concluded that she was as happy as she had ever been in her life. She was in a stable relationship, she had a future career that she knew was right for her, and a group of friends that she had become closer and closer to, especially in the last few days when they'd been together 24 hours a day. She was awoken from her reverie by the familiar 'ding' of a text message, as Gabriel's phone came to life. The first message was shortly followed by another, and then another. There must have been about 40 of these in quick succession. When reflecting in bed later on that evening, Donna was convinced that it was not a deliberate act on her part; she had no interest in reading Gabriel's messages, it was simply an involuntary movement of her head towards Gabriel's phone, which stubbornly refused to shut up. It was obvious instantly that all − or nearly all − of these messages were from Lily, meaning that she had been texting him upwards of ten times a day, despite getting no response. But it wasn't this that grabbed Donna's attention. In a pause between texts, she quite clearly saw the words: 'that bloody Donna'. She turned quickly away, not wanting to invade Gabriel's privacy anymore or, indeed, not wanting to read on. What the hell did that mean? Was Lily jealous of her? Did she think that maybe they were secretly seeing each other?

When Gabriel returned a few moments later, Donna watched his face carefully as he read. But there was nothing, no sense of surprise or indignation, just a blank expression. When he finally finished reading, he casually called to Matt to get him another drink and started talking about something else.

Surgery

'So, everyone. On the journey here, I told you that this week's Surgery will be an opportunity to voice what you have learnt from these three days. Now that we are on our way home, I'd be very interested to hear some of your reflections.'

There was a brief silence whilst everyone, presumably, waited for either Matt or Jamie to talk about lessons learnt and growing up, but their quietness and bowed heads spoke as loudly as any words would have done. Eventually, it was Gabriel who spoke.

'When I was 11, I went on a school trip to one of those activity centres where trained staff get you to try a variety of new things, such as archery or even jumping off high poles, and trying to cling on to a slippery handle. I really enjoyed it and we had lots of fun. But I don't think it was a patch on this. What I've learnt most from this trip is the importance of organising things for yourself, and of being active with the children, rather than letting strangers do everything for you.'

'Thank you, Gabriel. I think that's probably the main message that I wanted to get across to you. Don't take the easy way out and book some activity centre; plan things yourselves. That doesn't mean that you can't get a professional to teach the kayaking or whatever; there's a huge difference between that and simply handing the children over. Anything else?'

'I think I've learnt,' began Kathryn, 'just how tiring all of this is. I'm not just talking about physical tiredness, it's more the fact that you are with people for 24 hours a day. I can imagine that that would be completely draining if looking after children. I've − I've got a lot on my mind at the moment, and even though this was a great distraction and I enjoyed it, all the demands of the trip seem to be weighing me down just a little bit more.'

Martin noticed the slightest of glances from Anna to Kathryn as she spoke, and he wondered. What was going on there?

'You're right, Kathryn. These trips are exhausting, and it's important that the parents know just how much you are giving of yourself looking after their offspring all week. I could tell you some stories there… Anyway, I think we're all tired and can probably do with a quick pick-me-up before we get home. Callum, fancy sharing some more of your delightful songs?'

Chapter 16

Miriam

'God, what a day. I do feel for Nathan – you know that – and I can only imagine how his parents cope with his ADHD, but he's such hard work. D'you wanna know what he did today? Okay, so you know how he hates my TA, right? Well, she was trying to calm him down after something wound him up, and he just looked at her, yeah, and then shouted right in her face… Martin? Are you okay? You seem to be miles away?'

'No, it's okay; just a few – you know. You were telling me about Nathan?'

'Sod Nathan. What's up? You were so full of things when you got back from Derbyshire on Tuesday but now you seem – I don't know – like you've got the whole weight of the world and all that. What's the problem?'

Martin sighed. 'You know I told you just before we were going away that Kathryn had asked to see me after Surgery? And I also said that I thought she sounded worried? Well, when we spoke, she seemed to hesitate for a while before banging on about being concerned about going away for the weekend. Once we'd smoothed that over I asked if there was anything else. She'd said that there wasn't, but I didn't really believe her. I felt that there was nothing more that I could do, but I knew that there was something else on her mind.'

'Yes, I remember you talking about it. Why, has something happened?'

There was a pause before Martin spoke again, 'Jo came to speak to me today. She's just started marking their essays and was concerned about one of them. She said it just didn't feel right. As you know, we're supposed to mark them anonymously, but if there is a potential issue, we need to see who's written it. The essay was Kathryn's, and after reading it, I had no doubt at all that it wasn't her work. I assumed that someone had probably helped her, so I called her in, ready to give her a bit of a ticking off…'

Martin paused again as he remembered and repeated their conversation:

'Thanks for coming to see me, Kathryn. I'll get straight to the point. We're a little bit worried about the essay that you wrote for Professional Studies. Both Jo and I have looked at it, and it doesn't really seem to have your "voice" to it. I just wondered – and I want you to be honest with me, Kathryn, did anybody help you to write it?'

Martin expected either a furious denial or something along the lines of, 'Well, Mary helped me a bit, but it was my work really…' He was therefore completely unprepared for what happened next. It was as if someone had flicked a switch. Kathryn responded by bursting into tears; a loud, uncontrollable and pitiable outburst of pent-up emotion, which continued for a full minute before she managed to stammer out the words, 'I'm sorry. Such a stupid thing to do. I should never have agreed to it.'

'Agreed to what, Kathryn? What's going on?'

There are times in most people's lives when a combination of shame, embarrassment, and guilt prevent them from talking. All Kathryn could muster, over the next couple of minutes, was, 'I can't. I can't. I'm sorry.'

'Listen, Kathryn. We all know what you've been through, and how you must be feeling. There's nothing that can't be sorted out.'

And so, Martin listened as, between sobs, Kathryn eventually explained how she had been unable to focus on her assignment and had used one of the online essay-writing services to write it for her.

'Thank you, Kathryn,' Martin said eventually. 'That must have been a hard thing to admit. Is there anything else that you want to tell me?'

But Kathryn was resolute in her silence. In the end, all he could do was to send her away, advise her not to mention this to anyone, and tell her that he'd contact her again soon after they'd decided what should happen next.

'Oh my God,' said Miriam eventually. 'So, what's going to happen now?'

'God only knows, Miriam. This is the sort of dilemma that really gets me down sometimes. On the one hand, it's a no-brainer. My duty is to report this to the academic misconduct officer, and to let justice take its course. Indeed, Kathryn is unlikely to get anything more than a reprimand – first offence and all that. What's more, if I didn't do this, what the hell would I tell Jo, who's marking the essay? I'd then be at the mercy of anything she either does or doesn't say to anyone, and even ignoring what she might think of me, sooner or later the truth will out and I'll get it in the neck. As I say, it's a no-brainer.'

'But?'

'But, indeed. This is Kathryn, for God's sake. We know what a state she's in at the moment. Whilst she'd happily accept a rap on the knuckles, I just wonder how she'll cope with other people's reactions. What's Mary going to say to her? What's she going to think about her mum and her nan looking down on her, knowing that she's been shamed? I just think that this might push her under.'

'I get that Martin, but ask yourself this: would you have any hesitation in reporting this if it were, say, Jamie or Anna as the accused? And if your answer is different, can you, on any level, justify not reporting this?'

'Of course I can't bloody justify it. I know that. It's just… it's just… It's just that sometimes I care more about the students than I do about the system. Is that so wrong?'

'Only you can answer that, Martin, but for what it's worth, I think – what you've just said there – well, I think that's why I love you.'

'Thank you, but that actually makes matters worse.'

Miriam smiled. 'Sorry about that, but I think there's another worry here. You mentioned something about Kathryn saying that she shouldn't have agreed to it. That rather suggests that someone might have put her up to this. Any ideas?'

'Several. There's no way that Kathryn would have dreamt this up by herself. But, quite frankly, Miriam, finding that out would open up another can of worms, and I don't really need that at the moment.'

Martin

Martin looked again at the email in front of him. Both he and Miriam had always prided themselves on their open relationship – one where neither kept secrets from the other, yet he could not really articulate why he had not mentioned the email, despite having received it some 48 hours previously. Perhaps it was simply the fact that, ultimately, he knew deep down that he would reject the offer. Yet, now, after pondering what to do about Kathryn for most of the day, he wondered.

Dear Martin

How are you? It's been too long, and we must get together for that promised round of golf sometime very soon. It may also then give me a chance to talk you through a proposition that I have for you. You may remember Tracey Saunders, head of PE? She told me last week of her intention to retire in the summer, and of course she will need replacing… Tracey was quite brilliant at her job, and I'm absolutely determined to get someone who I know will fill her shoes ably – and I thought of you. Clearly, I'm going to need to advertise the post officially, but you know what I think of you, Martin. Say no more. Have a chat to Miriam, think it over, and perhaps we can meet for a pint or that round of golf, if you'd like a bit more information. Suffice it to say that you wouldn't suffer financially if you were to join us.

I look forward to hearing from you soon – hopefully with some positive news.

Best

Phil

Martin had worked with Phil Williamson several years ago and was not surprised when Phil eventually became headteacher at a private boys' school. Martin had always thought that it was unlikely that he'd go back to being a primary school teacher and was certain that he'd found his niche inspiring the next generation of teachers. But now, he looked again at Phil's offer through a different lens. As head of PE, would he ever have to make the sort of moral decision that was plaguing him now? And whilst he loved this job, there wasn't quite that magical sense of wonder when a child finally achieves something, or that sense of camaraderie at a collective victory. With his eyes now firmly looking through a rose-coloured lens, Martin reminisced about such wonderful memories, including the time when an impromptu invitation to a lacrosse tournament at a prestigious school led to his untrained girls, against all the odds, lifting the trophy. The scenes of unbridled joy from both the girls and their parents were firmly implanted in his mind. And then there was Kate. Martin had taught Kate over 20 years ago, and was both amazed and delighted when, out of the blue, she had recently tracked him down and emailed him. Apparently, a visit to the zoo with her daughter had sparked memories of a trip led by Martin, and she'd felt moved not just to contact him but to tell him just how much she'd enjoyed being in his class. This email had sparked a lengthy set of further emails, where both had fondly reminisced about her year group. As Martin smiled at the memory, it occurred to him that it was extremely unlikely that one of his students would contact him in over twenty years…maybe it was time to have that chat with Miriam, and for that round of golf.

Perhaps it was Karma, or perhaps it was simply one of those strange coincidences that happen to everyone occasionally, but Martin was awoken from his reverie by the arrival of a new email, this time from Gabriel.

Dear Martin

You are cordially invited by us, the undersigned, to an evening of exquisite food, fine wines, and entertainment. Dress to impress.

Please join us at the Pizza Palace (!) this Friday 28th April at 8:15 p.m.

RSVP

Gabriel, Donna, Mary, Anna, Callum, and Matt

P.S. You will be frisked at the door, and if you have brought a wallet with you, it will be confiscated for the evening.

Several things went through Martin's mind as he read and reread this email. The first was the simple conclusion that his students wanted to thank him for taking them on a residential visit, and for that he was truly humbled. Next were the names of the students, notable both for who was included and who was to be absent. It also occurred to him that if the balance of fate had been beginning to shift towards a change of job for him, some sort of equilibrium had now been restored. And finally, he was far from sure that he was going to like the sort of 'entertainment' that was likely to be on show…

But what this day of reflections, conundrums and choices had cemented in his mind was that he was not in the right frame of mind, at present, to make important decisions. He needed to think. He would speak to Miriam, send a non-committal email to Phil later, but Kathryn's absence from the invitation made him realise just how she must be feeling at present, and if nothing else, he needed to send her some form of holding email.

Dear Kathryn

Thanks again for seeing me today and for your honesty in our meeting. I think it unlikely that any decision will be made about where we go from here until early next week, but I think it probable that the worst-case scenario for you will be some form of warning, and a need to rewrite the assignment, which would, of course, have the grade capped at the minimum mark. I hope this offers some sort of reassurance for you at what must be a very difficult time.

Martin

Anna

'Hi, Leah. How are you? Just thought I'd just touch base.'

'Hi, Anna.'

'Er, how are things? Everything ready for the wedding? Really looking forward to the final dress fitting next week.'

'Yeah, all good.'

'So, yeah, really looking forward to it. Assuming I'm not in jail by then, of course.'

Leah sighed down the phone. 'What's that supposed to mean?'

'Oh, it's nothing really. It's just − you remember that I pulled off that stunt at Christmas with the buying of the essay over the internet? The trick, incidentally, that you taught me. Well, I'm pretty sure I got away with it but − well it's complicated. You see, there's this other girl, right, and now she's done the same and been caught and − well…'

'Oh, for God's sake, Anna. What's the worst that's going to happen? You're hardly going to get kicked out. Naughty Anna, have a detention. If you remember, I survived bricking up the boys' toilets after Darren dumped me − with him still in them. I'm not really sure what you are worried about.'

159

'Yeah, I guess so. I just wanted – you know.'

'I know. Listen, Anna, nice as this is, I really must be getting on. I'll see you at the fitting. Oh, and Anna? I didn't like to say it when we were in Corfu, but I noticed that you seem to have put on a pound or two. I trust you'll be back to your fighting weight before my wedding?'

Anna put the phone down and poured herself a glass of wine. Leah was right. This wasn't a massive issue, and after all, Kathryn was a grown-up. She made her own choices. There really wasn't anything to feel guilty about. She'd even tried to persuade Kathryn to join them for the group pizza tomorrow. She didn't need to do that; Kathryn had got the same memo as everyone else. So, she wasn't in the mood for it. Again, that was her choice.

Martin

'First, and on behalf of all of us, can I reiterate our thanks to the guest of honour? Not only have you been there for us all year, Martin, and I think all of us, at one time or another, have needed your support, but taking us away for a few days – with all that goes with that – well, I'm sure that's not in your job description, and tonight is about our appreciation for that. I hope you have all enjoyed your pizzas, and we now come to the serious part of the evening, the entertainments. I had okayed it with the manager that we could begin with a three-legged race, but then he saw Callum come in and that was the end of that. He'd also agreed to let us cook our pizzas on one of Mary's famous homemade fires, but unfortunately, Matt thought he'd help by dumping an industrial-sized log on the proceedings. Please make your own jokes there.

'So, we are going for the more sedate – indeed, I might say cerebral – form of entertainment. Some of the games, as you will see, Martin, are known at present by only me, your humble host, and some, for reasons that will become apparent, have been pre-prepared. The first game is the limerick round. Each of you has five minutes to come up with a limerick with the starting line of: "There once was a teacher named Martin". Before we commence this, I want to make one final toast; to absent friends.'

'To absent friends.'

At this point all, eyes fell on Matt, who could only utter: 'Er, Jamie couldn't... Well, you know.' And everyone did know, and nothing more needed to be said.

Then Anna, in a rare moment of diplomacy, added, 'And Kathryn. Well, it's her mum's anniversary soon, and well, you know.'

And everyone did know, and nothing more needed to be said. But Martin knew that this was about more than the anniversary of her mum's death, and he was pretty sure that at least one other person in the room was also aware of this…

And as everyone started preparing their limerick, it occurred to Martin, not for the first time, just how articulate, warm, and witty Gabriel was. That young man was going places. It also occurred to him, as he watched them all pondering their lines, that he had probably never seen such a degree of concentration on their faces, and this, rightly or wrongly, pissed him off just a little bit.

'Time's up,' said Gabriel, after the allotted five minutes. 'Time to hand in your efforts to Martin, who will judge which one he thinks is the best.'

It took Martin less than a minute to make up his mind. 'So, I have a winner. And, perhaps, surprisingly, the winning entry is the only one to avoid the rather schoolboy tactic of rhyming "Martin" with "fartin'".' And I have to say, Mary, that you really need to wipe your mouth out with soap and water. Such filth. Anyway, many congratulations go to Matt, whose prize effort goes as follows:

> *There once was a teacher called Martin*
> *Who at first glance could seem quite enchantin'*
> *But he noticed that Matt*
> *Behaved like a twat*
> *And he crushed him with fiendish outsmartin'*

The spontaneous applause that greeted Matt's self-deprecating winning entry seemed to say, firmly, that he had finally been accepted into the group.

'Impressive stuff, Matt. Your shot is on the way. Okay, round two. A few days ago, I asked everyone here, including myself, to write a confession; something that they did or didn't do whilst on teaching practice. The six pieces of paper are in this bowl. Your job, Martin, is to guess which confession matches which student. The rules are that the confession must be true, and if you guess correctly, the guilty party must own up. If you are wrong, the real perpetrator can keep their secret forever. None of us know each other's secret.'

Martin took a deep breath, not sure where this was going to lead.

'As a dare, I once went an entire day at school without wearing a bra.'

As he looked round the sea of faces, the laughter, the sniggers, and the 'oohs' and 'ahs', he felt, a little sadly, that Kathryn would have been in her element here, and would have worked out whodunnit every time through her extraordinary ability to read body language. It didn't, however, take him long before coming up with a shortlist of one suspect…

'I've warned you about this sort of thing before, Callum. I'll see you in my office first thing on Monday morning.'

Martin had wondered, as Gabriel was explaining the game, exactly how Callum might feel about it, given his very public indiscretion earlier in the year, and hence felt that a bit of banter was the right way forward. If Callum was feeling slightly uncomfortable, he certainly didn't show it, and maybe it was the four pints of beer, but his subsequent portrayal of walking around without a bra on was pushing it, even by his standards. By now, the elderly couple sitting closest to them had hastily asked for their bill and seemed to have every intention of sharing a mutual heart attack.

'I once corrected a child's spelling, even though she had spelt it correctly the first time. When she questioned it, I panicked and told her that the TA had marked that particular piece of work.'

It seemed as though this whole game had been designed to belittle Callum, but his 5th beer had just arrived, and he seemed oblivious.

'Hmmm. This one's a little harder. I can see a few guilty faces in front of me but I'm going to plump for… Gabriel.'

'Wrong again! Next.'

'When listening to a child attempting to sing in assembly, I literally wet myself. I had to go home to change.'

'You've got form for this, Donna. I think this has your name all over it.'

'Guilty as charged. Am I really that transparent, in more ways than one!?'

By now, the competitive side of Martin was coming through and he was determined to get the last three correct. One out of three so far was hardly anything to write home about, although he was pretty certain that it was Anna's bra that had been missing that day.

'During assembly one day, and after a particularly vicious curry the previous evening, I let out a quite horrendous "silent but deadly", safe in the knowledge that nobody would accuse a sensible teacher, when there was a whole host of young boys to cross-examine. The headteacher, not known for her sense of humour on the smelly fart front, actually stopped reading her story and insisted that the guilty party confessed, or the whole school would miss their break. Needless to say, I wasn't needed for playground duty that morning.'

By now several people from nearby tables were looking and joined in with the shocked laughter which met this story. Out of the corner of his eye, Martin saw the elderly couple actually run for the sanctuary of the exit.

'I so want to get this right and completely shame the guilty party. It has to be a boy. You all look pretty shifty but I'm going to plump for... Callum.'

'Me? What an outrageous slur! As if? Sorry Martin, but it ain't me.'

'I was chatting to my TA one day during playtime about our favourite cocktails, and I mentioned, when asked, that my favourite was sex on the beach. A small child, who I hadn't realised was behind me, asked, in all innocence: "What's sex on the beach?" I might just about have got away with it if the TA hadn't, at that moment, let out a snort that actually measured on the Richter scale.'

'Mary!'
'No!'
'Bollocks.'

'I had been warned about a particular child in my class and when, at the end of the day, he offered my mentor one of his homemade cakes, she politely refused. I, on the other hand, was hungry. Within a couple of minutes, I realised that there was something other than cake mix in the cupcake and I started to feel decidedly lightheaded. For the next hour, I sat, with a lopsided grin on my face, as the headteacher tried to lead a staff meeting on assessment. On more than one occasion, she gave me a decidedly suspicious glance, before I excused myself and somehow managed to stagger home before passing out. It was the best staff meeting I've ever attended.'

By now, Martin was desperate to get this last one correct, and spent a full thirty seconds examining the faces of those around him. At one point, a young man from the next table shouted, 'I reckon it's the big guy drinking beer!'

'Right, I'm pretty confident about this one. Gabriel.'

'As I said, I was hungry. I now have the recipe if anyone's interested...'

It was a truly magical evening, although, no matter how often he asked, nobody would come clean about the assembly fart. Mary got one of the biggest cheers of the evening when she lived up to her growing reputation of being the 'dark horse' by resoundingly winning the 'first to down a pint' contest, much to Callum's annoyance and everyone else's amusement. It seemed to Martin, that in such a relaxed setting, the likes of Mary and Gabriel really excelled, and whilst they all appeared to have a good evening, Anna was a little quieter than usual and Donna − well, she was her usual charming self, but there were a few times that he noticed a correlation between Gabriel's phone pinging and Donna looking very mildly irritated. It was none of his business, of course. By the time that they had settled the bill, one which, despite Martin's protestations, was shared six ways rather than seven, Miriam had been quietly waiting for a good 30 minutes in the car ready to drive him home, and the manager was openly yawning and turning off the lights.

Surgery

'So, Martin, you can be the student trying to sort out a major dilemma or two, and I'll be you trying to nudge you into making some decisions. What are you going to do?'

'I'm going to sit on the fence, Miriam, squarely. I'll email Phil later today and arrange a meet but will be noncommittal. At the moment, after last night, I don't see how I can walk away, given that it's the expectation to see your Surgery Set through all three of their years. But who knows? Maybe tomorrow, I'll have a few more Kates nominating me for Teacher of the Century award and begging me to come back into the profession.'

'In your dreams. Before you put yourself on that particular pedestal, I could remind you of several times, when, as a teacher, you really were rather shit, or lazy, or lacking patience or – well, I could go on. What about Kathryn?'

'I'm going to go and see Jo on Monday and have a chat with her. She knows Kathryn well. Maybe we'll sort something unofficial out between us. And if that leads to me getting the sack, well, that will make my other decision nice and easy, won't it?

Chapter 17

Jo

'Over the course of this year, we've had many conversations with you about behaviour, whether that was during placement preparation, or when you had to think of times in your experience when behaviour was an issue. In this Professional Studies module, we are going to revisit this, but look at it in a bit more depth. We're going to think about why children misbehave and consider that they need to be in the right frame of mind when at school. We're going to look at how the attitudes and personalities that children bring in with them to school each day will have a massive impact on things, and we're going to think about our role in dealing with this. As you'll see, there is a word that is going to pervade through all of our discussions, and that word is, *choice*.

'So, let me start by showing you one of my favourite ever quotations, spoken by a well-known modern-day philosopher: *It is our choices that show what we really are, far more than our abilities.*

'And the name of this philosopher? That great wizard himself, Albus Dumbledore. I want you all now to take a minute to think about this quote. What does it mean to you? I want you to think of a choice that you have made recently. Why did you make that choice and what has been its impact? Would you have done anything different with the benefit of hindsight? This is a purely private moment − I want you all to stay quiet and be as honest with yourself as you can be. You can choose to discuss this later, but you absolutely don't have to.'

Jo looked around the lecture theatre as the first years contemplated this provocation. She'd rarely seen all 80 of them look so pensive, and it filled her with hope for what was always going to be quite a heavy module. She looked, especially, at some of the familiar faces in her seminar group and could almost hear them talk to themselves in their moment of reverie…

'That's an easy one. It was the worst choice I've ever made in my life, and the more I think about it, the more I don't blame Anna. That's too easy. She was actually just trying to help. She didn't force me to do anything, and it's time to accept that. I'm going to go to my meeting at the end of today with Jo and

Martin with my head held high, and happily accept whatever they say. And I'm certainly not going to blame it on my bereavement.'

'Too many bad choices to just pick one. God, what a horrible question. I never liked Harry bloody Potter, anyway. The thing is, I keep telling everyone that I'm going to grow up and stop being the rugby-playing bad boy, but maybe that's just harder than it sounds. Perhaps I just need to accept that I'm never going to be perfect − yes, okay, I have just spent the last five minutes trying to surreptitiously look down the top of the girl in front of me − perhaps there needs to be some sort of acceptance here − acceptance that I'll always be a bit of a lecherous arse, but that there are times when I have no choice but to rein that in − so no more teachers, TAs, mums or lollipop ladies for me. Well, at least while I'm actually at school. Perhaps a contact number for afterwards? Surely that's okay?'

'So maybe I've put on a couple of pounds − is that really a problem? I'll still fit in that dress. Sometimes I feel that I have to choose between my sister or my friends, and I'm not really sure why that needs to be a choice in the first place. I remember before Christmas saying to everyone that I need to stop listening to Leah, so why is that so difficult? Would Donna have made a snide comment about my weight, had I phoned her up for a bit of reassurance? Of course she bloody wouldn't. This whole behaviour thing, and how it links to choices that Jo's going to bang on about; not sure I'm going to like this. Feels a bit like I'm about to pull off a scab.'

'Wow, what a question! Where to start? What are some of the big choices over the last year? Taking the plunge to change careers at my age, jury still out on that one. Throwing myself into everything to the detriment of...not sure I'd be able to say this out loud at the moment but yes, definitely, to the detriment of my marriage. And while we're soul-searching here, choosing to belittle professionals because they are younger than me. But I've also chosen to relax sometimes, and I secretly now like my "dark horse" nickname. Winning at sumo wrestling, writing rude limericks or making a campfire from scratch: I've seen how others look at me in those moments and it feels really good. I promised myself a year ago that I would end up with a first − anything else would feel like failure. Was that a good choice? Does it matter that much? All I do know is that I'm putting myself first too much, and ignoring Simon, the kids and Kathryn as well. I think she's probably been crying out for help recently and I was too busy writing my essay to notice. Choices, choices...'

166

'Coming here was the best choice that I've ever made. When I first arrived, I felt like a little boy, and I could have easily just run when, Anna, in particular, thought it fair game to take the piss. Okay, memo to reincarnated self some time in the future − lay off the James Blunt Adulation Society for at least a couple of weeks. But I've won her round − we had a real laugh when we worked together in the Peak District, and everyone was slapping me on the back for hosting the pizza evening. I've got great friends, a great girlfriend, and I'm doing well in essays and in school. Not sure that I'd change anything.'

'So why have I chosen to keep quiet? I don't know if I can answer that. Maybe it's because it's none of my business or maybe I just don't want to bring up the phrase, "that bloody Donna" in conversation. But there's something not right here, and I think I owe it to Gabriel to speak to him. Not that I'm looking forward to it. Maybe that quote is saying that it's sometimes not easy to make the right choice, but that, when all is said and done, it's these difficult choices that shape you. God, where's Frank when you want him? I could be blissfully ignoring rants about the environment at the moment, rather than having to brace myself...'

As Jo had hoped, the students gradually began talking with each other, and it was clear that most of them were being very reflective, and certainly in some cases, they were clearly starting to open up. She wondered, not for the first time, whether the students ever thought about how the lecturers were feeling. She had made a choice, well within recent memory, to speak to Martin about Callum when she had clearly got the wrong end of the stick, and then not to speak to Martin when she patently needed to. She was also very aware of the choice that she and Martin were making regarding Kathryn; one which was at odds with university protocol. Were any of them thinking about this? *'It's all very well for you to go on about making the right choices; you're our lecturer, for God's sake'*. The thought made her shiver, even though each of these choices had been made with the best of intentions. It also made her next words feel very personal indeed:

'You see, much of this is linked to anxiety and how we deal with this. Some of you might be feeling very anxious at the moment because you've started questioning your choices, and if I'm honest, I'm also feeling a bit anxious about things at the moment. Is it ever a good thing to be anxious? If your answer is no, does that mean that we should always stay in our comfort zone? You can choose to stay in your comfort zone now during your coffee break, or you could choose to have conversations that might make you feel anxious at first. That's up to you. And what has all of this got to do with behaviour, and our understanding of why children misbehave and the choices that we then make when faced with that behaviour? We'll discuss that after break in your seminar groups, but, by all means, think about it over coffee. By the look on some of your faces, it looks like you need some caffeine.'

Donna

'Okay, Gabriel, I probably wouldn't be having this conversation with you if it hadn't been for Jo's session just then, so if it all goes tits up then we can both blame her. Okay?'

'Sure, yeah, what did you want to talk about?'

'You really don't know?'

'Well, er, something about Lily maybe?'

Donna sighed. This was going to be harder than she thought.

'Yes, Gabriel, I just wondered, really, if everything was okay between you?'

'Yes − fine − Lily's great. I mean I know that she can be a bit clingy sometimes − and I've seen the look on your face when her texts keep coming in − but isn't it a good thing to be wanted? You've got Dominic and I know that you two make a wonderful couple and all that. It's just − it's just that I've never really had a girlfriend who clearly thinks so much of me. It's really nice.'

'I'm sure, Gabriel, but − God, how do I say this? − I didn't know whether to mention this, and I've been beating myself up about it since Derby but − well, I accidentally saw something.'

So, for better or for worse, Donna explained to Gabriel how she had read part of Lily's text on their last night in the Peak District.

'I really wasn't looking at your private texts, Gabriel, I'm sure you know that, and the last thing I want to do is to come between the two of you, but I'm just worried that all of this feels a bit more than clingy. You clearly read the text when you got back and decided not to say anything to me − which is absolutely fair enough, it just felt a little − I don't know – aggressive? Is she jealous of me or something?'

Gabriel took a mouthful of his coffee before replying: 'I don't think so, Donna, although I wish you'd told me before that you'd seen this. She can just get a bit − well − possessive when she hasn't seen me for a while and if I haven't responded. It's no big deal.'

'So, does this kind of thing happen often?'

'Er, maybe a few times a − whatever. Actually, this will make you laugh. On Sunday we were at Sainsbury's and I went off to the biscuit aisle, and saw Mrs Evans, one of my Mum's best friends? I hadn't seen her for a while and we were chatting and laughing a bit, and then Lily came round the corner and

– well, she must have thought that I was chatting up some random stranger – so she stormed – er walked – quickly – over to us and grabbed the biscuits from the shelf with a "let's get a move on" sort of look. Well, anyway, you know how biscuits are often piled up in supermarkets? Well perhaps it was just bad luck or perhaps she grabbed a little forcefully but about 15 packets tumbled around us. Just our luck that we were getting digestives – well, you know how they break, especially the chocolate ones. Well, anyway, it was all okay. I introduced them and they both smiled, and I picked up the biscuits and we went on our way. It was all just a bit funny, really.'

'That's crazy! Did she apologise for making a scene or anything? She must have been embarrassed.'

'Well, it wasn't really a scene, Donna, just – you know. Er, I'm not sure that she actually said sorry but I'm sure that she was.'

Donna thought carefully for a full five seconds before speaking again. 'Listen, Gabriel, we know each other well enough to tell each other to piss off and mind our own business, and I'm more than happy to do exactly that if you want. But – I'm sorry Gabriel, but that's more than clingy; that's more than being a bit possessive. This feels more like being *ob*sessive.'

'Oh no, Donna, I mean you've not really met her to get to know her. Honestly, she's lovely and I'm just really lucky to have her. She might not have actually said sorry, but she was *very* attentive to me when we got home, if you know what I mean.'

Donna smiled to cover the frown. 'Lovely. That's an image that will be with me all day, thanks Gabriel. It's fine, let's just leave it. I was just trying to be honest. You know I'm here if you ever need to talk.'

Mary

Mary noticed a slight sense of unease as they returned to the more intimate setting of their seminar group. She had been impressed with Jo's performance before the break, yet everyone was aware that this was the first time that Jo and Callum, let alone the likes of Anna, had been together in such a small room since Callum's now-infamous exit before Easter. Callum, indeed, looked just a little sheepish, and Jo just a little awkward, but she regained her composure quickly, much to her credit in Mary's eyes, and began talking once more.

'Okay. Let's go back to where we first started our conversation this morning and focus again on children's behaviour. You'll understand in a minute why we've spoken in depth about the notions of choice and anxiety. Let me give you a scenario – one, indeed, that I have witnessed in one form or another, many times. A child has misbehaved – let's say he's been disruptive in class all morning, and the beleaguered teacher, perhaps not unreasonably, has had enough and has sent him to the headteacher. After hearing what's gone on, the head calmly asks the boy – let's call him Nathan – if he is going to make the right choice and go back to class and behave, or make the wrong choice and have to stay in her office over lunch. Nathan replies that he will behave, and skulks back to the classroom where an uneasy truce occurs until lunch. What do we think? Good behaviour management?'

Mary listened carefully to Jo's eloquent speech and felt compelled to respond. 'I think it is good management. She's being strong and not putting up with any nonsense but is also doing what we have talked about all morning, offering a choice.'

'Thank you, Mary. Anyone else?'

'I disagree,' said Anna, with a degree of vehemence. 'That doesn't sound like a choice to me at all. It just sounds like a veiled threat.'

'Yes, but it worked, didn't it?' continued Mary. 'I mean, he went back to his class and got back on with his work.'

'Jo didn't say that,' snapped Anna. 'she said he went back to an "uneasy truce". The child wanted his playtime, he'd been threatened that he might miss it, so he just kept his head down. The head has papered over a crack, that's all.'

'Remember we mentioned right at the beginning today about a child's frame of mind,' said Jo, gently. 'What was it that had made Nathan behave like that in the first place? What could we, as his teachers, have done here? That's what I want to explore in this module.'

Mary began to redden slightly as she started to feel that she had somehow given the 'wrong answer'. She rather hoped that someone would step in and move the conversation away from her, but Anna, for some reason, was now on one of her notorious high horses, and was getting genuinely worked up.

'Exactly. What's Nathan going to do over lunch? Play sweetly? Of course he bloody isn't. By now, he's probably so wound up that he's going to deck someone. Who knows why he was in that state of mind at the start of the day? I don't know, maybe he'd just witnessed Dad selling drugs or hitting Mum. Either way, veiled threats aren't going to help him, and they certainly aren't giving him a chance to make an informed choice. I'm sorry, Mary, but that argument's just bollocks.'

In the silence that followed, there were several things that were confirmed for Mary. The first was that however good a teacher Jo undoubtedly was, however eloquent her lecturing and whatever the skill she possessed in provoking a discussion, she was simply out of her depth when it came to adult conflict. Martin wouldn't have let those seconds pass, seconds that ticked like an unexploded bomb. He would have quickly stopped Anna in her tracks and moved the conversation on. But Jo just stood there open-mouthed, clearly not knowing what to say. And then there was Anna. Mary had always viewed her as a bit of an enigma: as someone who was both articulate and intelligent, yet also as someone who could erupt at the slightest provocation, even if that meant that others would suffer as a consequence. And Mary was suffering. What she actually wanted to do, after such a personal affront, was to simply get up and walk out of the room. That's what Callum had done, but she was better than that. So, she just sat there, head down, waiting for the excruciating moment to pass. It was left to Donna to uneasily pick up the conversation and steer it in a slightly different direction, and gradually the moment passed. But the damage had been done, not just to Mary but to the mood in the room, and the session limped to an unsatisfactory ending. At its close, and with as much dignity as she could muster, Mary stood and quietly left the room.

Anna

Anna left the seminar room on her own, feeling the gaze of accusing eyes around her. She knew what she had to do, and it felt as if it would be a defining moment for her, assuming that Mary would accept her apology and offer of a coffee. She found Mary, as she knew she would, in the library and already starting to work on her computer. Such was the simplicity of Anna's apology that Mary accepted her offer of a drink readily enough. She seemed, Anna thought, somewhere between grateful and relieved as she packed away her computer quietly. There was an unspoken agreement between them that there would be no words as they walked to the café; indeed, they must have looked a strange sight to anyone who had been in their previous session.

'I really don't know where to start. Of course, I'm sorry that I laid into you like that and I shouldn't have sworn. It's too easy to say "I don't know what came over me"; the harsh truth is that this is just who I am occasionally. You know, Mary, when we were asked to think about choices this morning, I rather thought that something might happen, but I wouldn't have ever guessed I'd have opened up my soul to you. After all, for whatever reason, we've barely ever spoken really. Are you okay with this?'

'I am, and I might end up reciprocating, if it's all right with you.'

'Sounds fair enough. God, this is hard. To think something, to have it at the back of your mind – well, it's kind of safely hidden. It's only when the words come out of your mouth that things actually sound real. Sorry, I'm not making sense. Here we go: the words I've never spoken aloud. I think – I think for just about all of my life, I've felt alone and insecure and – yes, I'll say it – a bit frightened. You might know that I'm one of five. I have an older sister, Leah, who you've probably heard me talk about and then three much younger brothers. My parents are both busy people and we were rather left to bring ourselves up. Naturally then I've always looked up to Leah, and I suppose I've just always needed her seal of approval and also her affection. The thing is though, Mary, the more that I've thought about this, especially since moving away from home, the more I've begun to realise that she actually isn't very nice – at least, not to me. That may sound a bit rich coming from me, but believe me, she makes me look like a saint. And I suppose the subconscious part of me has always thought that if I'm a bitch as well, then she'll accept me. Coming out of my mouth like that it makes it sound ridiculous, but maybe you can see where I'm coming from. I'm not making excuses for anything I've done, I'm really not, I'm just trying to rationalise it. And I'm also trying to rationalise just why I got so irate this morning, and maybe the answer is that I saw myself in Nathan; some deep memory of times where nobody stopped to wonder why I was such a cow at school. God, have I really just said all that? You should be a psychiatrist, Mary; you'd have been paid a shedload for just listening then. I've always thought that was a totally overrated profession. Come on Mary, you know you want to say those immortal words; *"Tell me about your mother?"* You could then be paid another fifty quid as I rattle out more tripe. I'm going on a bit, aren't I? Maybe I'm just delaying the moment when I have to hear what you're going to say…'

Mary

Mary had always considered herself to be a good orator and her previous career in the City had demanded such a skill. She also considered herself to be adept at constructing an argument which she could skilfully debate, yet within the last hour or so, both of these qualities had been put to the test by Anna, and she was now struggling to phrase what she wanted to say.

'Wow!' she said at last. 'How do I follow that? I suppose the first thing to say is that I fully accept your apology, and – and this next bit is spoken through gritted teeth: I think I actually agree with you. My argument *was* a load of bollocks, and you wiped the floor with me. Believe me, Anna, I've never uttered such words to one your age before, so please take it as the compliment it's meant to be. I'm also rather humbled that, whether by design or by luck, it was to me that you chose to open up, and I really hope that you feel some sort of weight has been lifted just by articulating this out loud.

'So, while we're in the mood for baring our souls, let me also say something out loud for the first time. I've been married now for 25 years, and for the first time really in that marriage, I feel that it is under threat – and it's under threat totally due to me. There have been so many times since September, where I've just felt that I've got to prove myself by working stupid hours, and it's often Simon who's suffered, by my lack of attention or due to my last-minute cancellations. I don't know if you remember, during our presentations after the last school experience, me telling you about a big-shot lawyer friend of ours who clearly thinks that all this is beneath me, and I suppose our psychiatrist friend might think that I'm overcompensating by trying to prove to everyone just how much work needs to go into this and to prove to myself that I am, after all, cut out for it.

'Anyway, it all came to a head a couple of weeks ago, on the day that we were due to hand in this latest essay, which was also my birthday. I'd planned to spend the evening proofreading everything and doing my usual trick of trying to outdo myself, when Simon announced that he had booked a surprise meal out. My reaction, and I'm so ashamed to say this, was one of − and there's no other word for it − irritation. I'd finished the bloody essay, for God's sake, and yet I made it really clear that this restaurant booking was an inconvenience. What a cow. We went for the meal, but the atmosphere was soured and when we got home, I went straight back to my computer. The thing is, Anna, that I know that my obsession with perfection is causing a genuine rift between us, but I'm not sure that I'm going to be able to do anything about it.'

'Shit, what a pair, eh? Let's make a pact, shall we? If you ever see me being a cow, or if I ever see you overworking, we have each other's permission to stone the other to death. Sound fair?'

'Definitely. And the other thing I must do is to have a chat with Kathryn. I feel like I've been really neglectful to her recently and I think that there might be something wrong − beyond the obvious.'

'Ah, yes, Kathryn,' said Anna with a rueful grin. 'Well, as we're in the mood for being honest…'

Surgery

'Thanks very much for coming to see us, Kathryn. Jo and I have spent some time thinking about what's the right thing to do here, and I hope you agree that what I'm going to suggest is the best course of action. Clearly, you're going to have to rewrite your essay and we'll have to cap it at a basic pass, but neither of us can see any reason why this needs to be taken any further. If you can complete this in the next couple of weeks − and Jo's more than happy to help get you started − then we can still mark it in good time and say that it's been capped because it was handed in late which, technically, it will have been.'

173

Martin had anticipated tears of joy and relief from Kathryn in response to his words, therefore he was slightly taken back by her response:

'But I thought you said that it would need to go through a disciplinary panel because of what I did?'

'Well, yes – technically – maybe it should. But we all know what you have been through and these seem like extenuating circumstances. The thing is, Kathryn, that if we go down that road, it will be much harder to gently put this to bed. It will then be "official", and with the best will in the world, it will inevitably come out and your friends will learn that this is what you did. No, we think it's best if…'

'I don't care.'

'I'm sorry?'

'I said I don't care who knows. In fact, I'm going to tell everybody in our next group Surgery. Jo has been talking about choices today and this is my choice. It's bad enough me imagining about what Mum and Nan would be thinking as it is. Maybe they'll now feel as though I've done the right thing by not sweeping this under the carpet. Maybe they can be proud of me again.'

Chapter 18

Martin

'Welcome back! I really hope you've enjoyed your day in school and I'm looking forward to hearing about all your tales. Let's just remind you about why we sent you out just for a day in a completely new environment for you. The first and most important reason, of course, was that we wanted you to "test all the theories" that we have hurled at you during this Professional Studies module. We've talked a lot about children's engagement, their motivations, and how these link with both behaviour and learning, so we wanted to send you to schools to observe for a day; schools which we know have a heavy focus on getting to know children very well, and ones which underpin everything that they do with a focus on well-being and developing children holistically. But these approaches are all different, and I know that the schools that you visited apply vastly differing strategies to achieve this aim, and it will be really interesting to hear all about these. As you know, you start your final teaching experience in a few days' time, and hopefully part of what you've seen in school last week will also rub off on you then. The second reason for doing this was to give you the opportunity to work and observe at a totally different school – with all that entails – and also pairing you up with somebody who you haven't worked with in school before seemed to make sense, for reasonably obvious reasons.

'Now what we've asked you to do – give a summary of the day but focusing on your partner rather than yourself – well, we've never done this before so I've no idea whether it will work, or whether, indeed, you'll end up killing each other. We shall see. Finally, we decided that it would be more intimate if we did this in your Surgery Sets, rather than in your seminar groups, so I hope this works. Right, who'd like to go first?'

Callum

'Okay, so I don't like dogs. I never have. Horrible smelly things with teeth and fleas and worms and who-knows-what. Now whenever anyone asks me why I went into teaching, I always give them the usual "making a difference" stuff, but I could also justifiably add that it's a profession in which I can reasonably be assured of not coming in to contact with bloody dogs. Well how wrong was I? "Puppy cuddles"? Really? Do I look like someone who wants to cuddle a nasty mutt, for God's sake? No, I don't, and let me say right away that it was horrible. Don't get me wrong, I can do touchy-feely-wanky stuff like the best of them − my name's not Anna, after all − but when I finally go for my first interview the first thing I'll say is that I won't sign anything until I have written assurances that no canine monsters will ever darken my classroom door.

'Okay, let's go back a step. When we first arrived at the school, we were told that they had recently acquired a pet dog as part of the "nurturing process" for some of the needier children in the school. Apparently, research has suggested that children who lack empathy and the ability to form relationships and develop trust can channel these feelings into the caring of a dog. So, they look after it, walk it, play with it, ensure it has all its tablets, and even phone up the vet to book in routine visits and injections. Can't argue too much with that. But also, apparently, some do-gooder of a researcher has also computed that children develop love and affection from cuddling dogs, and so, once a week, each group of children that this is relevant to, have a "puppy cuddles" session, and the idea is that when it's their turn, they have to talk about something nice, or something that makes them happy, while they are becoming infested with fleas. And d'you know what? Even that sounds okay, and I sat in the circle, knowing that all I had to do was to grin inanely, say "ooh and aah" in all the right places, and wait until the session finished, before locking myself in a darkened room and phoning up my shrink.

'So, the first little girl, Sasha, took hold of the puppy and started talking about a holiday she had with her grandparents the previous summer, whilst stroking the unfortunate animal a little too firmly in my opinion. The dog was to be passed to the left, and I was on Sasha's right, so all was fine there. The "nurture teacher", or whatever they're called, was next to Sasha on the other side and Donna was somewhere in the middle. When the dog was passed to Miss Peters, I rather assumed that she would pass it straight on to Abdul and was therefore horrified to see her not only start stroking poor Fido, but also begin talking about the day her daughter was born. Apparently, if these children really want to find empathy, then they need to see their teachers get involved with the process. But not only their teachers, so it seems, but any other adult who is in the room. At that point, I tell you, I nearly got up and left, citing some allergy or other, but the look on Donna's face said categorically that she would never let me live it down if I did. Bastard. Sorry Donna, but bastard is the only word for it.

'I know the idea of this is to talk about the other person, but I kind of needed to get that off my chest first. Eventually the dog found its way to me, and I think I got away with it, but I'll leave Donna to talk through that. Needless to say, she took to it like a seasoned pro. In fairness to her, she didn't do the obvious and talk about her boyfriend or just how bloody perfect she is – sorry again, Donna, but you are – no; instead she talked about nearly having to leave university soon after she'd started and how upset that had made her, but how wonderful she felt when she was allowed to stay. The moral, she'd said, was that no matter how low you are feeling, there is always some good news around the corner. By now, Fido was sticking his paws down his throat, but in fairness, it was really rather a good speech and the children lapped it up. No pun intended. So, come on then, Donna, do your worst. Remember I've just said something nice about you.'

Donna

Donna had really been looking forward to this. She was very fond of Callum, but – and she wasn't sure who she blamed most for this – she was even more fond of gently taking the piss out of him, and, boy, did she have ammunition today. But then she'd got the phone call late last night and her whole world had been rocked. It was only after Gabriel had dropped his bombshell, after she had tried to reason with him, and after she had finally hung up in complete frustration did it occur to her just how much she relied on him, primarily as her closest friend, but also as someone to whom she could bear her soul. She remembered what he'd said, almost word for word – it was so embedded on her mind:

'I want you to be the first to know, Donna. I've just come back from Lily's, and she's told me that she is pregnant. I'm going to be a dad, Donna. Me, a dad! I still haven't taken it all in; it's certainly not what we'd planned, and I'm far from sure it's what I want at the moment, but it is what it is and we'll make it work, I'm sure of that. It's just – well, it's just that neither of us have got much money, and she's going to have to look after the baby and stuff and – well – she sort of suggested that I leave the course – perhaps not forever – but for a year, so that I can earn enough for us to live on and look after the baby. I know this is a bit of a shock, and well, if it were up to me, then I'd carry on with my studies and work, but well she was adamant, and they really must come first. I'm sorry, Donna, I know we'd always said we'd be there for each other till the end. Please don't say anything to anyone at the moment. I'm going to complete the year, and I might wait until after our last placement before telling Martin, unless, of course, Lily insists that I tell him now. As I say, it is what it

177

is, and I will make sure it works out for us, despite the sacrifices I'll have to make. Tell me you're happy for me?'

How could she tell him that she was happy for him when, patently, she wasn't, and on so many levels? It was abundantly clear to her that this wasn't planned by them both, but she was far from convinced that it wasn't planned by Lily. It was also pretty clear to her that Gabriel was still trying to come to terms with this, despite attempting to sound upbeat. And then there was his use of language: "she was adamant" and "Lily insists", for instance. If she had been concerned about Gabriel before, she was now desperately worried about a relationship and a woman that she simply didn't trust. Yet there was absolutely nothing she could do about it, especially now that Lily's pregnancy would tie them together for the rest of their lives.

'Of course, I'm happy for you, Gabriel, I just don't want you to leave the course, that's all.'

But that was then and whilst it was impossible to clear it from her mind, six faces were now turned to her, and she knew that she had a job a do; a speech that was well-prepared, but needed gusto in its deliverance for it to work. She could do this.

'Ladies and Gentlemen of the jury. You have just heard from the accused who stated, and I quote: "Eventually the dog found its way to me and I think I got away with it." I shall let you make your own mind up about the veracity of this assertion when you have heard the prosecution's evidence. I know Callum well enough to have been sure, from the outset, that he was not going to like the puppy cuddles. From my perspective, it was a brilliant notion, and it really opened my eyes to the importance of finding a vehicle, whether that be a dog or anything else, which allowed vulnerable children to channel their emotions and to develop empathy. But as soon as it became clear that we too were to be part of this process, well, any remaining doubts that I had about his hatred of the situation completely disappeared. So, Pippin (not Fido) gradually worked his way around the circle as child after child enjoyed stroking him and sharing a fond memory. I could see a definite sheen on the brow of Callum as his moment of reckoning got closer, and eventually Bobby carefully handed Pippin over. There was a moment when the two of them eyed each other, before Pippin, in an ill-judged moment of affection, turned to give Callum a friendly lick on his cheek. To say that Callum dropped the unfortunate beast at this point would be an understatement. It was more like a chuck, as Pippin fell unceremoniously to the floor with a clunk and a yelp. That should have been the end of it, but rules is rules, and Miss Peters was clearly not one for bending them so she carefully picked Pippin up and placed him back on Callum's lap. By now, they were both looking at each other with something approaching mutual hatred until Miss Peters, ever the stickler for the rules, said: "So then, Mr Williams. Tell us something that makes you happy."

'"What? Really? Now? Er – okay. Er, well, you know. Er, Brexit."

'"Brexit?"

'"Yes, Brexit. And er, that makes me happy because, well, it means – er – that we can control our own borders and regulate immigration."

'The silence following this revelation was eventually broken by Abdul, who asked, in all innocence, what Breck sick was. Miss Peters, clearly concerned that Callum was about to weigh up all of the economic arguments for and against to this group of six-year-olds, quickly brought an abrupt ending to the proceedings. It was priceless, definitely a "bring back the stripper story, all is forgiven" moment. Oh, and next time, I really am going to make sure that I bring some TENA Lady. It happened again. And there, your honour, rests the case for the prosecution.'

Anna

Such was the level of hilarity that greeted Donna's speech that Anna was really rather peeved that she had to go next. Indeed, she needed to wait until Callum and Martin completed the mock trial, but she had some ammunition of her own…

She was still just a little fed up by Mary's late-night call yesterday, even though much of Mary's argument had centred around the fact that she felt that Anna was the better speaker, and better at making last-minute adjustments to speeches, which, coming from Mary, was high praise indeed. Yes, Mary had had a tough weekend, but so had she. Mary had eventually asked her about the dress-fitting and had seemed genuinely shocked by her revelations, but after all, it was she up here about to speak and not Mary.

Despite all her soul-searching with Mary the previous week, Anna had still been looking forward to the dress-fitting at Leah's flat, not least because she knew just how much prosecco had been ordered. It was supposed to be a girlie event, but Michael was not to be thrown out of his own home and had lurked in the background. Anna couldn't quite put her finger on the rationale for her reservations about Leah's fiancé. Perhaps it was simply that he seemed to look down on her in the same way that Leah did. But now, it felt slightly different. She had gone to the spare room to change back out of the dress and was feeling slightly self-conscious anyway, due to it being decidedly tighter than it had been at the initial measuring. (The upside of this, of course, was that when she'd recently bought her wedding bra, she'd also gone up a cup size. Oh well, swings and roundabouts.) She hadn't paid too much attention when the door had opened with her in her underwear, but most certainly did when she'd seen Michael standing there. Of course, he'd quickly apologised – hadn't realised she'd been in there and all that – but, and here, of course, she was only really surmising, it seemed to have taken him a second or two longer than he should have done to retreat. Again, she couldn't be sure, but when she did notice him, it also seemed that he too was weighing up that extra cup size. Mary's view, as indeed Anna's, was that there was nothing that could be done or said – that could end in disaster in so many different ways – but she now felt both reserved and slightly sickened. But such deliberations would have to wait. She had a speech to make.

'Thanks very much for that, Donna. If you had told me this was a stand-up round, then I would have prepared accordingly. Anyway, in the school that Mary and I were in, they practised something called "Philosophy for Children". I still haven't got my head around the concept, but I know that it's something to do with promoting curiosity and encouraging children to ask questions. One of the straplines of the school was: "This is a safe place to ask and a safe place to tell", and our teacher was telling us how she had spent the whole year trying to create an ethos in her classroom where children wouldn't judge each other in these "safe" moments. I can see your faces – yeah, that's what I thought as well, but actually this really seemed to have worked. We witnessed a session where they were talking about moral dilemmas, and this led to a child asking what she should do if someone told her a secret, but she felt she needed to say something, even though she'd promised not to. We both really learnt from listening to how the teacher responded to this; how she didn't preach, and how she skilfully got the children to justify their own responses to the scenario. Eventually, Archie put up his hand: "I don't know what I should do, Mrs Roach. I overheard my Mum on the phone to someone. She didn't know that I was listening but when she saw me standing there, she made me promise not to say anything to anyone."

'"Well, Archie, I'm sure you made that promise to your Mum, and of course you might want to keep it, but if you ever want to talk to me confidentially then you know that I'll listen."

'"Thanks, Mrs Roach. It's just, well, it didn't seem that bad. She just said something about a smack, and I thought she was telling about how she'd smacked my little brother when he took some money from her purse, but then she said something about a couple of grams and that didn't seem to make any sense."

'At that point, both Mary and I looked at each other with ever-widening eyebrows, and still the children – they were only seven and eight, looked on earnestly at their teacher, who quickly muttered something about it probably not being very important, and that her advice was for him to forget all about it. The conversation very quickly moved on. We chatted to Mrs Roach afterwards, and she said that this was one of these really difficult situations that they had to deal with a lot. On the one hand, it's "a safe place to ask and a safe place to tell", and on the other, the mother of one of her eight-year-olds might be a drug dealer. Her advice to us was that if we ever hear anything like that, go straight to the headteacher and let them deal with it. She also said that on no occasion should we ever promise a child that we will keep a secret for them. I tell you: you learn something new every day in this job. It was really quite scary.'

Mary

When eventually Anna finished explaining all they had learnt from their day, Mary finally spoke. 'Anna's right. We were both totally shocked upon hearing something clearly drugs-related come out of the mouth of one so innocent. Martin, I know you said that we were to tell this from each other's perspective, but as we both witnessed the same thing, it felt like we'd just end up repeating each other, so I was more than happy for Anna to do the talking. I hope you don't mind.'

Of course, Martin didn't mind, and Mary sat down again very quickly but she sensed a slightly quizzical mood in the air. It was so unlike Mary to shirk any responsibility, and it was clear that they all thought that something was going on. But it was much more preferable for her to just accept a few awkward moments rather than explain the reason for her silence.

At the end of their day in school on Friday, they had briefly agreed how they would share the load, and Mary was more than happy to plan her piece during her weekend away. Her family's spring weekend to Southend had been a regular fixture since the children had been born, and it was a family rule that everyone would always make it: a rule which had become harder to maintain since the children had grown up, but they were still yet to miss a year. Mary saw no reason why she shouldn't take her computer with her and steal a couple of half hours to prepare, and was rather shocked by Simon's vehemence on the subject.

'It's just not happening, Mary. This is family time, as you are so keen on telling us all, and quite frankly, we all need a break from your studies.'

She'd tried, half-heartedly, to argue but it was clear that this would have been a very ill-advised choice, and so she had finally accepted. She was even stymied by the horrendous Sunday evening traffic, and eventually had no choice but to phone Anna to ask if she'd do the talking. For all her oratory skills, presenting without adequate preparation was not something she did well, and she'd noticed a slightly off-handed tone in Anna's voice. If she'd felt bad then, she felt decidedly guilty when Anna had talked her through her weekend, which rather put an enjoyable family excursion as an excuse not to do her homework well and truly into perspective. Mary began to feel that she was owing rather a lot to several people, and it was a feeling she didn't like. And she was still to tell Kathryn about her conversation with the school placement organiser…

Gabriel

'When you first mentioned, Martin, that we were to report this back from each other's perspective, I think both Kathryn and I couldn't really see the point of the exercise. However, as it forced us to observe each other, rather than just what was going on in the lesson, we both quickly found out that we can learn so many different things from looking at the situation holistically.

'We were with a group of six-year-olds, and the teacher was reading a picture book called *Granpa* by John Burningham. The story is about the relationship between a young girl and her grandfather and explores all the things that they did together. On the very last page, it shows the girl sitting by an empty chair, soon after being told that he was unwell. The teacher explained that she regularly used stories to explore feelings, and after reading the story, she skilfully led a discussion about loss. She'd told us that one of the children had recently lost a grandparent, and wanted to let him either join in or just listen, so that he could see that some of the others were also suffering some sort of bereavement, even if it was for a pet. The boy opted not to speak until near the end of the conversation, when he commented that he hoped his granny and the girl's grandpa could now be friends. It was powerful stuff.

'Kathryn and I agreed on what I would say before this meeting; indeed, she was insistent that I did say this. Clearly, this discussion was close to home for her, and I could see that she was struggling, even listening to a group of very small children talking about dead hamsters. I was both surprised and impressed, then, when she put her hand up near the end and spoke about her nan and how much she missed her. She was clearly holding back the tears, but there was an amazing moment when one of the children came and gave her a hug.

'For whatever reason, Kathryn and I have never really worked much together, and it was so good to be put in a school with someone else for a change. No offence, Donna. I think maybe the main thing that I learnt from this session is that we aren't robots when it comes to being in a classroom. There are times when things are going to affect us as much as they affect the children. We might choose to hide behind our feelings in such a moment, but we might also choose, as Kathryn did, to share something very personal indeed with them and that this can help to strengthen the relationship between us and the children in our class. I shan't forget that hug for a long time.'

Kathryn

Kathryn was still far from sure what she thought about Martin. She had assumed that this was to be a serious discussion, and she was very glad that her talk followed the more sober words of Gabriel, rather than some of the initial presentations. That Martin played along with Donna's and Callum's antics, felt, on one level, to be quite wrong. Maybe she was old-fashioned, but she rather thought that there should be professional distance between teacher and child, or indeed, between lecturer and student. Yet, as well as today's episode, he had played silly games with them all in the Peak District and, according to Mary, was happy to guess who had broken wind during the pizza evening.

But here was Gabriel talking about the power of someone opening up, of being themselves, and showing vulnerability to children. Was not that, to some extent, also crossing the 'professional distance' line? Was there really anything wrong with Callum and Donna enjoying a joke whilst making important points? She had been laughing with the others when Donna was telling of the mutual hatred between Callum and the dog. Was Martin actually just being very skilful in creating a culture where learning was taking place whilst they were also enjoying themselves? She really didn't know, and it was something she vowed to herself that she would think about when developing relationships with the children during School Experience Three next week.

She was, however, very sure about one thing. Martin had been incredibly supportive of her over the last few months, both after her bereavement and after making such a terrible mistake, a mistake that she was bracing herself to speak to everyone about during Surgery immediately after their break. As always, Kathryn kept her presentation as brief as she could, as she discussed how she had felt knowing that Gabriel had been observing her, and how awkward he had looked whilst doing so. It made her reassess things. Up until now, she'd never really considered the effect of her misery on other people; it was all about her. So maybe now was the time to start smiling again, whilst still accepting that there would be moments; moments such as listening to a story about a grandparent passing away.

Surgery

At Kathryn's request, Martin allowed her to speak to all of them first about why she needed to retake her Professional Studies assignment. They all saw her speak with her head held high and blew a collective sigh of relief when Martin added that the disciplinary committee had accepted that this was a first offence with extenuating circumstances, and that no further action was to be taken, beyond having her new essay capped at a basic pass. Anna noticed Mary glance slightly towards her as she, too stood to get things off her chest:

'Kathryn is far too loyal to say this, but she wouldn't have done that if it hadn't been for me encouraging her to do so. In my defence, I thought at the time that I was trying to help her, but I see now that that was just really crap advice. I'm sorry, Kathryn.'

'As far as I'm concerned, the matter is now over,' said Martin, 'and there's no way that Anna's revelation needs to go beyond the sanctuary of this Surgery Set. What was it you said, Anna? "A safe place to ask and a safe place to tell?" I rather like that.'

So, Anna sat down with a slightly rueful glance at Mary. She'd promised her that she was also going to mention that she had done the same thing before Christmas, but in the end, just couldn't do so. *Quite frankly*, she thought to herself now, *that would just be a bloody stupid thing to do. I got away with it; I've learnt from it. Let's move on.*

And so, Martin reminded them all about their final teaching experience of the year, to commence the following week. 'The main differences between this placement and previous ones are that you are now in a different school and a different year group, albeit with the same partner that you've had before. We're going to expect you to teach more this time, plan a few lessons for yourself and really reflect on how far you've come this year. Also, we've put you back in the same class as your partner this time, so that you can plan, teach and reflect together. You've now got the rest of this week to touch base with the school and start to plan. And finally, one thing you don't know yet. Last time you all had me for your tutor, visiting you and your mentor in school, but that's changing this time. Donna and Gabriel, you'll be looked after by Richard, Anna and Callum will have Grace overseeing them, and Mary and Kathryn, er, you'll be with Frank.'

Chapter 19

Mary

'Okay, Mum. Sit down and tell all. I've been looking forward to this all day.'

Mary sighed, knowing that Alice was ready to partake in her favourite pastime – gently taking the piss out of her mother. And of course, it was her own fault. As she and Kathryn had been in the same school for the past two placements, Mary was adamant that she needed a completely new challenge this time, and had asked the school placement organiser if she could be placed in a totally different type of school for her final teaching experience of the year. She'd felt slightly guilty about not mentioning this to Kathryn, as of course it affected her as well, but she reasoned – without too much conviction of thought – that Kathryn would surely benefit from something diverse as well...

And so Mary and Kathryn had found out, shortly after their last Surgery meeting with Martin, that they were to be placed in a Hare Krishna school – a school with 60 pupils, sporting just one Key Stage 1 and one Key Stage 2 class.

'I spoke to Amadesh, who is the headteacher and your mentor,' explained the school placement organiser. 'Whilst they have never had any of our students in their school before, he was very keen to help to train you and has invited you both to a visit, of their temple as well as the school, before you start your placement next week. This will be an incredible experience for you.'

'Go on then, Mum. Tell me all about your visit. Was it an incredible experience?'

'It was certainly – interesting – and we were both made to feel very welcome, as promised. We were invited to join an organised visit of the temple and the surroundings before going to the school, as the whole environment plays a huge part in the daily life of the children. The temple was beautiful and there was a genuine sense of peace in the air. There were yoga sessions and wisdom workshops, which we briefly saw, and then there was a visit to the farm. Amadesh spoke to us all about how spirituality and belief in the Krishna way were central to everything that they stood for, and everything that was central to the school. He explained the importance of austerity and of meditation. We ate the vegan lunch provided for us with our fingers, as was the norm, in a sort of stunned silence. In the afternoon, we visited the school and learnt that we were both to be placed in the Key Stage 2 class. Kathryn had barely said a word to me all morning – we were both just a little taken aback by everything – but when we were told that we would be teaching in the Key Stage 2 class, when we both saw the size of some of the Year 6 boys, the look she gave me was a mixture of horror and disgust. I'm going to have my work cut out there, Alice. The children seemed nice enough; apparently much of the curriculum centres around topic work, and they were engaged on a project about space. It's difficult to put my finger on why, but it just seemed to me that there didn't appear to be a lot of structure to the session. When I asked Amadesh what the learning objectives were for the session, he looked at me slightly oddly and said that they were learning about space. We both left feeling rather overwhelmed, if I'm honest. But you know me, Alice, I'm not one for pre-judging; this could be an amazing experience.'

'It could, you're right, and it might also be a nightmare. Not because of the religion, the yoga, or the vegan lunches, but because you saw fit to ask your mentor about learning objectives on your first visit. I take it you also asked him to explain how the session linked to the National Curriculum and got him to justify his methods of differentiation? One day you'll learn.'

'Okay, point taken. We're meeting Frank tomorrow. It will be interesting to see his take on all of this.'

Kathryn

It had all been going so well. Kathryn had felt like she had turned a corner after her school visit with Gabriel and their subsequent discussion had made her understand that her bereavement did not just affect her and that it was time to look positively at the future. And when she had spoken to her Surgery Set with the sort of quiet authority that had eluded her for most of her life, it had seemed a defining moment.

And now this. Indeed, not just 'this', but 'these'. Not only was she having to teach the whole of the Key Stage 2 class in a school with an ethos so outside from her own experiences, but she was to be tutored by Frank. Kathryn remembered clearly, when, at interview, she had made it abundantly clear that she was only interested in teaching in the Early Years. The interviewers, both local headteachers, had mumbled something along the lines of 'I'm sure that will be okay', and now her vague misgiving about this rash statement was becoming a reality. When Martin had told her this week that, in order to train all students thoroughly, everyone needed experience in different key stages, she could hardly cite a half-remembered statement from nearly a year ago. But she was now terrified that these huge 11-year-olds would walk all over her. And then there was Frank.

When Kathryn and Mary went to visit him yesterday for a preliminary chat, Kathryn was literally shaking with fear. For here was a man who had shouted at her when she was at her most vulnerable and who had then been humiliated for his actions. Whilst none of this was her fault, she doubted that he would see it that way. She needn't have worried. His opening speech suggested that he had absolutely no idea who they both were, which, in itself, spoke volumes.

'Hello ladies. You must be Mary? No? Kathryn, then? Good. Which by process of elimination means that *you* must be Mary. Ha-ha. My name is Frank, and I will be supervising your placement. I'm sure you'll find me very fair. Let me say first of all that the things that I value most, especially at your stage of training, is order. Nicely-ordered files. Nicely-ordered lesson plans. Nicely-ordered evaluations. Nicely-ordered targets; indeed, nicely-ordered you.

'Now, I've never been to the temple and the school, but I have to say that I think they both sound fantastic. You may have heard a little rumour that I'm rather obsessed with the environment, and it seems to me, at a first glance, that the school has a wonderful ethos. Austerity, veganism, and total respect for all living creatures – that's my kind of a good school. Ladies, we're going to have a ball...'

Mary

In many ways, everything was going well. The first two days had been enjoyable enough. Mary and Kathryn had largely been observing, and they had seen a class that seemed very happy. They'd seen children keen to ask questions and children on task, and Amadesh had smiled his way through the two days to children who seemed in awe of him. Yet Mary was still concerned about the 'planned learning'. They had had it drilled into them all year that clear lesson objectives and success criteria were non-negotiables for any lesson, yet Mary had yet to see any evidence of either. Mindful of Alice's comments and her own reflections from previous placements, she couldn't bring herself to mention this again to Amadesh, even when he had asked her and Kathryn to plan a joint lesson.

'You choose what you would like to teach tomorrow, but I'd like you to focus on writing. Be creative, be enthusiastic and the children will learn.'

And so the two of them had spent ages trying to think about what they could do, how they could justify the learning, how they could differentiate, and Mary had got more and more wound up until Kathryn had said, simply: 'Do you know what, we could just teach.'

And in those words, Mary experienced something vaguely cathartic. Everything that she had done this year had had to be perfect and she knew that this seeking of perfection was affecting her marriage. It was all very well admitting as much to Anna, but this was not a theoretical discussion, this was actual practice.

'But what will we say to Frank? How will we justify the...?'

'Why don't we think about that *after* the lesson, eh?' said Kathryn. 'Why don't we get the children to write some poetry, and then think about what they've learnt afterwards?'

'There's a lovely poem by Pie Corbett called "I want to paint",' began Mary slowly. 'We could get them to write something in that style. I think it would work just as well for 7-year-olds as it would for 11-year-olds.'

And so that is what they had done. There were no lesson objectives, no success criteria. As Amadesh had asked them, they just taught. They taught with passion and they taught creatively, and the children produced some fantastic poetry. When Sam, all five feet ten inches of him, called Kathryn enthusiastically to read out one of his lines and Kathryn smiled and did so with gusto, it was a moment of revelation for Mary, and it made her realise that there was more to good teaching than to plan to the nth degree, fretting and sweating along the way. Sometimes, the best lessons are based on a gut reaction and on enthusiasm, and Amadesh had praised them greatly after they'd delivered it. Whether Frank would see it like that, of course, was a different matter...

Kathryn

Kathryn was very aware that she did not have too much of a sense of humour and was more than happy to let other people make the jokes. However, when she saw the likes of Donna or Callum tell stories that had everyone in fits of laughter, a small part of her thought that it would be rather nice to possess such a skill. Anna was in one of her good moods when Kathryn came into their communal kitchen and she poured Kathryn a glass of wine.

'How's it going then, Kathryn? We had our first formal observation today, and all seemed to be well. Though I say so myself, I think that Grace was really impressed by what she saw. It does annoy me slightly, though, that she seems to be spending nearly all her time with Callum. It's almost like: "Yeah, you're fine; but if you need me, I'll be talking to him." Which is fine – I take that as a compliment, but even so. Actually, to be fair, she is making a massive difference to Callum. I don't know if you know that she's dyslexic as well, but she has been giving him loads of ideas and his confidence is soaring. Fair play, although it's a bit disappointing to report that he hasn't, as yet, made a complete arse of himself. Plenty of time. I'm sorry; I vaguely remember asking you how you're getting on a minute ago. How's Frank?'

'Er, well, talking about making an arse of yourself...'

'Oh, Kathryn, this I must hear. Fire away.'

Buoyed by Anna's interest, Kathryn − with ever-increasing confidence − began to tell her story:

'Well, we obviously knew that he was coming in to observe us today after break, but what we didn't know was that Amadesh had invited him in for the whole morning, as he wanted Frank to get a sense of the whole ethos of the place. The motto of the school is "All together", and part of the idea is that everyone joins in and everyone learns together. It's a good motto. Anyway, what Amadesh forgot to mention to Frank before the visit was that the Key Stage 2 class had their weekly yoga session this morning.'

'Oh, please tell me you saw Frank doing yoga. Please tell me that you've got photos.'

'Well, not photos exactly but − er − it's actually even better than that. Mary and I knew about the session and turned up in our loose clothes. Frank clearly didn't and turned up in his suit− a suit which was probably bought when he was a few sizes smaller. As soon as he'd arrived in the class at the beginning of the day, he seemed different somehow. He was still very much Frank, but he had turned in to a sort of Victorian teacher, very stiff and upright and not really knowing how to talk to the children. I actually heard him say to one of them, as he ruffled their hair, "Right then, Sonny Jim, what are you up to, then?" The child didn't know whether to laugh or call the police and ended up just looking awkward and shrinking into himself.

'And then came the yoga. Amadesh told him that he didn't need to join in if he didn't want to, but Frank was adamant. "No, thank you, anyway, but when in Rome, do as the, er − Krishnas do." Neither Mary nor I had done yoga before so we sat at the back on our mats and tried to do some basic moves whilst keeping out of the spotlight, but Frank, clearly thinking that it was important to show willing, was prominent in the middle and tried to do every movement in a sort of exaggerated fashion and keeping a facial expression that I suppose tried to show some sort of meditation. When he tried to do something called "Halasana", a move which basically involves sticking your bum high in the air, he broke wind – loudly. But that wasn't actually the funny bit. He had got the idea that you need to breathe in heavily through the nose when practising yoga and − well − it rather looked like he was trying his best to smell it.'

As Kathryn paused, Anna burst out laughing and clapped her hands. She couldn't possibly know just what this natural reaction to a story did for Kathryn. It lifted her more, maybe, than she had ever been lifted before, and for the first time in many months, she felt a surge of happiness, albeit at Frank's expense.

'Oh Kathryn, that's absolutely brilliant. I'd have paid good money to see that.'

'And his armpits were still sweating when he came in to see us teach.'

'Hilarious. How did it go?'

'Hmm, well the lesson went okay; we were doing an investigation in Maths and tried to organise it so that they could all work at their own level. Frank gave us some good feedback, but then, as we knew he would, he started asking us about the lesson objectives and how the session fit into a sequence – all the stuff that's been drummed into us. Mary explained, as carefully as she could, that that's not really the school's way.'

'I bet Frank loved that.'

'He really couldn't cope with it. When he'd arrived at the school in the morning, he couldn't get enough of it and kept telling everyone who'd listen how the school's values echoed his own. But when it came to a lack of order, he couldn't accept it. The conversation between him and Amadesh was excruciating. Frank told him, in no uncertain terms, that if he was taking on the university students, they had to comply with the university's expectations. Amadesh replied that we are guests in his school, and therefore need to adapt to the school's ideals. He reminded Frank that the number one ideal is the joy of the spiritual experience, and that it was this, rather than anything else, which dominated how they planned and delivered the curriculum. It was a pretty horrible standoff, if I'm honest, and Mary and I just wanted out of there. Anyway, the upshot is that we are now in an awkward position – we've been told by Frank that we must give context to our lessons, even if there isn't one for the rest of the sessions that we aren't teaching. When Frank finally left, Amadesh clearly looked taken aback by the whole exchange. Doesn't bode well for the rest of our placement…'

Frank

Frank had handed in his notice a few weeks before being informed that, for the first time in three years, he was to supervise two first-year students in their final teaching experience of the year. When he had informed the Dean of his intention to retire, he had received what was, from his perspective, a mixed reaction. He had no doubt whatsoever that William Ranch had been itching to get rid of him for years, but he was also aware that, currently, the university was not replacing retiring lecturers for economic reasons, and a small part of him looked forward to the moment when Ranch would have to tell everyone else that they would have to absorb Frank's work.

The Hare Krishna school had seemed, initially, to have sound values, and the two ladies that he was to supervise seemed pleasant enough. But it was only when they had left the initial meeting that he realised that he had met Kathryn before, albeit fleetingly. Whilst he didn't blame her at all, she was the cause of his public humiliation and the catalyst for his decision to retire this academic year. Frank did not believe in coincidences. If this was their game, to rub salt into his wounds by making him supervise Kathryn, then so be it. He would throw himself into the role, he would support both Kathryn and Mary to the best of his ability, and he would keep his head held high. So, when he had been invited into the school for the whole morning, he readily accepted and was happy to embrace the culture of the school, even if that meant him pulling a muscle or two along the way.

His primary concern, though, was to ensure that his students had the best possible experience, and this meant that the planning, teaching and paperwork needed to be robust. He had soon realised that this was not the case, and it was very evident to him that the reason for this was the lack of adherence to National Curriculum objectives that characterised the school. Maybe he shouldn't have spoken quite so vehemently to Amadesh, and maybe discretion was not his strong point, but quite frankly, if they wanted to complain about his monitoring methods, then that was up to them. He could hardly be sacked. No, if nothing else, he would make it his mission to see that Kathryn and Mary did things by the book in a school that did things how they pleased.

Amadesh

Amadesh had followed the Krishna way all of his life, a life that was undoubtedly better because of his faith. He had been headteacher at the school for nearly a decade and was immensely proud of the well-rounded children that emerged after being educated in the Krishna faith. The school's values, centring on developing a spiritual and moral compass, as well as self-esteem, had stood both him and his staff in good stead for many years, and he had no doubt that his children left the school with enquiring minds and were well-prepared for future academic challenges.

At least he *had* felt this, but events over the last few weeks had made him question things. Having two students had been a good thing for the school in many ways. The children were not used to having different teachers, and this, in itself, had been good for them. Both of the teachers had done well, and he was proud of his guidance here. Kathryn was clearly terrified initially, but once she realised that the children listened to her and respected her, then she had quickly settled. Similarly, Mary had thrived when she had been given licence to express herself. But the spectre of Frank's interventions was always at the back of his mind, and it had made Amadesh question his own methods.

And then last week, he had got the phone call from Ofsted to say that they were coming in to inspect the school. And of course, they, as Frank had done before, had interrogated and probed about progress and about how this was documented and proved. He knew that, when interrogated that way, he struggled to provide concrete evidence, and now he was left waiting to see the report that would arrive in the near future. If developing free-thinking enquiring minds with a sound moral compass was not enough, then so be it. He would cross that bridge.

Surgery

'There'll be an opportunity to have a chat with all of the Surgery Set very soon, but I thought it important, at least initially, to chat to just the pair of you on your own. After all, I haven't really been privy to things over the last four weeks. How do you think things went?'

'We heard a rumour that Frank is retiring, soon. Is that correct?'

Martin pulled a wry grin. 'Does your answer to my question depend on this then, Mary? You don't need to answer that. Yes, Frank is leaving in a few weeks' time.'

'Okay, and I'm not going to Frank-bash here. I've actually learnt quite a lot from him. From my perspective, I think I've learnt a lot from this placement, and more importantly, it's made me realise, for certain, that I'm going to continue with the course next year. I think perhaps the main thing that I've learnt is that I've always been one for extremes, and that, for me, that's not the way forward. Frank and Amadesh could not have been more different in their approaches, and this was frustrating at first, until we looked at it through the lens of trying to learn from it. Yes, Frank is absolutely right that there should be order and clarity about what the children need to learn, and that's probably how I went into the process. But the freedom of Amadesh's approach was also incredibly liberating for me, and I suppose, if you're asking me how this has shaped the sort of teacher that I want to be, I think that it would be somewhere in the middle of these two extremes.'

'Interesting, and fantastic to hear that you are definitely staying on. I'll get you to sign for that in a minute. How about you, Kathryn?'

'Well you know that I've always wanted to be an Early Years teacher − at the absolute most Key Stage 1 − and that view hasn't changed. I was both terrified and angry in equal measure initially to have to teach the whole of Key Stage 2, but I think the most important thing that I've learnt is that I can work well with older children, and that they can respect me – I really never thought that this would be the case. The Ofsted inspection was interesting. It was patently obvious that they picked up on all of this. They weren't there to inspect us, but they definitely noted the difference between how we had to approach things and how the school did, and Frank should take credit for that. I actually really liked the school and am going to go back in a couple of weeks after we finish here to volunteer – in Key Stage 1, of course.'

'Good for you. When I heard that you were going to this school, I have to say I was a bit concerned, and if truth be told, I was a bit annoyed with the placements organiser for agreeing to this without speaking to me first. But, actually, what I've just heard is, if not a ringing endorsement, a sense that you learnt a huge amount from experiencing such a different approach. I think we'll use them again. I'll see you all again on Friday, briefly, for our final session of the year before the Summer Ball in the evening. I take it you're both going?'

Chapter 20

Kathryn

Kathryn was on a high. Martin had been so full of praise for them all in their final session of the year, and she'd felt genuinely excited when he'd talked about summer preparation for Year 2.

'I just want you both to know, I have every intention of getting drunk tonight. I'm not really sure how that will pan out, but I don't care. I just heard from Martin today that I've passed my retake, and so, like all of you, I've officially passed the year. Cheers!'

'You do realise that this is a pre-pre, don't you, Kathryn? That means vodka here, vodka when we get to Donna's, and cheap shots and vodka for the rest of the night at the ball. I'll put you to bed later, unless of course you pull, but I have standards. I'm a lady, after all, and I don't clear other people's puke. Sorry, Kathryn: bit of a rule.'

'Fair enough, Anna, but I'm sure Mary will clean me up if necessary, won't you?'

'Sorry, Kathryn, but I've done my time there. Wait until you have teenage children. Anyway, Anna, I haven't seen you since the wedding. How did it go?'

And so, Kathryn listened to Anna retell the tale of her sister's wedding the week before. Kathryn had always labelled people's demeanour in terms of something akin to material. When she'd first met her, when Anna delighted in shaming Gabriel or laying a volley of abuse at Callum, well Anna's material had been hard. Perhaps iron or steel. Yet, perhaps for the first time since they had known each other, Kathryn viewed Anna's current demeanour as verging on softness.

'It was actually lovely. Leah looked stunning and Michael was charm-personified, and everyone was just − well− happy. I don't know if it was the occasion or the drink, but Leah made an effort to come and speak to me towards the end of the evening. D'you know what she said? She said, "Thank you for being such a great sister." I'm quite sure she's never said anything like that to me before, and she'll probably be sneering again when she gets back from South Africa but − I tell you − I'll take that. So, if we are all in the mood for celebrating and drinking, then count me in. Cheers!'

Donna

Donna had been looking forward to this evening for a long time. The Summer Ball was a fabled event at the School of Education; just about the whole of the cohort would be there and everyone would be in the mood to let their hair down. Martin had given a wonderful speech on their last day today and had seemed genuinely proud of all of them as he had wished them a wonderful holiday. But then, just half an hour ago, she'd got a phone call from Gabriel, who, perhaps inevitably, had said that he would give the pre in her room a miss to stay with Lily. At least he'd still be at the main event, unless of course, some other drama unfolded in the meantime. She'd had time to be resigned to the fact that he was to take a year off − at least he'd still be local − and the more maternal side of her was now beginning to actually look forward to eventually meeting his baby.

Any potential downer was soon put to one side, as she opened her door to both the familiar and the unfamiliar. Anna was already giggling about something, and, perhaps surprisingly, so were Kathryn and Mary, whilst Callum was more or less unrecognisable in his bow tie.

'I knew that drugs were big on this campus,' began Anna enthusiastically, 'but I never thought I'd see the day when someone would try to peddle some coke on Kathryn. Mary and I had stopped to get some cash out, and Kathryn merrily wandered on towards the halls. The next thing we know she was chatting amiably to some smooth-looking guy, who was leading her surreptitiously towards a Vauxhall Corsa. The irony is that he may just as well have had the words "I am a drugs dealer" tattooed to his head, and here was Miss Body Language Expert happily walking along with him. If Callum hadn't have arrived at that minute, looking like some bloody bouncer, Kathryn would now be out of it.'

'He just seemed nice,' said Kathryn, laughing. 'I don't get many good-looking guys smiling at me and chatting. How the hell was I supposed to know what he wanted?'

'It was a Vauxhall bloody Corsa, Kathryn. What other clues did you want?'

'You lot don't live on campus,' said Donna. 'Sometimes I think that Gabriel and I are the only ones who aren't on something every night, if you don't count the natural high of listening to James Blunt on repeat. Thank God we're moving out of here permanently next week. Anyway, you all look like you are well ahead of me on the drinking front. Somebody pour me a large glass.'

Gabriel

It wasn't often that two major life-changing events happened in one day, and Gabriel had woken this morning feeling a mixture of both excitement and trepidation at what the day would hold. He knew that he was prone to procrastination at the best of times, and it was clear that Lily was beginning to get exasperated.

'This is your last day, Gabriel. How much longer are you going to give it before you go and speak to your tutor?'

And so, Gabriel had finally plucked up the courage to speak to Martin, during the last minutes of their last day, and told him of his intention to defer his place for a year. To Martin's credit, he had not tried to talk him out of it and had even offered him a tutorial at any point of the following year to ensure that he didn't feel left behind.

'You're a fantastic student, Gabriel, and a quite charming young man. You've just had an excellent final placement and your grades have been good all year. I have no doubt that you will fit seamlessly back in next year.'

One down.

But the second life-changing event, his intention of asking Lily to marry him upon his return from seeing Martin, just seemed a slightly harder proposition. It was definitely the right thing to do, of that he had no doubt. He was very proud of the old-fashioned values that he and his brother had been brought up with, and so he had reasoned that proposing on the day that he finally concluded his studies for the year seemed like good timing. Lily, however, was clearly feeling a little hormonal and agitated upon his return, and part of him wanted to defer the moment until a more conducive time. Seeing her face light up though when he finally took the plunge, seeing her rush into his arms and accept gleefully made him realise, once and for all, that he was doing the right thing.

Lily had been aware from the outset that the ball this evening was strictly only for the students, but now, several hours on from his proposal, as he prepared to leave her flat for an evening with his friends, her agitation had returned. This was, after all, the first time that he'd been out without her for several weeks, so it was only natural, what with the hormones and all that, that she might feel a little low. He'd read the book.

He'd already felt that he'd let Donna and the others down once tonight by missing the pre, and however much it might have been easier simply to cancel, his affinity towards his friends had not lessened, and he also felt, not unreasonably, that he wanted to celebrate the end of the year. Gabriel kissed Lily goodbye and walked out of the door. Apart from Donna, none of his other friends was even aware as yet of his intention to defer for a year; hence one other significant conversation was still needed today.

Callum

'Come on, then, Callum. What's the surprise?'

'You're going to find out any minute now, Donna, and I'm sure you'll be impressed.'

'Oh, God, you're going to make an arse of yourself again, aren't you?'

The evening was going well, everyone was in a good mood, and Callum was in his element as chief showman, especially now that the vodka was beginning to do its stuff. Teaching a distinctly tipsy Kathryn how to do the movements for the flossing dance had been one of the highlights, although she might not think so when she reviewed the video evidence when sober. She had reciprocated in kind by teaching Callum the Macarena, even though he couldn't cope with the timings, much to everyone's amusement, and Mary had yet again revelled in her dark horse persona by doing a very passable robot dance.

Callum could feel the eyes burning on him as he walked towards the stage and picked up the guitar. He could see Anna and Donna, heads in hands, just awaiting the moment when they could engage in their favourite pastime, and as he faced his expectant and somewhat dubious-looking cohort, he felt a surge of adrenalin pass through him, and knew that this was going to be a wonderful moment.

'I asked the band earlier this evening if I could sing and play the guitar for you tonight. It seems to me that this song just about sums up where we all are, and how we all feel right here and right now. So, this is for all you doubters out there, and especially you two in the corner. Enjoy.'

And so he played, and he sang, and the doubters listened open-mouthed at his talent and at his ability to hold the stage and gradually, a few, and then all of the students just completing their first year of teacher training, got to the floor and started to dance and to sing. And as the chorus began, there was an almighty surge of emotion as everyone joined Callum in belting out the words:

'I'm still standing, better than I ever did...'

'Where the bloody hell did that come from?' asked Donna, as the applause finally died down and he re-joined his friends. 'You kept that pretty quiet.'

'Oh, there's lots of things that you don't know about me, Donna. I've been playing the guitar all my life. Check me out on YouTube later. I've got all sorts of hidden talents and secrets; I'm not just an arse, you know.'

'Clearly. Though it pains me to say it, Callum, that was really rather good. But you're right. We don't know that much about you. I don't even know where you live.'

He didn't think that he was particularly ashamed or embarrassed about this, but somehow there had never really been a suitable time all year to state that he still lived with his parents. After all, he was still under 30, he was a poor student, and he got on well with his mum and dad. Yet even now, he paused before responding to Donna. Would they somehow feel different about him knowing that this beer-swilling, rugby-playing womaniser still had his clothes washed and his meals cooked by his mother? When he did eventually reply, he was gratified and slightly relieved that the response was simply one of interest, rather than one of teasing. Maybe his Elton John impersonation had just given him that extra bit of kudos.

'So, what else do you do on the music front, then?' asked Gabriel. 'Are you in a band or anything?'

'Not really. I've done some sessions and stuff, but I'm also a keen DJ. Another thing you didn't know about me.'

Anna's eyes lit up. 'Oh, yes. Callum the DJ. I've been saving up this story for a week or so now, but Callum's just set me up beautifully. Callum, you've got to let me tell them the story of the school disco.'

Callum put his hands up theatrically. 'Well, that didn't last long, did it? Go on then Anna, do your worst, you're going to anyway.'

'Oh, goody. But, as you say, Callum, I would have told it anyway. So, ladies and gentlemen, for the final time this year: *Callum makes an arse of himself.*

'Shortly before the end of our last teaching experience, the children had one of those horrendous discos, where nobody quite knows what to do. I don't know whether any of you have ever had the misfortune to attend one of these things – basically the boys spend most of the evening just running around the room for no apparent reason, and this just gets more manic as the evening goes on, as they fill themselves with ever more sweets. The girls shuffle in small groups to cheesy music, and at the end of the night comes the requisite "slow dance", usually to Celine Dion, where a few awkward-looking boys and girls hold each other at arm's length and turn around in circles.

'Anyway, Callum generously agreed to organise the music for the night and act as DJ, although what this really meant was him sticking on a few playlists, letting them run for three or four songs whilst he charmed a parent helper, then asking stimulating questions such as "Is everyone having a good time?", before sticking on a few more and finding someone else to talk with.

'There was a song that came out last year which has basically been banned by many radio stations and institutions because of its highly suggestive and offensive lyrics. In fairness to Callum, unless you really listen you might just think that it is a totally inappropriate song to play at a children's disco, rather than a downright offensive one, but of course, play it he did. He was busy chatting away with some of the girls when one of the teachers came up to him and suggested that this shouldn't be playing, but none of the children seemed to notice so he laughed it off. But I was watching by then and when the words *"I'll let you have it"* were sung, he started to look a little worried, especially given the title of the song and the clear links with rather aggressive sex. Any suggestion that maybe this was still vaguely okay at a children's disco was then completely shattered when the singer started to hint darkly about anal sex. At this point, Callum realised that he had to get back to the stage as quickly as possible to turn off the offending song, but didn't want to be seen blatantly running across the school hall. As luck would have it, a group of boys were charging around the outside of the hall at that moment, and Callum, in a moment of genius, tagged along unnoticed at the back before quickly nipping on to the stage and curtailing the singer's indecent proposals.

'Of course, the next problem, and one I don't think he'd considered, was that there was a sudden silence, and everyone naturally looked his way for some sort of explanation. Again, in a quite inspired moment, Callum picked up a shovel, started digging an even bigger hole for himself and spoke the immortal words: "Er, I thought it was time for a game so, er, I decided that we'd play musical statues, but that I wouldn't tell you we were playing as that would – er – spoil the fun. And we have a winner! Step forward Maisy who was – almost certainly – the first to be completely still. A round of applause for Maisy!"'

'But then of course there was another problem. Maisy came up with something approaching a snarl and looked at him, clearly expecting some sort of winner's prize. Still digging furiously, Callum looked desperately around before putting his hands in his pockets, picking out half a pack of chewing gum and offering her a piece. Maisy didn't quite say the words, "What the fuck are you doing, you stupid man?", but she might as well have done. Callum, clearly now worried about the lyrics in his playlists, hastily went totally the other way and tried to get this group of incredulous and stunned 7 to 11-year-olds doing the conga. Needless to say, nobody was interested. Even by Callum's standards, this whole scene was priceless. Donna, if you'd have been there you would have totally flooded the dance floor with your dodgy bladder. Thank you, Callum. Thank you so much.'

Callum had spent most of the year worried about who was going to be next to rip him to pieces but there was – as Kathryn might have said – a softness to this anecdote, and a definite sense that Anna was laughing with him, rather than at him, and that was okay.

'All right,' he said eventually. 'There's a pint for anyone who asks the band to play the anal sex song, and two for anyone who asks for the conga.'

Donna

Donna finished her pint of water, swallowed the Anadin, and looked out of the window of her room. She'd never liked the feeling of being drunk and had always managed her drinking pretty well, but she was very aware that she'd had too much vodka too quickly earlier on and was now beginning to notice it. She'd enjoyed Anna's story as much as anyone, but by the end of it had felt the room swim somewhat, and had announced that she needed some air. The walk back to her room had helped considerably, and she knew she'd be ready to return in a couple of minutes.

She thought back to the moment, at the start of the ball, when Gabriel had shocked everyone by telling them of his conversation with Martin earlier in the day, and had seen the way they'd all looked from him to her, as if needing some sort of clarification.

'I know,' she'd said holding back the tears, 'I know. Believe me, I've spent much of the last four weeks begging, persuading, and cajoling, but he wasn't having any of it. God knows how we both got through placement. The only thing that I can think of now is that we take it in turns to chain ourselves to him, and then drag him in each day.'

Part of her had always held out a little bit of hope, but now that it was official, she felt a touch more resigned to the situation. She'd still see him.

Donna picked up her jacket, took one last deep breath and started making her way back from her room to the hall where the ball was taking place. As she turned a corner, she noticed a girl, clearly the worse for wear, doubled up with her back to her, and holding on unsteadily to a railing. As she got closer, she could see a pool of liquid vomit and a small packet containing white powder, which had clearly fallen from the girl's person as she'd bent over.

'Are you okay? Can I help at all?'

'I'm fine, I just need a minute.'

But Donna recognised the voice of the girl who still had her back to her.

'Lily?'

The effect upon hearing her name was electric as Lily wheeled round instantly to face Donna.

'What the fuck do you want, Donna? Shouldn't you be inside, trying to chat up Gabriel?'

'I don't know what – I'm not trying to – Lily, what's going on? You're preg–'

'None of your fucking business what I do, is it? Don't you think I've watched you these last few months? Don't you think I know your game? Has Gabriel told you that he asked me to marry him tonight? No? Thought not. And I'm going to make him choose, Donna, between you and me. And who do you think he'll pick, eh? Who do you think he'll believe when I tell him of this conversation, and that you told me to piss off and leave him alone?' So, I've had a couple of drinks tonight – so what? I've just got engaged, for fuck's sake. Not that my fiancé is with me, of course…'

Donna looked at the snarling face in front of her, not knowing how to respond.

'Lily, listen. You've got it all wrong. I'm genuinely happy for you both. I really–'

'Fuck off! Happy for us? If you were so happy, Donna, why have you been trying so hard to get him to stay on next year when we need money? And you've written some very interesting texts, haven't you, Donna? Let me see if I can remember some of your words: obsessive, domineering, selfish – how about those for a start? Happy for me, my arse!'

'You've been reading my –'

'Of course I've been reading them. I've told you: I don't trust you an inch.'

There was a moment's stand-off, whilst both girls looked at each other, neither quite sure where this was heading.

'That baggy on the floor, Lily: coke, is it? You're pregnant, for God's sake.'

Lily bent down, picked up the packet and started to walk away. 'What baggy, Donna? I don't see any.'

Gabriel

Gabriel sat alone in his room, trying to rationalise the last 24 hours, as James Blunt sang wistfully about one so beautiful in the background. None of it made any sense. Donna had returned to the ball after going out for some air and immediately sought him out, telling him simply that Lily was outside and that he should go and find her. When he'd returned a few minutes later with Lily nowhere in sight, Donna had seemed very reluctant to elaborate, beyond saying that she'd seen Lily, who had looked unwell. Whilst he hadn't pushed her, it felt like she'd been holding something back.

Gabriel had returned home to Lily's flat before the end of the ball, to find her sitting at home, having clearly been drinking. All she would say was that she'd felt bored and lonely on the night of her engagement, and just wanted to feel close to him, which was why she'd come over to his campus, even though she knew she wasn't invited to the ball. But then this morning, she'd said that she needed some space, and that she was going to stay with a friend for a few days. Since then, she hadn't replied to any of his calls or texts. Had he done something wrong? Was it really such a crime to want to celebrate the end of the year with one's friends? Maybe he should have stayed at home with her or delayed the proposal until a time when they could enjoy the moment together. Yes, on reflection, that had been bad timing, but he remembered the look of joy on her face when he had asked her to marry him and felt reassured somewhat that this was just another hormonal blip.

Eventually, there was a knock on the door, and a rather sheepish-looking Donna stood there with a bottle of wine.

'Care to share this with me? I think we could both use a drink.'

After a moment, Gabriel gave her a wry grin, collected a couple of glasses, and poured some wine. There was a silence between them for several moments, until Donna eventually spoke.

'I'm not sure that I want to say what I need to say, and I really hope that this won't be the end of our friendship. You know how much I think of you. You probably worked out that I didn't tell you everything last night, but I just couldn't – I mean I was too shocked to…'

And so, Donna slowly and carefully described the confrontation that she'd had with Lily the night before, and when she relayed that Lily had said that she was going to make him choose between them, there was a definite crack in her voice. When she finished telling her tale, there was yet another silence as Gabriel just stared at the ground, as if in shock.

'Do you know that Lily has a brother, Gabriel?'

This, at least, got a reaction.

'A brother? But I've known her since Christmas. I know that she hasn't spoken of her family much – she said they're not very close, and I don't even know where they live. But a brother? Are you sure, Donna?'

'Gabriel, I've just spent the last half-hour on the phone to him. He wasn't hard to find. I know. I know. You might hate me for this, Gabriel, but I just felt that I had to find out more.'

'And?'

'Lily isn't well, Gabriel. Mark is two years older than her, and has tried to be the protective older brother, but the older she's got, the more she's retracted from her family. They are pulling their hair out. They know she's got a flat here, but they've barely seen her for a year. Ultimately, she hasn't committed a crime, so if she wants to be estranged, then that's up to her.'

'You say she's not well. What's wrong with her?'

Donna sighed. 'She's a diagnosed schizophrenic, Gabriel, and a fantasist. She spent much of her teenage years seeing a psychiatrist, but she also turned her back on that support. It seems she's spent the last few years with boyfriend after boyfriend, getting more and more possessive as the relationship develops, and then turning nasty when it ends. Apparently, her last boyfriend had to get a restraining order out against her. Highly complex issues with relationships can be common with schizophrenic people. We both know that Lily has an incredibly charming and seductive side to her – you wouldn't have been so smitten otherwise – but in her case she can't sustain a relationship and things just crumble around her.'

'But you didn't see her face when I proposed last night, Donna. I've never seen anyone looking so happy.'

'And I'm sure she was. But let's not forget that a couple of hours later, she was practically stalking you and being sick outside our hall, certainly as a result of drink and possibly of drugs too. Let's not forget the venom with which she spoke to me. You know that I haven't done anything wrong.'

'But the baby. What am I going to do about –'

'Lily isn't pregnant, Gabriel. One of the symptoms of schizophrenia is that it can make the sufferer delusional, which might explain her attitude towards me. I don't know whether this is a delusion or if there is another motive behind everything. She clearly wanted to be tied to you, but the fact that it would soon become obvious that she wasn't pregnant wouldn't have been an immediate concern to her; she lives very much from day to day.'

'But how do you know? How does Mark know? Okay, I get that she has issues, but that doesn't mean for certain that she's not pregnant.'

'Lily contracted ovarian cancer at 13. Mark said that there was almost certainly a link between this and the psychological problems that she has had since then. It's strange how we change our perception of people. When you first introduced her to me, I thought she was lovely and just right for you. I then gradually began to get more and more wary of her and last night it was something close to hatred. But now I just feel for her, as I feel for you.'

'But that doesn't mean that she definitely isn't –'

'Lily can't have children, Gabriel. The treatment that she had for the cancer has left her infertile. Whilst she is now completely in remission, she has paid a heavy price for all she went through. I'm so sorry, Gabriel.'

It took Gabriel several seconds to try to take this all in, and he needed several gulps of wine before he could speak again.

'So, what do I do? I've just asked her to marry me, for God's sake.'

'I can't tell you that, Gabriel, but Mark made it very clear that history has told him that she won't be the same person now that you know all about her and her mood swings may well intensify. She'll hate you one minute and stalk

203

you the next. Sooner or later, she'll accept and move on, which is what you need to do, Gabriel. You do see that, don't you?'

'I suppose so. I just don't know what to do.'

Donna went over to Gabriel and gave him a massive hug.

'Let's hold fire for a couple of days, Gabriel. So much has happened to you recently that you just need a weekend, your friends, and copious amounts of alcohol. We'll get there.'

Martin

'So then, Rich, looks like it's a draw.'

'A draw?'

'Remember our bet, back at the programme social? You went for Kathryn and I plumped for Donna as the one not to last the distance. It's strange, but both could so easily have left for totally different reasons, but now I would put my mortgage on both of them thriving over the next two years and becoming excellent teachers. I'm really proud of them.'

'As you should be, Martin, although it's such a shame about Gabriel. I really didn't see that coming. Do you think he'll rejoin next year? They so often don't.'

Martin took a large swig of beer before continuing.

'It *was* a shame about Gabriel, but it's not now. That's one of the reasons I wanted a drink tonight, mate, to share the good news. Gabriel came to see me this morning with Donna in tow, and basically asked if he could change his mind. I think my grin gave him his answer. It seems that there have been issues with his girlfriend – ex-girlfriend now, I gather – and he's keen to carry on. I can't tell you how happy I am, Richard. As you know, I've got rather a soft spot for that boy, indeed I've got a soft spot for all of my lot. No, Richard, they started off as six of them in our Surgery Set, and that's how they'll stay.'

Epilogue: 6 weeks later

Donna

Donna carefully seals the last envelope and begins the short walk to the postbox. She can't actually remember the last time that she physically posted something by hand, but this is far too special for an email. She's been on a natural high since Dominic asked her to marry him last week, and it didn't take long to persuade him to celebrate with an engagement party. Apart from Gabriel, she hasn't seen her university friends since the end of term, and this has given her the perfect excuse to catch up with them before they start Year 2 in a few weeks' time. It hadn't taken too long to win Dominic around, and already now she is pretty confident about who's going to wear the trousers when they move in together next week.

'I thought that the idea of this was to get together to celebrate with our close family and friends? Of course you need to invite Gabriel and Anna, but the others? Do you really know them that well? I'm not going to win this argument, am I? Okay I get it, but your tutor? I mean, I know he's helped you a lot this year and all that and I know he fought your cause at the beginning, but isn't that just a little bit weird? A tutor at your engagement party? Hang on whilst I go and find the number for my cub scout Akela. Stop looking at me like that; I'm making a valid point here. There's only space in the pub for 40, and we're already pushing it, and now you want to start being plain weird and… I'm losing this one, aren't I? I'm never going to win, am I? I've been sentenced to a lifetime of being henpecked, haven't I? God, I hate it when you're this stubborn.'

Mary

Mary looks at herself in the mirror and smiles a rueful smile. She's really not that bad for 50. Alice comes up behind her with a gin and tonic, and gives her Mum an affectionate hug.

'Okay, Dad's gone to bed. How did it go?'

'It's Anna, Alice, she is the devil, I'm sure of it.'

'What's Anna got to do with anything? Didn't you and Dad just go out for a nice meal?'

'Well, yes, we did but − er − it was a bit more than that.'

'I'm intrigued. Go on.'

'You know I'll talk to you about anything, don't you, Alice, but I'm not absolutely sure that you'll want to hear −'

'Oh, shut up, Mother, and get on with it. You went for a meal with Dad and you both came back grinning. How can I possibly not want to know about that?'

'As I said, it's Anna. She sidles her way into your life. She oozes charm and God-knows-what, and she just sows ideas. That's all, Alice, she just sows ideas… Look, you know that this year has taken its toll on your father and me. That's no secret, and it's totally my fault. I've thrown myself into the year to the detriment of you lot − I know I have.'

Mary thinks back to the conversation that she had with Anna a couple of weeks ago, not quite knowing how much of it to relay to her daughter. There are some things…

'So, what you need, Mary, is to spice things up a bit. Yes, yes, yes, let's cut the crap. Half of this problem is that you're both too irritable and tired, and therefore you're not getting any. Tell me I'm wrong? Thought not. Have you ever tried, you know, a bit of role-play? "Doctors and nurses" and that sort of thing? It's amazing what that can do. I know! He can be the headmaster, and you are the NQT, right. He's interviewing you and asking what you can offer. At this point, you flutter your eyelids, loosen your… No? Oh well, just an idea. How about a date night? Why don't you suggest that you meet up at a restaurant on a blind date? You can be whoever you want to be and just let the evening take its course…'

Alice listens with something approaching incredulity as Mary offers a watered-down version of Anna's suggestion, before continuing the story.

'I don't know what came over me, Alice, I really don't, I just thought it might be a bit of fun, that's all. So, I arrived at the restaurant looking a bit − glam − and we sort of flirted for a bit, that's all really, and we had a nice evening. Well, we did have a nice evening until the last few minutes. As I say, Alice, she is the spawn of the devil.'

But it is with affection, rather than anger or even embarrassment, that Mary remembers the text exchanges with Anna at the end of that evening:

OMG, Mary, what are you wearing? We didn't recognise you!!

What are you on about? I'm at the restaurant with Simon.

I know! But the length of that skirt? At your age? And what is that wig? It took us a while. We really thought that he had stood you up and had chosen some blonde bimbo instead!

You're not...? You complete bastard! Never, ever again will I talk to you. Bastard!

Turn round!

So, Mary had turned around, and there, in an obscure part of the restaurant, were Anna and Callum, showing no semblance of shame or regret. Their laughter had just intensified as Mary had murmured something to Simon and shuffled up to them in heels designed for one younger than her own daughter.

''Allo, darlin'. How much do you charge, then? D'you do threesomes?'

She'd wanted to scream and point accusatory hands, but somehow Callum's impersonation of a punter, together with Anna's howls of hilarity swept her on board.

'You knew that I was coming here tonight, and you bloody followed? You complete bastards! Incidentally, how do I look?'

'Like mutton dressed as lamb, Mary. I think you need some more lessons. Tell you what, let's have a coffee tomorrow, and I can...'

'Oh no you can't, Anna, you absolute bastard. Now, if you'll excuse me, I've just pulled a rather handsome young man and he's invited me back to his place...'

Alice rubs her ears theatrically as Mary concludes her anecdote.

'Oh my God, Mum, where's the wig? No, on second thoughts, I don't want to see it. I'll need therapy. Jesus, Mum, Dad's just gone up to bed. Do you need me to go out for an hour? No! Don't answer that, I'm off. If I'm not back in a few hours, then I've died of alcohol poisoning. Yuck!'

Callum

Callum slowly and deliberately rubs suntan cream into his well-toned torso. He can't help himself; it is almost an involuntary action that makes him position his body in such a way that as many people as possible around the pool can now see him, can see those muscles ripple as he works his arms. He shamelessly looks around and counts at least three girls, their focus hidden behind dark sunglasses, who he naturally assumes are watching his every move and planning how to sidle their way into his life. Not that he's interested. Not now. He watches as she slowly finishes another piña colada at the pool bar, drifts to the edge of the pool on the lilo, shakes her hair and walks back towards him. She really does have a very nice figure indeed. He'd never really appreciated that until now. Would it work? Was this really the start of something long-term or just another holiday romance? Girlfriends come and girlfriends go, but even with the shakiest of foundations, he somehow feels that there is a genuine chance here…

Anna

Anna towels herself down and lies on the sunbed. Without needing to be asked, Callum squeezes some oil on to her back and begins to massage it in. He's pretty well trained already; a few more weeks, and he'll be complete putty in her hands. Anna tries to remember the exact point when she began to view Callum in a different light, as someone more than just a friend. She'd been so angry at him when they'd first had any real contact; the physical contact of his falling chair knocking her over at the programme social and ruining her evening. But now, nearly a year on, she can see that this accident was nothing to do with him, it was her deep-rooted anger that needed so very little to ignite. She shivers. Callum had done his best all year to hide behind his blokey exterior and had almost been at his most comfortable when he was making an arse of himself. But people change, and now she is really rather proud of the way that he has battled so hard all year to overcome the quite considerable hurdle of becoming a primary school teacher whilst coping with dyslexia. Maybe it is this that made her view him in a different light, maybe it was the way that he held the stage so impressively at the Summer Ball, or maybe it is just the gradual realisation that he is, fundamentally, a really nice guy. She thinks ahead to next year, about living arrangements, and about the prospect of how their relationship will pan out in such close proximity to each other. At least it won't be just the two of them in the house; she's quite sure that without the others there, it would have been too much, too soon, but at least with the four of them there together, any potential tension might be diluted somewhat. Time would tell.

Kathryn

Kathryn places the flowers between the twin graves and sits down on her favourite bench. The silence is absolute, and she feels completely at peace. For the last eight months or so, she has both haunted and motivated herself with the perennial question: *Are they proud of me?* And now, perhaps really for the first

208

time, she is sure that they are, and as she looks up to the sky, she can almost see two heads nodding in approval. She had been terrified upon moving away and embarking on her studies and had been terrified and lonely when her nan had died. But she now sees, with crystal clarity that, whilst still dreadfully sad, her nan's death has been the making of her. It has forced her to fully enter the world of adulthood, to take responsibility and to develop independence; an independence that was almost non-existent a year ago. She is almost ready to go home, to face the emptiness of the house that had been made for three and then two, and now just for one. She knows it will be horrendous initially, but Alice has offered to come and help her redecorate throughout, and this feels like yet another moment in the start of her new life. Her lease in her shared flat soon expires, and there are another few weeks before she can move in with the others, so this journey back home has always been inevitable, only now she is actively looking forward to it.

Kathryn remembers the moment, less than a week ago, which finally persuaded her that things were going to be okay. Several months ago, she had agreed to move in next year with three of the girls who she knew vaguely from the Christian Society. This had seemed a sensible thing to do: the girls were all quiet, well-ordered and pleasant enough, but as time had gone on, she'd been far from certain, perhaps ironically, that this is what she wanted. And then had come the news, just last week, that the move had fallen through: one of the girls was leaving, one now had a boyfriend and − well, it didn't really matter. So, it was a state of both panic and self-pity that Anna had found her in when she'd returned briefly to their shared house last week to pick up some things.

Anna had been adamant: 'Move in with us. Go on, Kathryn, you know you want to. More to the point, I need you to. Now that Donna has jumped ship and is selfishly moving in with Dominic, we've got a spare room, and quite frankly, I need another girl in the house, if only to redress the balance.'

'But what about Gabriel and Callum? Won't they mind?'

'You leave them to me, Kathryn. Can you really see either of them standing up to me over this? I'd bite their bloody heads off.'

Kathryn had accepted there and then and in a moment that she was certain that she would never forget, Anna had given her a huge hug.

'You'll be okay, Kathryn. We'll see to that.'

Gabriel

'You really are serious, aren't you?'

'A bet's a bet, Mark. There's no way that Lily can come now, and even Donna's managed to get out of it by going on her honeymoon, so it's got to be you.'

'But I'll never live it down! I agreed to your stupid bet because I didn't think I could lose – there was no way England were going to win that game – but now the true horror of the situation is fully dawning on me.'

Gabriel laughs and takes another swig of his beer. Things are good. He'd been to see Lily several times over the last few weeks, and although he never really knew what to expect, he always felt better for going. Just knowing that she'd agreed to start seeing a psychiatrist again was enough, even if he still had to sometimes bear the brunt of her extremes of moods. She'd been signed off from work for an indefinite period and so had much time to fill, and Gabriel was happy to help her to fill this time, even though he was acutely aware that their relationship was now permanently over. A wonderful by-product of the whole affair had been meeting up with Mark and developing a firm friendship almost immediately.

'So how was she today, anyway?'

Gabriel thinks, before responding.

'I think perhaps the word I would use to describe her at the moment would be placid. She doesn't say a lot when I go round but actually that's okay. She seems happy that I am there and today we just sat watching television for a while and didn't talk much. She's certainly calmer now than she was a few weeks ago.'

'I agree, and you don't know how grateful we all are that you haven't just abandoned her. That would have been more than reasonable, given what you've been through. Actually, Gabriel, my parents are coming down in a couple of weeks and I know they'd love to meet you. Would you be up for another beer?'

'Absolutely. I never turn down alcohol, you know that, Mark.'

'Excellent, I'll arrange it. Oh, and I've just thought of something. I'm sure Mum's really into James Blunt. Maybe she could go along to that concert with you, instead of me...'

Martin

Miriam pours the coffee and settles down on the settee with Martin.

'Was it really that bad?

'God, Miriam, it was awful. Half the School of Education weren't there – many take annual leave at this time of year – and the other half certainly didn't want to be there. Ranch is a bit crap at speeches at the best of times, and he knew he had to try to say something nice and all of us – including Frank – knew that he didn't want to say anything nice and the whole thing was simply excruciating. If Richard and I hadn't had a side bet about the amount of times that William would say the words "grateful" and "service" – which I won, incidentally – I would have fallen asleep. There was loads of food and people were just expected to mingle, but as soon as Frank had said his thanks and opened up a disappointingly small set of gardening vouchers, everyone seemed to just quietly go back to their offices, leaving all the food virtually untouched. God, I hate leaving dos.'

There's a moment of quiet before Miriam changes the subject.

'So, you've been invited to Donna's engagement party? Are you going to go?'

'Of course I will. Donna's asked us all to get there a bit earlier than the other guests so that we can catch up, and well, you know.'

Another moment of silence.

'And are you going to mention…? You have definitely, definitely made up your mind, haven't you?'

'I have, Miriam, yes, and yes, I will find time to have a word. You know how much affinity I have for all my students, especially my Surgery Set. But over the last couple of months I've begun to realise that they are going to be fine whatever the circumstances. However much I'd like to think that they do, they actually don't need me. Grace will do a brilliant job with them. I know you've been reluctant to push me, but I finally took the plunge today and went to see William after Frank's do.'

'What did he say?'

'I think he was shocked, perhaps not as shocked as some of the students will be, but hey, we've all got to move on, don't we?'

'We do, and as you say, they'll be absolutely fine. Head of PE at a posh boys' school, eh? Who'd have thought it?'